Glass Slipper Press

Captain Casey stepped closer and raked his eyes over her, taking in her disheveled appearance. With surprising gentleness, he swept her hair from her forehead. When his fingers touched her flesh, her breath froze in her lungs, and every muscle in her body coiled. Shocked by the electricity in that brief touch, her knees buckled, and she sank back down to the sofa. When he hunkered down in front of her and took her chin in his strong hand, her breath caught in her throat.

"You really are hurt. What happened?" The deep timbre of his softly spoken question was like the man himself—sexy.

She met his probing gaze before lowering her eyes to the floor. "My horse threw me and ran off. I don't know what spooked him, and I don't know where he is."

He rose to his feet and curled his lip. "Where are your trunks?"

"They're due to arrive from Pecos later this week," she said, unable to meet his gaze.

"Why would you leave your trunks in Pecos and travel alone on horseback? Why not wait at the hotel for the next stage to Canyon Creek?"

She was nervous enough without him towering over her, so she rose to her feet and forced herself to hold his intimidating gaze. "I felt a lot safer taking my chances on the road dressed as a man than I did staying in some skeezy hotel in Pecos where everyone knew I was a woman traveling alone."

It was a reasonable explanation. She was wearing jeans in a time when women didn't even wear slacks, and she had just shown up without taking the stage. He might have actually believed her if it hadn't been for her modern vernacular.

He raked his eyes over her with a quirked mouth and skeptical lift of his brows. "You couldn't fool a blind man in those clothes, and no man would wear an undershirt that color. You even smell like a woman," he added, sniffing the air around her neck. When his nose grazed the tender flesh behind her ear, goose bumps raced down her arms.

WINDS OF TIME

Lilly Gayle

Winds of Time
Copyright © 2018 Gayle W. Glass

Print ISBN: 978-1-7323904-1-6
Digital ISBN: 978-1-7323904-0-9

Contact Information: lillygayle@gmail.com
Https://lillygayle.com
Https://facebook.com/lillygaylebooks
Https://twitter.com/lillygromwriter
Https://instagram.com/lillygayleauthor|

Publishing History
First Edition 2018
 Published in the United States of America

Cover design: AGW Visual Alchemy
www.agwvisual.myportfolio.com
Cover model: Caroline Kelly ckblue21@instagram.com
Tornado image: ©rasica - stock. adobe. com, purchased from https://us.fotolioa.com/Fotolia_145285951_M. jpg
Locket image: ©abigail210986 - stock. adobe. com, purchased from https.//us.fotolia.com/Fotolia_73248369_M. jpg
Image in locket: Photoshop picture of author's son-in-law.

Dedication:

Thank you to everyone that made this book possible, from friends and family to my critique partners, editors, and beta readers. A big thank you to Laura Browning, Donna Steele, Jo-Ann Verlik, and Selena Newton. Yes, Selena, you finally get a heroine named after you.

Thanks also to Jennifer Kelly for her photography skills, my gorgeous cover model, Caroline Kelly, and Alexander Winston of AGW Visual Alchemy for the gorgeous cover. You rock, bro.

This book is dedicated to my little Paisley Pie.

Prologue
Canyon Creek, Texas. Friday, March 31, 1871.

Dylan Casey knew it was over when he heard Mary Tillman was engaged to Lieutenant Tommy Walters. Yet some perverse need to humiliate himself again made him saddle his horse and ride out to the Tillman farm a week after Mary's father died. He wanted to offer his condolences. He *needed* Mary to look him in the eye and tell him she didn't love him. With the colonel gone, he'd hoped she would have the guts to follow her heart and marry him instead of Walters.

He should have known better.

The tan sorrel tied to the hitching post proved she was no different from every other white woman of his acquaintance. Despite her declarations of love, she couldn't see passed the color of his skin. He might have been a fun diversion, but he was still just a half-breed—a half-breed who'd made the mistake of falling in love with the colonel's daughter.

Still, he shouldn't judge without proof. Perhaps Mary had ended the engagement, and Tommy had come to plead his case. His being here while her housekeeper was away didn't prove anything. That's how rumors started, and Mary had had her fair share of rumors already.

Determined not to jump to any wrong conclusions, Dylan swallowed his pride and stepped onto the porch. The windows were open, allowing a gentle breeze to blow in from the back of the house. It carried with it the heated sounds of desire.

Mary hadn't ended her engagement. She'd invited Walters into her bed.

Fury knotted Dylan's gut, and his fingers curled into fists at his sides. He should have paid attention to the whispers instead of listening to his heart. But everything in life came as a teacher, and he would learn. But could he walk away without hearing the truth

1

from Mary's own lips?

Indecision left him standing on the porch too long, cursing his foolish heart for wanting what he could never have. When movement inside drew his attention, he turned to leave, hoping he could escape before being discovered.

"Wait!" a strangled voice softly called from the open window.

Dylan's left boot hovered in midair. He lowered it to the first step and turned as Mary opened the door. With his right foot still on the porch, he crossed his arms over his raised knee and leaned forward. His heart beat like a war drum inside his chest.

Mary pulled up her bodice and stepped onto the porch. "Please, Dylan. Let me explain."

He eyed her kiss-swollen lips and whisker-scratched cheeks. Her enraptured moans echoed in his brain, hardening his heart. "I've heard enough."

She clutched her loose bodice to her chest and looked at him with beseeching eyes. "Shh. Keep it down. Tommy's asleep, but it's not what you think."

He ground his teeth against the furious words he wanted to spew, holding on to his temper by a thread. "It's exactly what I think."

"But you don't understand," she whispered through her tears. "I have to marry Tommy. I don't have a choice now that Papa's gone. If I don't marry him, everything goes to Uncle Ben, and I get nothing."

He'd never liked the colonel, but the man *had* loved his daughter. Forcing her to marry a white man was his way of protecting her. But why hadn't Mary confided in him?

Why did she let me find out from Tommy?

Pain tightened his throat. "We could have worked something out."

"No. We couldn't. Papa made sure of it."

Dylan heard the pain in her voice. He also heard resignation. For once, she was going to do exactly what her father wanted. In the past, she'd done as she pleased, believing the Tillman name and her father's reputation would protect her from scandal, but she'd underestimated the power of gossip.

He met her gaze, his heart in his eyes, holding back

nothing. "You could have married me."

She pursed her lips, but tears glistened in her eyes. "That wasn't one of the choices listed in Papa's will."

And there it was. The truth. She cared more for her home and reputation than she did for him. "There's always a choice, and you've made yours."

When he turned to leave, she grabbed his arm. Her eyes begged. Her voice pleaded. "You don't understand. If I don't marry Tommy, I'll lose the farm, and my reputation will be ruined."

"I understand perfectly." If nothing else, her betrayal reminded him of who and what he really was.

"Damn you," she cried. "I *don't* have a choice. It doesn't matter that you're Cherokee instead of Comanche or Apache, and it doesn't matter that your father is Irish. You're still a half-breed, and I can't marry you. If you really loved me, you'd understand, and you'd *want* me to marry Tommy."

"So marry him." Unable to meet her gaze, he looked over her shoulder. She'd left the door open, and Tommy Walters stood in the darkened interior of the house, his posture taut with anger. Dylan sympathized. Mary had betrayed them both.

Keeping his eyes on Walters, he said, "You've made your decision. There's nothing more to say."

"But I love you," she whispered in a tight voice, obviously unaware of Walters' presence. "I'm only marrying Tommy because he's white. It doesn't mean things have to end between us. If we're discrete—"

"There is no us."

Dylan stepped off the porch and mounted his horse without a backward glance. And later that day, Mary Tillman disappeared without a trace.

3

Chapter 1
Friday, March 31, 2017

Selena Tillman turned off the main road and followed the rutted path through overgrown weeds and buffalo grass until the abandon farmhouse came into view. She'd inherited the property two years ago after her parents died within six months of one another, but it was in worse shape than she'd imagine. The paint was peeling, a section of roof was missing, windows were broken or boarded over, and the foundation sagged.

Her heart sank as she climbed out of the car, her fingers drifting to the antique locket that once belonged to her ancestor, Mary. The house had been Mary's before she disappeared without a trace a hundred and forty-six years ago today. On the anniversary of her disappearance, a half-Native American army scout accused of her murder came to the house, either to revisit the crime scene or search for clues to prove his innocence. Despite the lack of evidence against him, someone shot him and then scalped him with his own knife in a sort of vigilante justice.

Captain Casey bled out on the porch, and the house had been haunted ever since.

Some said Mary's ghost sought justice. Others claimed the scout's ghost sought revenge. But for some reason, both of their spirits haunted Selena's dreams, and she lived in Virginia.

Her cousin, Jeff, believed an attachment spirit haunted her through Mary's necklace. If that were true, then the disembodied energy originated here—where Mary and the scout died. Dangerous or not, Selena was going inside the house. If she didn't find some way to communicate with Mary, the dreams would continue—or the spirits would become more aggressive. As long as she dreamed of Mary, she'd never find peace. As long as she dreamt of Captain Casey, she'd compare every man she dated to the fantasy man in her dreams.

It had to stop.

Taking a deep breath to calm her nerves, Selena climbed the first step. It held her weight, but the second step had completely rotted away. It wasn't too big of a gap, so she reached for a porch column and stretched her leg over the missing step. As she was pulling herself up, the wood beneath her back foot gave way, and she started to fall. To avoid a face plant or broken wrist, she drew her arms to her chest, tucked her chin, squeezed her eyes shut, and dove for the porch.

Her shoulder hit first, and she rolled into a ball, coming to a stop on her right side. When she opened her eyes, a dark stain was mere inches from her face. It looked like a bloodstain.

A shiver raced down her spine, raising the fine hairs at her nape. She rubbed her neck to ease the prickling sensation and rose to her feet, but her gaze drifted back to the dark stain. "That's where Captain Casey died. They never washed away the blood."

No wonder the house was haunted.

Earlier in the day, Selena had stopped in Canyon Creek to get gas at the only store still open in the dying town. The people she'd talked to about the Tillman house claimed they'd seen strange things over the years. One man said he'd seen the murderous "half-breed" on the porch. Another swore he'd seen Colonel Tillman's ghost, while the clerk claimed he'd seen ghostly storms and weird weather patterns most locals attributed to paranormal activity.

Selena had the cell number for Jeff's paranormal investigator friend, but she wasn't quite ready to place the call. Despite feeling strange since stepping off the plane yesterday, she'd wanted some sort of proof that ghosts from Texas were invading her dreams in Virginia. Rather than driving straight to the Tillman house this morning, she'd gone to Fort Davis first.

Mary's father and Captain Casey had led a regiment of Buffalo Soldiers from the army garrison at the foot of the Davis Mountains. Eerily enough, Selena had felt the same sense of overlapping time at the fort. It was almost as if remnants of the past lingered in the shadows of the present, but the feeling was even stronger here at the house.

The skin between her shoulder blades prickled, as if someone was standing behind her. She spun around, but she was alone.

She rubbed her arms through the sleeves of her denim jacket, but the chill persisted, and it wasn't just from the gathering storm clouds that now blocked the sun. The chill went soul-deep.

Selena shivered and looked at the door. The hinges were rusted shut, but the doorframe was no longer flush with the door, leaving a gap wide enough for her to squeeze through. As she slipped through the space between the edge of the door and the doorjamb, she snagged her shirt on a rusty nail and nearly fell as she stumbled inside. She quickly righted herself and touched her side. The skin along her ribs throbbed, and there was a small tear in the fitted green t-shirt she wore beneath her denim jacket, but the nail hadn't broken the skin.

"At least I won't have to go to an urgent care for a tetanus shot," she said aloud as her eyes adjusted to the gloomy interior.

The oak floors were warped and worm-eaten, and the foundation sagged low enough in the parlor that one wall was separating from the floor, exposing rotten floor-joists beneath the house. Collapsed beams and other rubbish were strewn about, and the wind blowing in through the cracks and crevices stirred up a century of dust, deepening the shadows.

At the end of the hall, feeble light shone through a hole in the roof, calling to Selena like a beacon to a trapped miner. Unable to resist its pull, she picked her way over rotten planks and sloping floors until she made it to the kitchen.

Dirt and debris camouflaged whatever color the room had once been, and nothing remained of the cabinets or appliances but a cast iron woodstove—the same woodstove Selena had seen in her dreams.

The air thickened, an oppressive weight that made it difficult to breathe. Selena inhaled sharply when the weight settled between her shoulder blades like an unseen hand, nudging her forward.

"It's just a drop in barometric pressure due to the approaching storm." It was certainly not the *proof* she needed before calling a paranormal investigator.

Knees shaking, she stepped over a fallen beam to reach the filth-encrusted woodstove. When she touched it, the air crackled around her, and a cold, electric tingle raced from her fingertips to her shoulder, setting off an explosion of light behind her eyes.

Then a faded image flickered before her like the remnants of a dream.

> *Mary stands at the stove. She's wearing a thin gossamer wrapper. Her long, dark hair is unbound. It's early morning, and the sun is shining through the kitchen window.*
>
> *Dust motes float in beams of dappled sunlight as she turns from the stove holding two steaming cups of coffee. She smiles and walks toward the table. Her hips sway gracefully.*
>
> *When she leans forward, the deep V in her dressing gown exposes her breasts as she sets her cup on the table and offers the other to her lover. His large, bronze hand takes the cup and places it on the table next to hers. Then he reaches for her, and she falls into his arms.*

"I never meant to hurt him," a voice whispered in Selena's ear—a voice coming from over her left shoulder and not from the hallucination playing like a movie clip inside her brain.

"Shit!" Selena jerked her hand from the stove and spun around. The air stirred as if someone had passed behind her, but she was still alone.

She released a pent up breath and turned back to the stove. Her hand shook as she reached for it again, touching it with hesitant fingers. She quickly tapped it as if checking a hot iron before placing her palm flat on the rusted surface. When the vision failed to reappear, she allowed her fingers to linger.

If she'd simply remembered a dream, it didn't explain the voice whispering in her ear as clearly as if someone had actually spoken. Any doubts she'd had before vanished. The house was definitely haunted. She'd just seen Mary Tillman and Captain Casey's ghosts.

Yet even if ghosts did exist, they were nothing more than fingerprints of the past left on the fabric of time. They would be fleeting images seen from the corner of one's eye, not holographic movie clips played on the back of the eyelids, but she had seen something. She just wasn't sure if it was real or her imagination working overtime, and she wanted proof the house was haunted— not empirical evidence she was crazy.

She stepped away from the stove, and the floor sagged under her weight. If she left the way she'd come in, she could fall through the floor before reaching the front door, but the path to the kitchen door didn't look any safer. It was just closer.

Keeping an eye on the floor, Selena made her way to the back door. Like the front door, the hinges were rusted shut, so she put her shoulder against it and pushed. The wood groaned, but the gap widened, and she was able to step onto the back stoop.

While she'd been inside, the sky had grown increasingly dark, and storm clouds swirled overhead. Thunder rolled and lightening sizzled just before a wind gust ripped the door from her hand and sent it tumbling end over end across a waving sea of sun-dried broom straw.

"Holy crap!" She jumped back and nearly fell off the porch as a section of tin roof flew over her head and chased the door across the field until the door toppled to the ground two hundred yards away. The sheet metal wrapped around a scrub oak, creating an eerie sawing sound that accompanied the moaning wind as rain mixed with hail pinged the tin roof in a rapid staccato that sounded like gunfire.

Selena pressed her back against the house, trying to escape the rain and hail stinging her cheeks. Before she could turn around and dash back inside, it stopped raining. There was a brief moment of calm before the wind began to gust, whipping her hair across her face. When she raked her hair from her eyes, her heart lodged in her throat. The swirling, dark clouds had sprouted a white, funnel-shaped-finger that ripped through the field of sun-dried brook straw on the other side of the creek bed, eating it up like a hungry beast.

Fear tightened her chest, making it difficult to breathe. Trying to outrun a tornado in a car was suicidal, and the house was a deathtrap—unless it had a storm cellar.

She jumped to the ground and ran around the house, searching for a basement or some sort of underground shelter. The remains of a barn were to her left, and a pile of rubble that may have once been a foundation was on the other side of the dry creek bed. The house didn't have a basement or underground shelter, but several yards away, Selena spotted what might be the partially buried entrance to a storm cellar.

A surge of adrenaline sent her running toward it, her legs pumping like an Olympic sprinter, but the opening was no bigger than a rabbit burrow. One door was missing, but weeds and thick roots blocked the entrance, and the earth had reclaimed the remaining door years ago. It would take a shovel to get inside, but Selena was out of options. Heart pounding, she dropped to her knees and began digging as thunder rumbled, and lightening charged the air with static electricity.

Earth and tangled roots scraped her knuckles and broke her nails, but Selena didn't stop digging until she heard the telltale sound of a roaring freight train. Only then did she stop long enough to look over her shoulder.

"No," she whispered, fear tightening her throat.

The tornado had almost reached the house, but before she could resume digging, a dark-haired woman wearing a long skirt rushed out the back door and started running toward the storm cellar. The Victorian-clad apparition looked like Mary, and the house from which she ran no longer resembled a weather worn relic. It looked like the Tillman house, perfectly restored to its former glory.

As her ancestor drew closer, Selena reached out to her, but her fingers passed through Mary's body as though she were made of smoke. Then the ghostly figure glanced over her shoulder. When she turned back around, her mouth opened in a silent scream, she reached for the storm cellar door—a door that was no longer missing. Like the house, the storm cellar was now intact, and it had *two* doors.

Staring in disbelief, Selena watched Mary jerk open the previously missing door as the wind pulled against her—a wind Selena no longer felt.

Mary's eyes widened, the color leaching from her face as the twister lifted her feet from the ground. Her grip on the door tightened, her knuckles turning white mere seconds before the twister sucked her and the cellar door into its swirling vortex. Then the wind returned along with Selena's fear. Before she could react or even offer up a prayer, the tornado took her just as it had taken her ancestor one hundred and forty-six years ago.

Chapter 2

Selena was lying face down with the sun warming the right side of her face when she opened her eyes. The ground beneath her was dry, but her clothes were damp, and there was an abrasion over her left eye. She touched the raw, sticky wound and then pushed herself to a seated position. When she blinked to clear her vision, a horse came into focus. It grazed in a corral next to a small barn, but neither her house nor rental car were anywhere in sight. Then she remembered the howling wind and darkness, and her heart thumped against her sternum.

A tornado had struck, lifting her off the ground and tossing her around like a rag doll. Her ears had popped, and she'd been unable to breathe. The pressure on her chest had been so intense she'd passed out, but at least she wasn't dead. She didn't seem to have any broken bones either, but she could still have a concussion.

She reached for her cellphone, but it was no longer in her back pocket. Nor could she find it when she searched the ground around her.

So much for calling 911.

When her head stopped spinning, she slowly pushed to her feet. Her denim jacket and jeans were dirty, and her shirt had a small tear in the side. She was also missing one earring and her locket. The earring wasn't valuable. She'd bought it in Odessa yesterday, but the necklace was her strongest connection to Mary. Even if Jeff's theory was a bit whack-a-doodle, she'd hate to lose a family heirloom.

The house to her left looked like a restored version of the Tillman farmhouse, and the storm cellar was in a similar location. It was even missing a door—only it wasn't old or overgrown with weeds.

A quiver started in the pit of Selena's stomach and worked its way up her spine. If she were no longer on Tillman land, then she shouldn't have the exact same view of the Davis Mountains behind a house that looked like hers, only restored. There was even a guesthouse fifty or sixty yards away, located the same distance from this house as the pile of rubble she'd seen behind the creek bed at the Tillman house. The only difference between the landscape here and the landscape at the old Tillman house was the creek. This one had a steadily flowing stream within its narrow banks.

It was an eerie coincidence, nothing more. The tornado must have carried her beyond its path of destruction because this house was relatively undamaged. Aside from the missing storm cellar door, it didn't look as if there'd been a storm here today. Even the roof was undamaged, but oddly enough, it didn't have a vent pipe.

How can a house have plumbing without a vent pipe?

There weren't any power lines or utility poles overhead either, and Selena could no longer hear the sounds of traffic in the distance. Then again, the tornado had probably carried her away from the interstate, and the power lines were most likely buried. It didn't matter. Even if the house didn't have electricity or a landline, the owners were bound to own a cell phone.

Pushing crazier thoughts aside, Selena strode across the yard, but as she climbed the undamaged steps to the porch, her legs began to tremble. If she'd seen a bloodstain, she would have freaked. Yet even without the stain, she knew this was Mary's porch. She'd been seeing it in her dreams for years.

Impossible. This couldn't be Mary's house, but knowing that didn't stop the fear from coiling in Selena's gut when she knocked on the door. No one answered, but as she turned to leave, the eerie screech of creaking hinges drew her attention. When she turned back around, the front door stood ajar.

Selena took a shaky breath. "Hello?"

Silence greeted her.

"Is anybody home?" She poked her head inside, and a nudge from behind sent her stumbling over the threshold.

She yelped and caught her balance before spinning around to face her attacker, but no one was there. She was alone in the house—a house she'd been in before. The foundation wasn't sagging, and there were no holes in the roof, but it was the same

11

house—or at least—it had the same layout as the house she'd inherited.

Her heart beat faster, her pulse drumming in her ears as she hesitantly entered the living room. There were no electric lights and no television—just Victorian style furniture that didn't look antique—just eerily familiar.

An overwhelming sense of déjà vu slowed Selena's steps as she walked toward the kitchen, praying someone would grab her and demand to know what she was doing in their home, but no one did. Like the rest of the house, the kitchen looked familiar. There was even a woodstove in the kitchen like the one she'd seen in Mary's house. Only this stove didn't produce ghostly images when she touched it.

"This is still the twenty-first century, and this isn't Mary's house." To believe otherwise was crazy, and she wasn't crazy. Concussed maybe, from a blow to the head, but *not* crazy. So, there had to be a rational explanation.

Trying to control her rising panic, Selena closed her eyes and took deep breaths—in for two out for two. She was a third shift x-ray technologist at a level three-trauma center in Richmond. She didn't panic. By keeping calm, she could provide the doctors with diagnostic quality images, even under less than ideal circumstances. She could handle a crisis, and this was definitely a crisis. She just needed to stay calm and think.

A quick search of the premises didn't reveal a phone or electricity. There wasn't even an indoor toilet. There was a small metal bathtub in a hall closet, but the only sink was in the kitchen, and it had an iron hand pump and no hot, running water.

In one of the bedrooms, she found Victorian era dresses and old-fashioned underwear. In the other bedroom, a picture of Mary sat on the dresser. It wasn't old and faded like the one in Selena's locket, and in a drawer beneath the frame, she found a stack of cash. The bills were unbelievably crisp with dates predating her existence by more than a hundred and twenty years.

Her mind raced as fast as her pulse. Captain Casey hadn't murdered Mary. No one had. A tornado killed her, and Selena had witnessed it in real time. Somehow, a phantom storm from the 1870's had jumped forward in time to pull Selena into its swirling vortex before ejecting her into the past. Maybe it had taken Mary forward in time—or perhaps Mary's body had been lying undiscovered in the desert or some rocky crevice in Limpia Canyon for the last century and a half. Either way, it proved Captain Casey was innocent of murder.

No wonder the Tillman house was haunted—a violent death and an innocent man murdered for a crime he didn't commit. Jeff had been right all along. Mary's spirit was attached to the locket. But that didn't explain the tornado—unless Mary's ghost had somehow been responsible for that as well.

Yet, even if Mary had found a way to send Selena back in time, Selena couldn't clear Captain Casey's name. It wasn't as if she could march into town and announce she was from the future and had witnessed Mary's death while time-traveling on a tornado. They'd lock her up in some nineteenth-century insane asylum, and she'd never find her way home. Then again, if time travel was a supernatural phenomenon she couldn't duplicate, she couldn't go home, and she had no idea how she'd survive.

In this century, she had no friends, no family, and no place to go. She was knowledgeable of the past but ill equipped to live in it, and her only job skill was in a field of medicine that didn't yet exist. The German scientist, Wilhelm Conrad Roentgen, wouldn't discover x-rays until 1895, so she was definitely out of the current job market. Unless of course, she was on a historic farm, and the real world was just outside her door waiting for her to stop acting crazy.

She didn't have a phone or a car, but there were horses in the corral, and she knew how to ride. She'd just saddle up a horse, ride into town, and find a phone. Then she'd take a cab or an Uber back to the hotel. From there, she'd pack her bags and hop the next plane back to Virginia. But she was sure as hell getting out of Texas.

She'd left her job and apartment in Richmond, and her parents and grandparents were dead, but she still had family in Fredericksburg, Virginia. Besides Uncle Robbie, Aunt Jane, and Jeff, she had Uncle Pete, his wife, Carol, and their two sons, Lance and Larry. Jeff was the only one who was still single, but one of her relatives would let her stay with them until she found another job and a place to live. She'd even go back on third shift if she had to. She just wanted her life back.

Lilly Gayle

With a new and saner plan in mind, Selena opened the front door—and came face to face with the living legend of her childhood fantasies.

Chapter 3

Selena yelped, and her legs nearly buckled. The man standing on the porch was tall and broad shouldered with longish black hair, high cheekbones, and a strong square jaw. He looked Native American, but his eyes attested to the fact he wasn't full blooded. They were a piercing blue.

"Ma'am," said the man standing next to the Native American. Until he spoke, Selena hadn't even noticed him.

He was shorter and heavier than his companion was and not nearly as good-looking. He wore a blue cavalry uniform with a plumed hat, and a bushy brown mustache covered most of his lower face.

His companion wore a double-breasted red shirt and buckskin britches with a gun holstered to his right leg and a long bladed knife strapped to the left. He didn't need to give his name for Selena to know it was Captain Casey. He'd been haunting her dreams since she was ten.

"Ma'am?" the Cavalry officer said again. "Are you ill?"

Selena shook her head and swallowed bile. Either she'd lost her mind or she really was in the nineteenth century.

"Are you Miss Selena Tillman?"

She nodded, unable to speak.

The cavalry officer smiled and swept the plumed hat from his head. "I'm Major Andrew Davis, and this half-breed is Captain Dylan Casey, an Injun scout for the army."

The room spun. She wasn't dreaming, and she wasn't crazy. Proof she was no longer in her own time stood before her as alive and real as she was. Her legs shook. So did her voice. "I am Selena Tillman, and this is my house. I inherited it, and I have a right to be here."

She just wasn't Mary's first cousin...more like her tenth cousin or second cousin five times removed or something, but for now, this *was* her house, and she wasn't leaving. She had nowhere else to go.

"We're not here to evict you," The major said after a brief pause. "The army is still investigating the disappearance of your cousin, and we've been keeping an eye on the place until your arrival, but your cousin has been gone nearly a year. What took you so long to get here?"

"A year?" Her stomach dropped. If a year had passed since Mary's death, then it was the spring of 1872, and Captain Casey's life was in imminent danger.

"Yes ma'am. We expected you a couple months back, but why did you come here before going to the lawyer's office? The telegram Mr. Dudley sent your father clearly stated that you were to contact his office immediately upon your arrival to legitimize the claim. Were his instructions unclear?"

Selena had never even heard of Mr. Dudley. A deed search of the Tillman house had shown that it passed from Colonel Tillman to Mary and then to Mary's uncle, Ben. Ben then gave the house to his illegitimate daughter, Selena, the ancestor for whom Selena was named. When the first Selena died *en route* to Texas, the home then went to Ben's son, William, who was the first Selena's half-brother and Selena's great, great, great grandfather. Nearly a century later, Selena's father inherited the property.

And he left it to me.

But if this *was* 1872, then the house rightfully belonged to William Tillman. He just didn't know it yet.

Although the first Selena carried her father's name, he'd never officially recognized her as his daughter, so more than a year went by before he learned of her death. Now, Selena was hoping he'd never discover the truth because she needed a home until she could figure out what had happened and why. She also needed a reasonable explanation for her untimely arrival and her disheveled appearance.

"I was on my way to the lawyer's office when my horse threw me and knocked me unconscious." That would explain her dirty clothes and the cut over her eye, but not the delay in her arrival. "I would have been here sooner, but after taking the train from Richmond to Louisville I got sick," she said, recalling that the first Selena died in Louisville. "It was a couple of months before I recovered enough to take the train to...um...Fort Worth.

Then . . . I . . . eh . . . took the stage before buying a horse at the last stage stop. When the horse threw me, I was closer to the house than to town, so I came here to freshen up. That's when y'all got here."

The major beetled his brow. "You rode? By yourself? From Pecos? Why didn't you just take the next stage to Canyon Creek?"

Selena's heart hammered in her chest, and her palms started to sweat. She wiped her hands on her jeans and tried to think of a rational explanation, but her throat felt as if it were closing.

Dear God, she couldn't do this. She couldn't make up enough lies to explain the unexplainable, and the truth wasn't an option. She wasn't even sure of the truth herself. For all she knew, none of this was even real, and she was standing in an abandoned farmhouse having one hell of a hallucination.

It was more than she could bear. Sinking to the floor with her back pressed against the door, she broke down and cried. The major quickly dropped to his haunches and gently pulled her to her feet. Then he tucked her under his arm and guided her into the parlor.

"Come now. It can't be that bad," he said as he lowered her onto the floral, Victorian-style sofa and took his seat beside her. He gave her hands a brief squeeze and then slid over, leaving a respectable distance between them.

Captain Casey entered the room behind them and stood with his arms crossed over his chest. His expression was about as readable as a rock.

Selena hiccupped, and the major handed her a handkerchief. "There, there my dear. You just take your time. "

Captain Casey grunted, making it abundantly clear he wasn't the least bit sympathetic. "If you rode a horse from Pecos, then where is it?"

Selena swiped a tear from her cheek and looked up at his stern, handsome face. "I don't know. I don't know anything right now."

Major Davis glared at the captain before turning back to Selena. "Don't worry, Miss Tillman. It doesn't matter why you got off the stage in Pecos. You're safe now, and we'll find your horse."

"You can't possibly believe this nonsense," Casey groused.

17

Davis' eyes filled with hate before he turned to glare. "Remember your place, Casey, and don't ever speak that way of a white woman again."

Selena looked from one man to the other, feeling as if she'd fallen down the rabbit hole. Major Davis's dislike for Captain Casey was obvious, and the knowledge wasn't lost on the captain. It was evident in the pained expression that briefly flashed across his handsome face before he carefully schooled his features.

Tension crackled the air before the major turned back to Selena. He gave her hand a firm squeeze and then rose to his feet. "Why don't you rest while we look for your horse? Then when you're feeling up to it, I'll escort you to the lawyer's office so you can sign those papers."

"Thank you." Selena stood on shaky legs and faced Captain Casey. She couldn't very well save his life if she antagonized him. "I'm sorry I snapped, but I've been a bit confused since I woke up on the ground with a busted eye."

Casey stepped closer and raked his eyes over her, taking in her disheveled appearance. With surprising gentleness, he swept her hair from her forehead. When his fingers touched her flesh, her breath froze in her lungs, and every muscle in her body coiled. Shocked by the electricity in that brief touch, her knees buckled, and she sank back down to the sofa. When he hunkered down in front of her and took her chin in his strong hand, her breath caught in her throat.

"You really are hurt. What happened?" The deep timbre of his softly spoken question was like the man himself—sexy.

She met his probing gaze before lowering her eyes to the floor. "My horse threw me and ran off. I don't know what spooked him, and I don't know where he is."

Dylan Casey rose to his feet and curled his lip. "Where are your trunks?"

"They're due to arrive from Pecos later this week," she said, unable to meet his gaze.

He grunted. "Why would you leave your trunks in Pecos and travel alone on horseback? Why not wait at the hotel for the next stage to Canyon Creek?"

She was nervous enough without him towering over her, so she rose to her feet and forced herself to hold his intimidating gaze.

"I felt a lot safer taking my chances on the road dressed as a man than I did staying in some skeezy hotel in Pecos where everyone knew I was a woman traveling alone."

It was a reasonable explanation. She was wearing jeans in a time when women didn't even wear slacks, and she had just shown up without taking the stage. He might have actually believed her if it hadn't been for her modern vernacular.

He raked his eyes over her with a quirked mouth and skeptical lift of his brows. "You couldn't fool a blind man in those clothes, and no man would wear an undershirt that color. You even smell like a woman," he added, sniffing the air around her neck. When his nose grazed the tender flesh behind her ear, goose bumps raced down her arms.

"Casey!" the major snapped. "You will keep your distance from white women, or you will suffer the consequences."

Captain Casey took a step back and stood ramrod straight as if standing at attention. The major cleared his throat and turned to Selena. "Don't you fret, now, Miss Tillman. I won't let the same thing happen to you that happened to your cousin, and once we find your horse, I'll escort you into town to sign those papers."

Naturally, they never found any sign of her non-existent horse, but Dylan found the missing earring she'd purchased in Odessa yesterday—more than a hundred and forty years in the future. It defied logic, but somehow, it was true.

She *had* travelled back in time.

Chapter 4

Dylan grunted and tightened the cinch on the Appaloosa's saddle. Major Davis had wanted Miss Tillman to ride in front of him, but she insisted on riding Mary's horse into town. She also refused to change into something more suitable than the odd colored undershirt and dirty denims she wore, but as she'd so aptly pointed out, her trunks were still in Pecos. He just didn't believe her.

"Allow me." Davis nudged Dylan aside and helped Miss Tillman into the saddle. Then he cast a brief, hostile glare in Dylan's direction and added, "And don't you worry about Captain Casey. I'll protect you."

Miss Tillman didn't respond. She didn't even glance in Davis's direction. There was no coy chin duck or fluttering lashes, and the look on Davis' face made Dylan smile. And it had been a long time since he'd actually smiled.

Again today, he and the major had spent the better part of the afternoon fruitlessly searching for clues into Mary's disappearance. Had it been a legitimate search, he wouldn't have been so angry, but his superiors thought he might confess to Davis if they were alone because he and Andy had served together during the war, but he had nothing to confess.

He'd had nothing to do with Mary's disappearance, but it was easier to blame the savage Indian scout than admit a white man may have killed her because she'd been with a half-breed. Yet Mary's fiancé, Lieutenant Walters, wasn't even a suspect.

Dylan ground his teeth and climbed into the saddle. He didn't know why Miss Tillman was lying, but she was definitely lying. Nothing about her story made sense. Even if she'd felt unsafe at the hotel, it was safer than traveling alone. She wasn't even armed. Maybe if she'd had a gun or even a knife in her boot, he would have believed her, but her jeans and that shirt hugged every luscious curve of her lean body, and she damn sure wasn't hiding a weapon in her jacket. Even that was snug fitting.

Hell, for all he knew, she was lying about her identity. Even if she weren't, she was lying about something, and he was damn sure going to find out what it was.

As they made the half-hour trip into Canyon Creek, Andy would occasionally remark on the landscape, but otherwise, they travelled in silence. Miss Tillman kept her eyes open and her mouth shut, but as they neared town, she became increasingly agitated.

Dylan rode up beside her and cast a sideways glance in her direction. Color drained from her cheeks, and a thin film of perspiration beaded her brow. If she was lying about her identity, the attorney would discover her duplicity, and she'd be out on her ass. Maybe then, she'd tell the truth.

As they passed Holloway's Dry Goods and Peterson's Mercantile, Miss Tillman began to visibly shake, and when Andy helped her dismount, her knees buckled.

Andy grasped her elbow to steady her. "You must be exhausted after sitting a saddle for so long, but don't worry. This won't take long, and then I'll escort you home."

Miss Tillman nodded but said nothing. Andy cast a warning glance in Dylan's direction and guided Miss Tillman into the lawyer's office. Dylan followed them inside and stood at attention when a tall, thin man with dark, slicked-back hair rose from behind a desk and shook Andy's hand. "Ralph Rawlings, at your service. I'm Mr. Dudley's secretary."

Andy nodded and released his hand. "Major Andrew Davis, and this is Colonel Tillman's niece, Miss Selena Tillman."

Mr. Rawlings ignored Dylan and cast Miss Tillman a dubious look. "Have a seat. I'll let Mr. Dudley know you're here."

Miss Tillman sat on a leather couch next to Andy while Dylan remained standing. She shifted in her seat, looking everywhere but at him. Mr. Dudley cast another disapproving glare in Dylan's direction and left the room.

Dylan knew he wasn't welcome in the lawyer's office, but he'd been ordered not to leave Andy's side. He was still a suspect in Mary's disappearance, and his superiors feared he'd run off before telling anyone what he'd done with the body. If not for Colonel Harper, Andy would have arrested him already, but even without a body, it was just a matter of time.

His fingers curled into his palms as the old, familiar rage bubbled beneath the surface, threatening his self-control. Feeling like a caged lion, he began to pace, until he caught Miss Tillman watching him from beneath lowered lashes.

Her silky blonde hair fell forward, hiding her face, but he'd already memorized it. Her fair skin was flawless, her lips full. Except for the color of her eyes, she looked nothing like Mary.

When Miss Tillman caught him staring, her cheeks flushed. She shifted on the sofa, her eyes straying to the calendar on the wall. Her breathing hitched, and the color drained from her face.

"What's today's date?" Her voice trembled.

Dylan narrowed his gaze. "March seventeenth. Why? You got another appointment?"

She shook her head and said nothing, but her storm-gray eyes were wide and glassy, as if she were about to cry. Then she clenched her hands together in her lap, and Dylan was more convinced than ever that Miss Tillman was an imposter.

#

Selena bit her lip to stop it from trembling. The calendar was proof she'd travelled back in time. It was the only explanation. She refused to entertain the possibility she was crazy for a minute longer, which meant she'd been sent back in time for a reason, possibly to save Dylan's life.

Besides her ancestor's restless spirit and Dylan himself, she was the only person who knew he hadn't kill Mary. In order to save him, she'd have to prove his innocence without revealing she'd come from the future. If she didn't, someone would murder him on the anniversary of Mary's death, which gave her two weeks to save his life. Then maybe after she saved him, she could find a way back to her own time.

Her gaze roamed over the granite hardness of his firm jaw and deep-set eyes. Tension knotted her stomach, and it was several minutes before her heart rate slowed to a normal rhythm. Then Mr. Rawlings came back into the room and led her and Major Davis into an inner office, leaving Dylan alone in the waiting room.

The lawyer rose to his feet when she entered, but his smile was disingenuous. "Miss Tillman, please be seated."

Once she and the major sat, the lawyer spouted some legal

jargon and shoved a stack of papers across the desk for her to sign. Then he handed her an envelope containing two hundred dollars in cash. It was old but new-looking currency.

The lawyer cleared his throat and curled his thin lips. "Now, if your cousin turns up at any time during the next six years, she has the legal right to reclaim her property. Colonel Tillman's estate didn't go to his brother, Ben, until after Mary was presumed dead. As Ben Tillman's illegitimate daughter, he is giving you the house and a two hundred dollar-a-year allowance for the next ten years, which more than fulfills any familial obligation he might have. He expressly stated that you are entitled to nothing more either now or upon his death. Is that understood?"

Selena wasn't concerned about the legalities, but at least she now understood the lawyer and his secretary's derisive attitudes. They thought she was a bastard and a moneygrubber. She clenched her hands in her lap, trying to still her trembling nerves.

"I understand perfectly." Too perfectly. If anyone found out she wasn't Ben Tillman's illegitimate daughter, she'd go to jail—a nineteenth century jail.

After signing the last paper, the major escorted her to the bank across the street while Dylan remained outside. There, a middle-aged man with thinning hair and round, wire-rimmed glasses handed her some forms so she could open a bank account.

"You'll need to date and sign all four pages." He slid a small black bottle and steel-nib pen through an opening in the teller's window.

Selena reached for it with a trembling hand. It wasn't a ballpoint. They didn't exist. Nothing she relied on in her daily life existed. Her pulse raced, and she was on the verge of hyperventilating.

"Do you need help filling out the forms?" The major's question prevented an all-out meltdown.

She took a deep breath and let it out slowly. She had to get her shit together. "I'm good. Thanks."

She dipped the nib of the pen into the inkwell without a problem, but stopping her hand from shaking was impossible. Except for her name, she answered every question with a lie. But if she confessed the actual year of her birth, no one would believe her.

With a stress-releasing sigh, she signed the papers and handed them back to the teller along with the two hundred dollar advance on her annual allowance. Since she had no idea what the value of a dollar was in the nineteenth century, she didn't deposit the two hundred dollars she'd found in the colonel's bedroom.

"One more stop." Major Davis took her elbow once more and led her from the bank.

As they walked passed Dylan, Selena made eye contact but said nothing. He straightened and stepped away from the post he'd been leaning against to follow them inside the sheriff's office next door.

"'Bout time you showed up, Miss Tillman," the sheriff said after Major Davis made the introductions.

Wilbur Hobbs was an overweight man of about fifty who stood when Selena entered the room. He quickly returned to his seat and leaned back in his chair. "I'm real sorry 'bout your cousin, but you mark my word, her body will turn up one day, and when it does, we'll get the man what done it to her."

"There's no proof she was murdered," Selena said, hoping now was her chance to clear Dylan's name. "If you searched the property, I'm sure you'd find—"

"Miss Tillman," the major interrupted, "the army did a thorough search for your cousin and turned up nothing." He cast a sliding glance at Dylan who appeared restless.

"We searched too," Hobbs added as he leaned forward on his elbows. "Didn't find nothing. Not a trace, but that don't mean you're in danger. We'll find the man who killed your cousin."

"I'm telling you, she wasn't murdered," Selena insisted. "There was a tornado and—"

"Where are you getting your information, Miss Tillman?" Major Davis cut her off midsentence. "You just got here. Or did you arrive earlier in the week?"

His suspicious gaze set her pulse to pounding. She couldn't tell the truth, but the more lies she told, the harder it would be to keep track, so she opted for sarcasm. "Don't you think I would have changed out of my dirty trail clothes if I'd been here any length of time?"

The major regarded her with suspicious eyes but said nothing. When Selena dared a glance in Dylan's direction, he appeared amused. The sheriff just looked uncomfortable. He cleared his throat. "Well, I reckon you ought to send a telegram to your pa then. Let him know you finally got here."

Her father was dead. But Ben Tillman wasn't. *Shit!* She never had been a good liar. If she was the Selena Tillman they were expecting, then her father was alive and well.

"Miss Tillman?" the sheriff said when she didn't immediately respond. "You want to send your pa that telegram now?"

"Of course." Her voice shook. So did her knees. Perhaps a telegram was all Ben Tillman needed to convince him his daughter had arrived in Texas. Then he wouldn't send his son, William, to look for her. And if William never went looking for his real sister, he might never learn of the first Selena Tillman's fate.

Selena sighed. She was safe for the moment, but she still needed to figure out how to save Dylan. Maybe then, whatever cosmic power had sent her here would send her back to her own time.

"Then it's settled." Major Davis took her elbow once more. "If the sheriff has nothing to add, I'll escort you to the telegraph office and then back to your new home."

"Thank you." She was grateful for the offer since she didn't know her way back, but she needed to convince the sheriff that Mary wasn't murdered. "Now about Mary—"

"There's no need to worry." The major firmed his grip on her elbow but spoke in a soothing voice, while casting an accusing glance at Dylan. "Since your cousin's murder, we've increased our patrols, and the army is not about to let another dirty savage harm any more white women."

As politely as possible, Selena extracted her elbow from the major's grasp and cast a glance in Dylan's direction. His jaw was so tightly clenched it was a wonder she didn't hear his teeth crack.

"I appreciate your concern, major, but I seriously doubt a war party is going to invade Canyon Creek." There'd been no historical documentation of an Indian attack in the area, so she felt relatively safe. "As for my cousin, she wasn't murdered. The tornado killed her."

Major Davis clicked his tongue against the roof of his mouth. "Don't be so naive, Miss Tillman. Your cousin was

25

murdered. Texas isn't Virginia. Out here, the Comanche and Apache have been known to brutally butcher young women such as yourself without provocation. Why, before we built the Fort to protect innocent whites from their kind, no one was safe from their bloodthirsty savagery."

"Are we not just as savage? The white man has been a threat to the Native Americans' way of life since we set foot on Roanoke Island. They're just defending their land and freedom. It's no different than when we fought the British." Of course, the land for which America fought had also belonged to the native people, but Selena didn't think the major would appreciate the irony.

His eyes nearly bugged out of his head. "Surely, you're not one of those misinformed people from back East with romantic notions about educating these savages so they can live peacefully among the whites. Are you, Miss Tillman?"

"I'm neither misinformed nor much of a romantic. I just haven't let unquestioning loyalty to *my* people blind me to the fact that it is the white man and not the Native Americans who started these hostilities. Nor do I believe in judging a person by the color of his or her skin. So, I think it unfair that everyone assumes—"

"Just where do you get your notions about, us, 'Native Americans'?" Dylan interrupted, speaking for the first time since entering the sheriff's office.

She refused to let him distract her. She had to convince them that neither Dylan nor any other Native American killed Mary, but before she could say anything else, the bell over the sheriff's door jangled, and a Hispanic woman entered the office.

The sheriff stood but quickly resumed his seat. Dylan inclined his dark head in her direction, but the insufferable Major Davis barely acknowledged the woman. With an irritated huff, he slapped his military hat back on his fuzzy brown head and turned to Selena.

"Miss Tillman," he acknowledged with growing disrespect for what she was sure he saw as her lack of feminine virtue. "If you'll excuse us, we must get back to the fort. Captain, mount up."

Selena's pulse jumped. He was supposed to escort her back to the farm. She wasn't just a stranger to Texas; she was a stranger to this century. She'd need road signs or GPS to get back, and they didn't exist yet. She was also used to 911, the highway patrol, and car doors with automatic locks. And horses didn't have doors. If hostile Indians or outlaws did attack, she was as good as dead.

Just as she was beginning to despair, Dylan stepped forward and whispered in her ear. "Don't worry. Anita and her husband will escort you back to the farm." He nodded toward the Hispanic woman talking to the sheriff. "Anita was your cousin's housekeeper, and she won't desert you—unless you want to get rid of her for some reason."

Despite the spike in her pulse his nearness caused and the brief surge of relief she felt knowing she wouldn't have to find her way back to the farm alone, the suspicion in his voice hurt. She raised her chin, meeting his intense gaze. "Thank you for relieving my mind."

"Don't be too relieved," he said with a snort. "The major might be satisfied with your answers, but I'm not. I'll be over in a day or two with more questions. You can count on it."

He turned away and after speaking briefly with the woman he called Anita, he cast one long last look in her direction and left without another word. With his departure, fear closed in around Selena, but before panic set in and she totally lost her shit, the sheriff introduced her to Anita Sanchez.

"I have been the Tillman's housekeeper and cook for years," she said in accented English. "We live in the old slave quarters behind the house. *Mi esposo*, Alberto, worked for the colonel as well, farming the land and caring for the horses." She glanced at the sheriff and then looked to Selena with imploring eyes. "We would like to stay, and it would be our pleasure to serve you as well."

From the desperate tone of her offer, Selena couldn't have turned her down had she wanted to, and there was no chance of that. She didn't know how to do any of the things people in this century took for granted, and maybe with Anita and Alberto's help, she could find a way to prove Dylan's innocence.

Chapter 5

Selena followed Alberto and Anita back to the house. After Alberto tied the horses to a hitching post out front, he followed the women inside.

"You must be hungry, no?" Anita said, turning to Selena.

Selena's stomach rumbled, but she wasn't sure if it was from hunger or nerves. "I suppose."

"*Mi esposo*, he speak little English. Do you speak *Español*?"

Selena smiled. It felt wobbly. So did her knees. "People seem to think I should, but my name is actually Greek."

The older woman spoke to her husband in Spanish and then turned back to Selena. "While I prepare your supper, Alberto will heat water for your bath. Then he will take care of the animals."

The water closet was a small room off the kitchen, and despite the language barrier, Alberto was able to show her how to pump water into the tub before adding hot water heated from the stove. When he left, Selena stepped into the tub and hurriedly bathed in the tepid water. Then she dressed in one of Mary's old gowns. When she walked into the kitchen, there was just one plate on the table.

A soul deep fear penetrated her bones. "Aren't you and Alberto eating with me?"

"We will eat at home," Anita said with a smile. Then she cleaned the kitchen while Selena picked at her food, but she no longer had an appetite.

"You look *fatigado*—tired," Anita said when Selena carried her plate to the sink. "You should go to bed. I will return in the morning to cook your breakfast."

Selena nodded, but her throat burned as Anita walked out the door, leaving her alone with her fears.

#

Selena awoke the next morning, stiff and sore, feeling as if she'd spent the entire night x-raying trauma patients and pushing a portable x-ray machine. Then she opened her eyes and nearly choked on a yawn. She wasn't in a hotel room in Odessa, and she wasn't in her apartment in Richmond. She was in her ancestor's bed, more than a hundred years before she was even born.

With a terrified cry, she pulled the covers over her head and prayed she was still dreaming, but it didn't change anything. Life went on no matter the century, and she needed to get on with hers. It didn't matter if time travel was logical or not. This was her reality now, and hiding from the truth was no more possible than going home. She just needed to get up, get dressed, and try to hold onto her sanity.

Mary had a wardrobe filled with clothes that looked as if they would fit, but Selena didn't know what to do about underwear. She couldn't wear the same bra and panties every day. She probably shouldn't wear her own underwear ever again—not in this century. Until she figured out what to do with them, she stuffed them under the mattress. Then she dressed in a sleeveless chemise, a camisole, and a pair of drawstring bloomers.

She liked the idea of not wearing a bra, but the drawers with the split leggings that hung to the knee and tied at the waist leaving the crotch seam open, were the damnedest things she'd ever seen. She was just thankful she fit into Mary's clothes without a corset since she didn't know how to put one on and wouldn't wear it if she did.

Once she tackled the underwear dilemma, she found a brown skirt and white blouse that weren't too ugly or uncomfortable, but Mary's shoes were two sizes too small. Thankfully, she'd been wearing her cowboy boots when the tornado took her. If she'd been wearing her multi-colored neon kicks, she would have had to burn them with her underwear. They would have drawn more attention than her teal tee.

The zipper in her jeans might go unnoticed, so she dropped

29

them and her denim jacket on the floor until she could ask Anita how to wash them. She seriously doubted the ringer washing machine had been invented yet. Even if it had been, she wouldn't know how to use it. She didn't know how to do much of anything in this century, but that was about to change.

Selena spent Saturday learning her way around a nineteenth century kitchen. In the absence of refrigeration, dairy products and other perishables were kept in the storm cellar or the cool pantry, a small room with a tiny screen window above the shelves that allowed heat to rise and cooler air to enter. Fruits and vegetables not stored in the storm cellar were canned or pickled, and meat other than poultry was salted or dried. Floors were swept, rugs were beaten, and the entire day was spent cooking and cleaning.

That night, Selena fell into bed, drained and exhausted, but sleep eluded her. She thought of her friends and family—people she might never see again—and she could barely contain the tears. She worried about her sanity and saving Dylan if she wasn't insane, and she didn't get to sleep until dawn.

Sunday was a day of rest, and Anita's day off, so Selena spent most of the day in bed. Anita had warned her that Monday was washday, and for the first time in years, Selena looked forward to Monday morning and the distraction physical labor would bring.

The time-consuming, labor-intensive process began at dawn, and despite Anita's objections, Selena insisted on helping. "You just have to show me what to do."

After stripping the sheets from the beds in both Selena's house and Anita's, they gathered the rest of the laundry. Anita placed most of the outer garments in a basket to be brushed or spot cleaned. She put Alberto's dirtiest work pants, the most soiled shirts and blouses, and the towels in another basket. In a third basket, they collected what Anita called body linens, which turned out to be chemises, petticoats, camisoles, and undergarments.

"Did you not help your mother with the laundry when you were younger, or did you have servants?" Anita asked as they carried the laundry baskets outside.

Selena didn't want to lie, but the truth was definitely off the table. "Um, it's been a long time since I helped my mother with the wash, and I, um, used a laundry service when I lived alone in Richmond."

Anita frowned, her eyes barely visible over the mound of clothes in her basket. "It is not good for a young girl to live alone. You are lucky to have me and Alberto to take care of you now."

"Trust me," Selena said, "you don't know the half of it. Now, show me what to do."

While they'd been gathering the clothes, Alberto had hauled two wooden tubs and a larger copper pot into the yard. He filled the wooden tubs with water and placed them on a bench. Then he lit a fire under the copper tub and left the women to their work.

Anita added lye soap and soda to the copper tub and threw all the whites into the water to boil. Then the two of them began the process of washing the rest of the clothes.

In the first wooden tub, Anita soaped and scrubbed a shirt on a washboard, twisting and turning it and scrubbing some more. Then she wrung it out and dropped it in the rinse tub where Selena dunked and twisted the shirt repeatedly to get out the soap. By the time she'd wrung it out and hung it on the line, Anita had dropped two more articles of clothing into the rinse tub.

Nodding to the water Anita said, "Everything must be rinsed in clean water. You do not want to wear lye-soaked clothing. So we will have to change the water soon. It is starting to turn gray."

Selena groaned, and Anita smiled. "And tonight, I will show you how to iron."

The day dragged on, and by midafternoon, Selena was aching in muscles she didn't know she had. She stood erect and arched her back, trying to work out a kink. "Man, this sucks. I thought I hated doing laundry before, but this is a beast."

Anita gave her the side-eye as she picked up a large paddle and removed a couple of items from the boiling water and dropped them into the first wooden washtub. Then she began the washing process all over again. Selena groaned and hunched over the second tub to start the rinsing process anew.

As Anita was scrubbing a ruffled petticoat, a horse cantered into the front yard. She paused, looking toward the front of the house. Selena wiped her hands on her skirt and stretched. "I'll go see who it is. I need a break anyway."

Worry lines creased Anita's brow. "Remember, Alberto has

31

gone into town." She reached for the paddle she'd used to remove the whites from the boiling water and held it aloft. "I am just a holler away. You need me, you call."

Selena nodded, praying she wouldn't need rescuing. "Yes ma'am."

Instead of walking around the house, she cut through the kitchen, grabbed a knife sitting on the cutting board, and slipped it into her skirt pocket. When she opened the front door and saw Dylan, her heart did somersaults.

He crossed the yard with an easy swagger that made her breathless with feminine appreciation. As he stepped onto the porch, his buckskins hugging his muscled thighs, her heart fluttered. "Hi."

Instead of answering, he brushed by her without a word and entered the house. His rudeness was unexpected, and it pissed her off, but this could be her only chance to save him. So she followed him inside and closed the door.

"Look, I know we got off to a bad start, but can't we move forward and maybe be friends?"

His eyes widened before his brows came together in a fierce scowl. "We can't be friends. I'm a half-breed, a violent savage, and your cousin is missing. For all you know, I abducted her and then scalped her. What makes you think I won't do the same to you?"

At the mention of scalping, a soul deep chill penetrated her bones. She hugged herself, trying to suppress the mental image of someone flaying Dylan's beautiful hair from his scalp.

His chiseled features hardened. "Relax. I didn't kill your cousin, and I won't scalp you. I'm here on official business."

Her cheeks burned. She wasn't afraid *of* him. She was afraid *for* him. She just couldn't say why, so she didn't even try.

"We can talk in the parlor," she said instead, and Dylan followed her into the room.

She sat on the sofa and demurely clasped her hands together in her lap. Despite her work-dampened skirt and the sweat rings under her arms, she felt very proper seated in the parlor wearing her green and white day dress—until she remembered she wasn't wearing shoes. She hadn't wanted to get her boots wet.

As Dylan sat in one of the mauve armchairs flanking the

sofa, he looked at her bare toes peeking out from beneath her skirt and arched his brows. Her face flushed.

"I wasn't expecting company," she said, wiggling her toes. Then she pulled the knife from her pocket and placed it on the table so she wouldn't accidently stab herself in the thigh.

His mouth twitched just before he threw back his head and laughed. The rich, rumbling sound warmed her heart. Her shoulders relaxed. "You should laugh more often. You don't look quite as fierce when your eyes crinkle up at the corners like that."

"You mean, savage, don't you?" The moment was gone. With his laughter still echoing in the room, the hardened expression returned.

His bitterness stung. "I meant no such thing. So, don't go putting words in my mouth."

He crossed one ankle over his knee and studied her in silence, as if she were an insect pinned to a block of wax.

She huffed out an impatient breath. She couldn't save his life if they couldn't even have a civil conversation, but his eyes could drag a confession from a priest, and no one in their right mind would believe her revelations. So she just sat there, staring at his handsome face, trying to discern dream from reality.

"You're a brash one, Miss Tillman, and you've got guts," he said at last. "But how far would you go to get what you want?"

He couldn't possibly know what she wanted. Even if she told him, he wouldn't believe her. "Why are you deliberately trying to bait me? Is it because of Mary? Does my being here reinforce your fears that she's never coming back?"

Her heart lurched just a bit, knowing he'd loved Mary and never had a chance to grieve. He'd spent the year prior to his murder trying to find her body and prove his innocence. Sympathy tugged at her heart. "I know you loved her, but she's gone."

"Love!" The unexpected rancor in his voice made her jump.

He stood slowly and clinched his fists at his side. Then he started to pace. After just a few steps, he turned to glare. "Your cousin didn't know the meaning of the word. Yes, we were involved, but she would never have married me. I should have known better, but I didn't kill her. I'm trying to find her before I'm hanged for a crime I didn't commit."

He was more than angry, and it went beyond proving his innocence. His pain was almost tangible. He might no longer love Mary, but he'd loved her once, and she'd hurt him deeply, as only a loved one could.

Selena sighed, forcing aside a confusing mix of emotions. Dylan had given her an opening, and this might be her only chance to save his life. She stood. "Why does everyone believe she was murdered? Was there evidence to suggest foul play? If not, then it's time to look at other possibilities. There was a tornado the day she disappeared."

He glared. "What's your point?"

"That doesn't strike you as more than a possible coincidence?"

"I don't believe in coincidences."

"Listen," she said, touching the sleeve of his blue flannel shirt. "I did some looking around after I got here, and I don't think Mary was murdered."

He glanced sharply at the hand resting on his arm until she lowered it. Her pulse hitched at the unexpected disappointment, but she took advantage of his momentary silence and continued.

"If she was murdered, then what was the motive, and where's the body? There was a tornado that day. Anita and Alberto were in town, and they took shelter in the livery stable. When they returned to the farm, the roof and storm cellar were damaged, and Mary was missing. Alberto fixed the roof, but he never found the storm cellar door, and no one's seen Mary since."

"That proves nothing," Dylan said with a shrug of his wide shoulders. Despite the disinterest in his tone, his posture was tense. Alert.

Selena leaned closer but kept her hands to herself. "So, I checked it out myself. The cellar door has a double sliding bolt. It didn't open itself, and the wind didn't blow it open. That means someone tried to get inside, and Anita and Albert weren't here. So, it had to have been Mary."

A vision of her terrified expression moments before the tornado pulled her into its vortex flashed in Selena's mind. She shut it out, concentrating on Dylan's face. "Don't you see? She was here alone when the storm hit. She ran to the cellar, but she never made it inside because the tornado got her. It took her and

34

the cellar door, and that's why they're both still missing."

A smirk raised one corner of Dylan's mouth. "Tornadoes don't hide their victim's bodies, Miss Tillman. Murderers do."

They might not hide them exactly, but they could dump them in places no one would ever find them. Selena had been the victim of a tornado, and she was damned certain no one in the twenty-first century was ever going to find her—not that she could tell him that. He'd never listen to her if he thought she was crazy.

"I've heard of tornadoes destroying one house and not touching the one right next to it. They can suck a cradle into the sky and drop it back to earth a mile away without harming a hair on the baby's head, and people go missing after storms all the time. Don't you think Mary could have been one of those people?"

Dylan grunted and turned his back on her as if he was about to leave. She touched his arm again and pulled on it until he faced her.

"What if I'm right? What if a tornado picked Mary up and hurled her back to earth several miles from here? Her body could be in the top of a tree or in the middle of the desert. Maybe it's wedged in a crevice in Limpia Canyon. It could be anywhere, but wherever she is, neither you nor anyone else is going to find her until you follow the tornado's path of destruction."

She hadn't meant to shout, but she was angry and frustrated. Without realizing it, she'd all but gotten up in his face, and he didn't seem to like it. His eyes burned and tension tautened his muscles. She couldn't tell if was angry or…

No way!

Her pulse jumped at the heat she saw in his steady gaze, sending white-hot desire rushing through her veins. Dear Lord, she was lusting after a man she'd dreamed of all her life—a man long dead in her own time—a man she didn't even know.

Knowing she had to calm her riotous pulse, she stepped back and took a deep breath. Before she could release it, Dylan reached out and pulled her into his arms. Taking advantage of her surprised gasp, he lowered his head and slanted his mouth across her parted lips.

His tongue stroked and caressed, coaxing her to respond as he pulled her closer and tunneled his left hand beneath her hair to hold her head in place. While he deepened the kiss, his right hand slid down her body, leaving a trail of heat all the way to the base of her spine. His left hand soon followed. Then he gripped the curve of her buttocks and pulled her hard against his hips.

Her body flamed, and her muscles tautened in anticipation of what would be the greatest orgasm of her life if she allowed him to do what they both wanted. And oh, how she was tempted. She'd dreamed of him most of her life, and now she had the chance to see if dreams came true or simply led to unrealistic expectations.

Heat pooled between her thighs, the throbbing pressure, making her ache—making her moan. Then Dylan slid his hand beneath the curve of her buttocks to touch her from behind, and she nearly climaxed. Even through layers of cloth, she felt the pressure of his probing fingers, and she wanted him inside of her. Deep. Hard.

Pulsing with need, she frantically moved her hands across his hard body, feeling the tightly corded muscles in his back and biceps. He was as solidly built as a weightlifter, but no workout on earth could have more perfectly sculpted a man's body, and she had no doubt he was well built in other areas too. She could feel the heat and length of him pressing against her, and she wanted him more than any man she'd ever met. The realization that he also wanted her was heady, but they were strangers. And she'd rather have his trust.

Dropping her hands to her sides, she reluctantly stepped out of his embrace.

"What's the matter?" he panted, making no effort to touch her again. "Did you finally realize it was a dirty savage making you wet?"

Reality washed over her, dousing her desire. Dylan wasn't desperate to make love to her. He was just horny, and by Victorian standards, she'd all but thrown herself at him with her light touches and direct gazes. She wasn't blaming him for making a move. She'd actually enjoyed it better than any make-out session she'd ever had, but she wasn't about to have wild animal sex with him in the living room when Anita could come into the house at any minute.

She rolled her eyes. "Don't be crude. The color of your skin had nothing to do with my second-guessing the wisdom of having sex with a stranger. It was common sense and self-respect.

Did you really think I was going to jump in the sack with you because you're gorgeous? Think again."

"Who the hell are you?" His eyes narrowed. "You claim to be Ben Tillman's illegitimate daughter from Virginia, but you don't act like any woman I've ever met from Virginia or anywhere else." Confusion colored his expression before he quickly masked his emotions. "I know you're hiding something, and I intend to find out what it is."

The intensity of his gaze sent a shiver down her spine. Captain Dylan Casey might be innocent of Mary Tillman's murder, but that didn't mean he wasn't dangerous. "Whatever secrets I may or may not be keeping are my own. Did you really think you could seduce information from me?"

Color suffused his cheeks as he lowered his gaze, sending Selena's heart into her stomach. He hadn't kissed her because he was overcome by sexual attraction. He'd wanted to use her.

The realization hurt. She might have dreamt of him for most of her life, but she didn't know him—not the real flesh and bones man. She'd grown up believing him a misunderstood victim of circumstance, but he was just a bitter man with a chip on his shoulder.

Disappointment twisted her stomach into a tight knot. She felt betrayed, but that was her problem. Not his. Holding her childhood fantasies against him wasn't fair. He might be the man she'd dreamt about, but that didn't mean he was the man of her dreams.

"I didn't lie to you about my name," she said at last.

"But you have lied. We both know it. You're no different from your cousin, Mary, in that regard. She also claimed my being a half-breed wasn't important, but when it came right down to it, she was no different from any other white woman. Your kind is all the same."

"And what kind is that, Dylan?" she asked, maintaining eye contact.

Her use of his given name startled him for only a second. "Prove you're different from Mary. Be my guest for the spring gala in town Saturday night. Show me you don't care what color I am," he challenged.

He expected her to refuse his invitation, thus proving him

right. But she had another agenda. She wanted to keep him safe. If she didn't, he'd be dead a week from Sunday.

She smiled. "What time are you picking me up?"

His eyes widened a second before he narrowed his gaze and took a step back, eyeing her from head to toe. His gaze lingered so long on her breasts, she felt exposed, but she resisted the urge to cross her arms over her chest. Since he intended to make her uncomfortable, she wouldn't give him the satisfaction of knowing he'd succeeded.

A smile stretched his handsome mouth, but it didn't reach his eyes. "Sorry, but I won't be picking you up. I'm with the ninth cavalry, and my unit is first on patrol. We won't get back in until early afternoon." His smile broadened. "But if you show up at the town square around one, I'll be a most attentive escort."

"Then, it's a date." Did he really expect her to shy away from a challenge? "I'm sure Alberto and Anita will be happy to escort me."

Chapter 6

The morning of the spring gala, Selena dressed in a blue gingham dress and matching spoon bonnet hat. She didn't normally wear hats, but she didn't normally ride in the back of a buckboard wagon or go without sunscreen either. The hat protected her face from the sun, and Alberto had spread a blanket in the back of the wagon to make the women more comfortable. The hat helped. The blanket didn't.

If there was a pothole in the road, Alberto hit it, and Anita didn't seem to notice. As they bumped along on a road that was little more than a narrow, rutted path, she talked about the history of Canyon Creek and the spring gala.

The town held the first spring gala at the start of the Civil War to show their appreciation to the soldiers. The next year, the troops abandoned the fort, and the Apache laid siege to it, burning most of the buildings to the ground. When the war ended, the fort reopened, and Canyon Creek celebrated by holding its second spring gala. Since then, it had become an annual event.

The festivities began at noon with a military parade through town followed by an earthen roast picnic, pie-eating contest, shooting competition, horse races, and dancing at the gazebo in the town square at sunset. For the soldiers, the day served as a much-needed reprieve from the tedium that often plagued them when not engaged in warfare. For the townspeople, it was the most anticipated day of the year.

Selena and her party arrived at noon. After Alberto unhitched the horses and led them to a makeshift corral set up behind the livery stable, he escorted Selena and Anita to a grassy area near the post office to watch the parade.

Barked commands and trumpet calls snapped the soldiers to attention, parade rest, and turns with military precision, reminding Selena of the reenactment she'd witnessed at Fort Davis in the future. Only this time, it was no reenactment. It was real, and she was still trying to wrap her mind around that unsettling fact.

In her time, visitors of all colors watched the parade together. In this time, white officers and their families watched the parade from the front porch of businesses alongside of Canyon Creek's more prominent citizens. The rest of the townspeople separated along the racial divide. After the parade, the Buffalo Soldiers and Indian scouts went on patrol while the white soldiers stayed behind to enjoy the festivities.

Business owners tended the fire pits where beef and buffalo roasted in the ground, and their wives uncovered the food laid out on tables set up next to the gazebo. When the food was ready, the people of color held back so the white people could eat first. Once the nonwhites got in line, the business owners and their wives sat down to eat with the white townsfolk, leaving the nonwhites to serve themselves.

Selena was white, but she knew no one in town, and she wouldn't have segregated herself if she did. So, she hung back with Anita and Alberto, despite the older woman's protest. "You should get a plate and find a spot near the gazebo."

"That's okay. I'm good," Selena said as she watched Sheriff Hobbs work the crowd. *Must be an election year.*

The rotund man moved with more grace than Selena expected. Smiling and shaking hands, he schmoozed with the more prominent members of society who sat at tables or spread blankets under or around the gazebo with the other white people. The nonwhites had gathered on the sidewalk in front of the livery stable with the Buffalo soldiers and Indian scouts who weren't on patrol.

The Civil War might be over, but segregation was alive and well, and Selena was getting the stink eye for standing on the wrong side of the road.

Panic crept into her chest. This wasn't real. It couldn't be, but the sun baking her scalp through the old-fashioned bonnet begged to differ. She felt every rivulet of sweat as it rolled down her neck and between her breasts, and she felt every curious eye that watched as she followed Anita and Alberta through the crowd.

"You shouldn't eat with us," Anita said when Selena nearly plowed into her back. "You should eat with the others in Town Square. Socialize. Get to know your neighbors. Alberto will bring you a plate."

Anita was her only friend here. She didn't want to leave her side, but Anita considered herself little more than the hired help.

The quivering panic in Selena's chest rose to her throat, threatening to choke her. She didn't want to be alone. She didn't even want to be here. She was fooling herself if she thought she could save Dylan. In her time, he was long dead, and he would most likely die again, as was his fate.

Choking back a sob, she forced a smile. "I can get my own food. It's just that. . ."

Anita's expression softened. "You will not be alone. You just need to see a familiar face. You know the sheriff, and the man next to him is the mayor, Floyd Huddleson. I'm sure if you go over there, Sheriff Hobbs will introduce you. Maybe you can ask the mayor about the tornado."

"Yeah. I guess." Selena took a deep breath and turned away.

Nerves twisted her stomach into knots as she crossed the road. She *should* talk to the mayor. If she convinced him Mary wasn't murdered, maybe he'd form a posse or something to look for her body.

But Mary's body was never found.

That was before. This was now. If the past couldn't be changed, then she wouldn't be living in it. Of course, there was always a chance the slightest change would create a butterfly effect and alter the course of history. Even if it did, she'd never know— unless she found a way back to her own time and discovered a world she no longer recognized.

Risky or not, she had to try. There had to be a reason she'd travelled back in time, and she couldn't bear it if Dylan died because she'd done nothing.

Keeping the mayor in her sights, she weaved through the crowd. Before she reached him, he and the sheriff carried their plates toward a group of men sitting under a tree.

"The idiocy of some women thinking they should have the right to vote," one man said as he wiped his mouth on his sleeve.

Another nodded. "They need to remember their place, and it's not at the polls."

"Women aren't stupid," the mayor added, sounding as placating as any modern day politician. "They just have more heart than brains, so they're not analytical enough to make political decisions."

Selena faltered. Approaching the mayor now would be a monumental waste of time. Without proof Mary wasn't murdered, he'd never listen to a woman with "more heart than brains."

Disappointed and more than a little disgusted, she walked over to the food tables, which were nothing more than old doors laid across sawhorses, and filled her plate. Then she grabbed a fork, napkin, and tin cup filled with lemonade and searched for a place to eat. All the tables were full, and those seated on blankets and in buckboards didn't seem to want her company. Not one person asked her to join them, and most avoided eye contact.

She felt like the class nerd, banned from the cool table.

How long before Dylan got back from patrol? He was supposed to meet her at the gazebo around one, and it was almost one thirty. He probably wouldn't even look for her when his regiment returned. He hadn't expected her to come. If she wanted to see him, she'd have to eat near the gazebo or risk missing him altogether.

With her cup in one hand and her plate balanced in the other, she turned toward the gazebo and bumped into a petite blonde.

"Watch where you're going," the young woman shrieked.

Selena's face flamed. "I'm so sorry. I didn't see you."

"I'm not invisible." The blonde shook lemonade from her hand and narrowed her eyes. "Do you have any idea who I am?"

Seriously, I'm on my way to the unpopular table and just happen to bump into one of the mean girls?

She forced a smile. "Afraid not. I'm new in town. My name's Selena. Selena Tillman."

The blonde snorted. "I know who you are."

Selena arched her brows. "Oh? Then you have me at a disadvantage."

"I'm Dolly Huddleson, the mayor's daughter." She gave Selena the once over and curled her lip as if smelling something foul. "And you're Mary Tillman's cousin, which is all I need to know."

Apparently, gossip travelled fast *without* the aid of telephones and social media. But Selena hadn't left the farm since riding into town with Dylan and Major Davis the day of her arrival. How could she have a reputation already?

She met Dolly's gaze and forced another smile. "So, what's to know?"

Dolly raised her chin. "You're both Indian lovers."

Selena's mouth gaped and shock rendered her speechless until Dolly nudged her elbow and knocked the plate from her hand. It tumbled to the ground, spilling food down the front of her skirt. "What the—"

Dolly harrumphed and swept her skirt aside to brush by Selena as if she were a leper.

"Bitch." The moment the words left Selena's mouth, the heat of piercing eyes bore holes into the back of her skull. She didn't need to turn around to know Dylan had finally arrived.

She turned, watching as he approached in full military dress. Distracted by the sight of his lean hips and muscular thighs encased in tight blue britches with gold stripes running the length of each leg, she failed to notice the angry lines bracketing his mouth. The she looked up. He'd obviously overheard her mumbled obscenity.

"What's the matter with you?" he growled in a harsh undertone. "If you cared about your reputation, you'd watch your mouth and socialize with your own kind."

"I am with my own kind," she said, unable to hide her snarky tone. "Human kind. Other than culture, our differences are only skin-deep."

"I doubt anyone here would agree with you," he grumbled. "And if you continue speaking to me in public, you'll hurt whatever chance you might have had of being accepted by polite society. The people of Canyon Creek may have eventually overlooked your being illegitimate, but they'll never overlook you whoring for a half-breed."

Just because she was speaking to a man in public didn't mean she was sleeping with him. People couldn't possibly be that stupid. She huffed out an annoyed breath. Of course they were. Idiots had always been around.

She crossed her arms and tapped her foot. "If you're so worried about my reputation, then why did you invite me on this date in the first place?"

He dropped his gaze and a flush stained his cheeks. "I never intended it to be a date. I was trying to make a point."

Anger quickened her pulse. "What part of 'I don't care about the color of your skin' did you not understand?"

"Damn it!" He raked a hand through his thick, dark hair. "Asking you here was a challenge I didn't expect you to accept. When you did, I never expected you to show up. To make matters worse, the gossips are already talking about Mary's bastard cousin riding into town with the very man accused of her murder. Now, you show up here and act as if I'm courting you. Are you loco?"

Quite possibly. But it wasn't because she didn't care if he was biracial. "I don't know them. I know you, and I care what you think. The gossips will think what they want anyway, so what does it matter?"

"It matters," he said softly, sounding more tired than annoyed. Then he sighed. "I don't know who's the bigger fool—me for inviting you—or you for expecting a half-breed to escort you without harming your reputation?"

She couldn't decide if his caring about her reputation was sweet or if she was annoyed that it mattered to him as much as it did. She went with annoyed. "If you're worried about my reputation, don't. I'm not running for prom queen."

"Huh?" His expression reminded her she wasn't exactly in Kansas anymore.

"Forget it. Let's just eat."

"Don't say I didn't warn you." He scooped her spilled plate off the ground and tossed it in a wheel barrel being used to collect dirty dishes. Then he took her elbow and escorted her to a grassy area next to the sidewalk and across the street from the livery stable.

He couldn't have been but so surprised she'd accepted his invitation because he'd spread a blanket on the ground as if awaiting her arrival. If he'd planned to eat alone, she doubted he would have gone to the trouble. Despite her previous annoyance, hope blossomed in her chest. Maybe he did like her—just a little bit. She hid a smile and looked up. He didn't meet her gaze.

"Sit," he commanded. "I'm going to get us some food."

Once she was seated, he stalked off, and she took the time to survey her surroundings. From the location he'd chosen for their meal, she could see the white families gathered next to the gazebo where a military band was setting up. She also had an unobstructed view of the non-whites and buffalo soldiers clustered across the road in front of the livery stable.

It didn't take a genius to see he'd chosen a spot halfway between the whites and non-whites. It wasn't a coincidence. He'd probably been stuck in the middle his whole life. As her gaze roamed over the town, taking in the people and the lack of cars and modern clothing, the unnatural quality of her life struck her like a blow. She blinked to clear her vision, but nothing changed. She was still sitting on a blanket in Canyon Creek, Texas in 1872 while a dead man she'd dreamed of her entire life handed her a plate.

"Thanks." Her voice shook and her hand trembled.

Dylan nodded and sat as far from her as possible without getting off the blanket. The silence stretched out between them, so Selena picked up a strip of meat, possibly buffalo, and took a bite. It was tender and juicy, but her emotions were so jumbled she could barely swallow.

She could no longer deny she was living in the nineteenth century, but accepting it left her no less confused. Her destiny had to be linked to Dylan's. It was the only explanation for her being in this century. He was meant to live, and she was the only one who could save him. She just had to find the mayor and convince him a tornado killed her *cousin* and not Dylan. Maybe then, the authorities would leave Dylan alone.

She searched the crowd as best she could from a seated position, hoping to spot the mayor or his horrible daughter. With most of the food gone, people had begun milling about, allowing Selena to catch snippets of conversation here and there. Most of the words were unintelligible, but one man's booming voice rose above the din as he stopped to talk with a group of soldiers standing just a few feet away.

"Them government agents ain't spendin' all that money on food. They're buying moldy flour and rancid meat for the reservations and then keepin' the rest of the money for themselves."

"That don't matter none so long as they keep the injuns on the reservations where they belong," a soldier replied.

A third man agreed. "And if the government's feeding

them, they won't need to go on buffalo hunts no more. That'll leave more hides for white folks."

Dylan shoved his plate aside and swiped his mouth with the back of his hand. "My people hunt only what they need while the whites take thousands of hides and leave the meat to rot. If they keep it up, there'll soon be no buffalo left to hunt, and my people *will* starve. That'll solve their Indian problem. Of course, they can always let that bastard, Custer, finish us off."

"The Sioux and Cheyenne will take care of Custer, but the buffalo are another matter altogether. It'll take another hundred years or so to bring them back from the brink of extinction." *Damn it!* She bit her lip to stop the word vomit. Her history was his current events. It would behoove her to remember that.

Dylan snorted. "Just because my people believe in visions, doesn't mean I'll believe you've had one."

The hostility in his voice startled her. She hadn't meant to imply she'd had a vision, but what else was he to think? It wasn't as if she could tell him she knew what the future held because she'd learned about it in history class.

"I never said I had a vision," she said instead. "I just meant that with a man as arrogant as Custer, it's inevitable he'll make a mistake, and when he does, the Sioux and Cheyenne will slaughter him. It's no less than he deserves, but it'll be a tragedy for those in his command who have to follow orders."

Chapter 7

Dylan stared at the top of Selena's head. She was an enigma who continued to fascinate him. Unlike most white women, she looked a man directly in the eye—except when she was lying. And so far, he'd known every time she had because she was unable to hold his gaze. Those smoky gray eyes *were* her best feature. They reminded him of the early morning mist high above the mountains in eastern Indian Territory where he was born. Every time he looked into their smoky depths, it felt like home.

What the hell? He shook his head to rid his mind of such a ridiculous notion. Selena's eyes reminded him of Mary's, but those smoke-colored eyes were the only physical characteristic the cousins shared. Mary's hair had been dark and curling while Selena's was as pale and straight as corn silk. From beneath the spoon bonnet she wore, those silky gold strands brushed her shoulders.

Unable to resist, he ran his fingers through the exposed ends. "Most women wear their hair up, but every time I've seen you, it's been loose. It's beautiful and as soft as corn silk, but why don't you let Anita style it for you?"

"It's baby-fine and straight. So unless it's braided, it doesn't stay up anyway."

She untied the bonnet and dropped it onto the blanket. When she shook those silken strands from her eyes, he felt an uncontrollable tightening in his loins. Yet despite the erotic gesture, she seemed unaware of the effect it had on him.

Her smile was innocence, her tone light, when she said, "I hate this stupid hat, but Anita made me wear it, and after the miserable ride over here, I'm glad I listened to her. The Texas sun about fried my brain even with the ugly hat."

"Don't you normally wear a bonnet outside?" Every white woman he'd ever known had.

"Not if I can help it. I'm not a hat person," she said, before quickly lowering her gaze.

He leaned forward and gently lifted her chin with his index finger. "What about your lovely white skin?"

"My lovely white skin is too white, thank you very much, and I happen to like getting a little sun as long as I don't burn when I lay out." She clamped her mouth shut and cringed.

Surely, she'd not meant to imply she lay down outside to tan her beautiful flesh. Why would she? Why would anyone?

"What are you hiding?" He looked intently into those storm-gray eyes. "I know you just revealed something you regret, but I can't figure out what or why. Tell me."

He gently cupped her chin until she met his gaze. She slapped his hand away and quickly stood. Dylan followed. He wasn't about to let her evade his questions. He wanted her too much.

What the hell?

He couldn't possibly want her. She was white, and he'd learned his lesson with Mary. Was he *unastisgi*?

Insane or not, it was true, and the realization stunned him. He couldn't trust Selena—or any other white woman for that matter—but he could no longer deny he was attracted to her. He had been from the moment he saw her. It was those eyes—so alluring—so familiar, and not just because they reminded him of Mary.

He'd had enough of her evasive answers. She was hiding something, and he needed the truth. He met her gaze and—

"Oh my God, he's choking!" a woman shrieked.

Dylan froze as chaos erupted near the gazebo, and Andy Davis ran by them issuing orders. "Everyone stand back. Sergeant Hines, run get Doc Adams."

"Daddy! Someone, please help him. He's choking. Do something," Dolly Huddleson squealed as her father frantically clutched at his throat.

Major Davis nudged Dolly aside and slapped the mayor between his shoulder blades. He staggered forward and nearly fell, but he was still clutching his throat.

Dylan rushed forward, and Selena was right behind him. Mayor Huddleson's eyes bulged, and his face flushed before slowly fading to white.

"Move!" Dylan said in a voice that demanded obedience, and damn if the white people didn't obey. "Give him room to breathe."

Andy stood slack-jawed, staring at Dylan as if he'd gone loco. He ignored his superior and cleared a path around the choking man. Then he stepped forward and loosened the mayor's shirt collar. Other than stifling Huddleson's daughter, it was the best he could do until the doctor arrived or the mayor coughed up whatever blocked his windpipe.

Dolly's hysterical screams continued until Dylan snapped. He turned, grabbed her about the shoulders, and shook her. "Stop! Your screaming isn't going to help. If anything, it increases your father's agitation. Now calm down."

The crowd inched closer, whether to rescue the mayor or save Dolly from a savage, Dylan wasn't sure. He quickly released her and turned toward Selena who'd stepped into the center of onlookers. "Please get Miss Huddleson out of the way." To his utter amazement, Selena nudged him aside and proceeded to take command herself.

It was the damnedest thing he'd ever seen.

#

Selena didn't doubt Dylan's ability to handle an emergency, but in this instance, she was the only one who could do what needed doing. She might be in a profession that didn't yet exist, but she was still a medical professional, and if she didn't intervene, Floyd Huddleson would die.

She didn't stop to ponder if saving his life would somehow alter the course of history or cause some cosmic time paradox. She just stepped behind him and wrapped her arms around his waist. Then she placed her fisted right hand beneath the tip of his breastbone and held it in place with the palm of her left hand. Pushing inward and upward against his diaphragm, she performed the Heimlich maneuver until a large chuck of phlegm-coated meat sailed from his mouth and freed his obstructed airway. But the mayor didn't respond. He slumped forward over her forearms, throwing her off balance.

He was no longer breathing.

Panic welled in Selena's chest before her annual CPR training kicked in. "Dylan, help me get him to the ground. He's not

49

breathing, and I'm not strong enough to lower him myself."

It took only a second for Dylan to process the scene and take charge once more. He took the mayor from her arms and lowered him to the ground. Then he patted the man's cheek in an ineffective effort to revive him. Before Selena could kneel down beside the mayor and check for a pulse, the doctor arrived.

He dropped to one knee and placed a stethoscope on the mayor's chest. His brows came together, concern shadowing his eyes as he placed two fingers on his patient's neck to check for a pulse. Then he shook his head and raised his chin. "It's too late." His sympathetic gaze sought Dolly's. "I'm sorry. He's dead."

"No!" Dolly shrieked, and the crowd gasped.

Selena dropped to her knees and shoved the doctor aside. "Move!"

He lost his balance and landed on his rear. Ignoring the physician's angry protest, Selena raised the mayor's chin and gave him two slow breaths before placing her hands over his breastbone and interlacing the fingers of her left hand with those of her right. Then she began counting off chest compressions.

"Stop that at once!" The doctor reached for her, but Dylan lowered a hand to his shoulder to restrain him.

"Leave her alone. She knows what she's doing." The conviction in his voice sent Selena's heart soaring.

She caught his eye and smiled. Then she counted off another cycle of compressions, trying to tune out her growing audience as they whispered about the crazy woman trying to bring the dead back to life.

After a third cycle of compressions, she leaned forward to check his pulse. The mayor gasped and heaved up the contents of his stomach. When she turned his head to prevent him from aspirating, he puked on her skirt, and the onlookers gasped in near perfect unison. Then Dolly Huddleson fainted at Dylan's feet.

Shock widened his eyes, and he didn't move quickly enough to catch her. Her face landed on the toe of his boot, and her dress billowed above her head, exposing layers of lacy petticoats and pantaloons. She looked like a toppled mushroom, and the look on Dylan's face was priceless.

Selena bit her lip, stifling hysterical laughter. She'd just saved a man's life—a man who should be long dead—using a technique that hadn't yet been invented. *How do I wrap my head around that and stay sane?*

Trying to hold on to whatever sanity remained, she raised the hem of her soiled dress and wiped vomit from the mayor's face. Dylan still looked a bit dazed when he dropped to his haunches and helped Mr. Huddleson into a sitting position.

The doctor knelt beside him. His shocked expression mirrored Dylan's, and his hand seemed to shake when he raised the stethoscope to the mayor's chest. He looked as if his patient might be a zombie or something. Selena stifled another giggle.

The doctor leaned closer to his patient. "How are you feeling?"

Mr. Huddleson tried to speak but coughed instead. The doctor patted him on the back and looked at Selena as if she might have a magic cure for coughing too. She bit her lip. If she started laughing now, she might never stop.

"Thanks Doc," Mr. Huddleson said when the spasms ceased. His voice was raw and raspy. "For a moment there, I thought I was a goner."

"Don't thank me." The doctor eyed Selena with a mixture of awe and disbelief. "This young lady is the one who saved you, and I would dearly love to know how."

The crowd erupted into chaos.

"She brought him back from the dead," one woman said.

"I thought she was trying to kill him," said another. "She *is* here with that murdering half-breed."

Fury fueled Selena's already frayed nerves. She pushed to her feet and addressed the crowd because she wasn't sure who had spoken. "How dare you condemn a man without a single shred of evidence for a crime that wasn't even committed. Mary Tillman wasn't murdered. She was killed by a tornado. Yet you people would rather blame an innocent man because his skin isn't as white as yours than search for the truth."

"Selena!" Dylan grabbed her arm and spun her around. She was still breathing heavily when she looked into his angry eyes.

Chapter 8

"That's enough," Dylan said in a low growl meant for her ears only as he steered her away from the crowd. "I don't need you or anybody else defending my honor."

Andy Davis sure as hell never defended him. They may have been comrades and friends once, but that was a long time ago. In those days, he and Major Davis were sharp shooters in the Special Services Unit of the Confederate Army. While most soldiers were lousy shots, he and Andy had been excellent marksmen.

Armed with a Sharps . 52 caliber rifle, a skilled sharpshooter was a deadly threat to the enemy but usually safe themselves. Thrown together under such stressful circumstances, the men in his regiment had become close, something that would never have happened in the infantry. Foot soldiers seldom lived long enough to make friends, but the men in his unit were together for two years.

Then Andy learned of his attachment to the Cherokee Regiment of Special Services and accused him of having ulterior motives for hiding his Cherokee blood.

The accusation hurt, but he'd never denied anything. He just didn't tell them he was half Cherokee. During the war, everyone's skin was burned, tanned, or dirty, and with his blue eyes and American name, the men in his unit accepted him as white from the start. He honestly thought things would be easier if he didn't mention his heritage. He *thought* if he were a good enough soldier—a good enough friend—the color of his skin wouldn't matter. He should have known better. The color of his skin would always matter. But it didn't seem to matter to Selena.

He glanced at the top of her head as he dragged her away from the crowd. She knew of his Indian heritage, and he'd supposedly murdered her cousin, but she insisted he was innocent and claimed a tornado killed Mary. It was a far-fetched theory, but even if it were true, he couldn't prove it. Finding Mary's body after a year would be nearly impossible, and then he'd still have to prove he didn't kill her before the tornado struck.

Rage simmered in his chest, burning and smoldering like an ember fanned to flame. He tightened his grip on Selena's arm and dragged her around the corner to an alley next to the telegraph office. If he wanted to find Mary and prove his innocence, he needed Selena to tell him everything.

She pulled her arm free and spun around to face him. "What in hell is the matter with you?"

Shock rendered him momentarily speechless. She had the manners of a lady but spoke as forthright as a man, and there wasn't a demur bone in her body. He looked down into those storm-gray eyes and lost all train of thought. "I—"

She flattened her palms against his chest and shoved. He didn't move an inch, and when he negligently leaned against the side of the telegraph office and grinned, she punched him in the arm and tossed her head to shake the hair from her eyes. Speaking in clipped tones, she punctuated every word by stabbing the center of his chest with her finger. "Don't you ever manhandle me like that again. You do and I'll tie a knot in your tail. You got that?"

His jaw dropped. Her hair was mussed, and the hem of her dress was soiled with vomit. Yet there she stood, defiantly jabbing him in the chest while threatening to tie his tail in a knot. If that was supposed to be a threat, he failed to see it. In fact, the more he thought about it, the funnier it seemed.

He chuckled. "Oh, really?"

"Don't you dare laugh at me." Her sexy pout was adorable. "I'm not kidding. If you ever grab me like that again, I'll—"

"Tie a knot in my tail?" He laughed some more. "Would that be my ass, or my spine?"

She giggled. "I don't know. Is your ass big enough to tie in a knot?"

He threw back his head and laughed. He'd been furious just a second ago, but she'd completely defused his anger. He stepped away from the building and draped an arm over her shoulders. "I don't know how big it is, but I've been told it's a nice ass."

She flushed crimson and flashed a devilish grin. "That's the best kind to tie up."

Her innuendo left him speechless—and aroused as hell. Once he recovered from the shock, he laughed again. They were still laughing hysterically about knots and tails when Andy and Doc Adams came around the corner. The doctor mumbled something about their behavior being a reaction to stress, but Andy eyed them with open hostility.

"Captain Casey," he snapped. "If you and the *lady* could refrain from your scandalous behavior, we'd like to have a word with her."

#

Selena loved the sound of Dylan's laughter. She loved the way his eyes crinkled in the corners and the rich timbre of his voice, and she loved having his arm draped around her shoulder.

Then Major Davis spoke again, ruining the moment. "I insist the two of you conduct yourselves in a civilized manner."

Dylan dropped his arm and stepped away. He stood at attention, facing his superior, but he couldn't disguise the glint of anger in his eyes.

Ignoring the pompous major, Selena turned to the doctor and smiled. "You'll have to excuse us. We were just letting off a little steam."

The doctor was tall and angular with slicked-back blond hair and a pencil thin mustache. His pointed nose was arrow-straight, and his lips were thin, but soulful green eyes softened his sharp features when he smiled and said, "Perfectly understandable." Then he doffed his bowler hat and added. "I'm Dr. Ross Adams, by the way, and it's a pleasure to meet you, Miss Tillman."

"Call me Selena." She extended her hand and to her surprise, he kissed it rather than shaking it, but he didn't call her by name.

His eyes lit with pleasure and a hint of excitement. "Young lady, I would love to know what technique you employed to revive the mayor and who taught you. Had he not stopped breathing so soon, I could have rushed him to surgery and performed the British inter-laryngeal procedure to remove the obstruction surgically, but you did it without a single instrument, and then you brought him back to life. I've never seen anything like it."

Selena twisted her fingers together in a nervous gesture she was unable to hide from Dylan's sharp gaze. "I, em, just forced air upward from his abdomen in an effort to dislodge the obstruction. Then I used a resuscitative technique that keeps blood flowing through the heart and forces oxygen into the lungs until the patient revives or there's no longer hope of survival."

As she attempted to explain the Heimlich maneuver and CPR, Dylan's dark brows drew together in an intimidating scowl. His constant scrutiny unnerved her but not nearly as much as Major Davis's probing question.

"How do you know so much about medical procedures the doc never even heard of?"

Selena's heart thumped against her ribs as she searched for a way to explain her medical knowledge. She didn't want to lie more than necessary, but neither could she risk jeopardizing her assumed role as Ben Tillman's daughter.

"Um, my mother and Ben weren't married, but after I was born, she married a doctor. I stayed with him when she died, and, um, helped him tend the wounded when the war ended." It wasn't a great story, but it was believable. The first Selena would have been fourteen or fifteen at the end of the Civil War.

When the major didn't comment, she started to relax—until she realized he wasn't even looking at her. He was eyeing Dylan, and there was no doubt in her mind he hated him. But did he hate him enough to commit murder?

"So, you became a nurse after the war," Ross Adams said, drawing her attention away from the major. "Doc Crowder here in Canyon Creek probably has need of a nurse. I could check with him if you'd like."

Selena shifted her feet, unable to meet his honest gaze. Even if she had been a nurse in her own time, she wouldn't know enough about nineteenth century medicine to pose as one now. "Um, I wasn't a nurse. I just helped my father."

The major huffed. "Ben Tillman never mentioned a stepfather."

"Why would he?" The man had barely acknowledged his own daughter, and he'd obviously never planned to live in Texas after his brother died and left him the house. So, he would have had no reason to mention an illegitimate daughter's additional family ties to people he'd never met."Before Mary disappeared, the only thing Ben ever gave me was his name. He was never a real father. Thomas Tillman was, and now that he and my mother are both gone, I have no real family left."

The tears shimmering in her eyes lent credibility to her story, but she wasn't acting. The pain of losing her parents within six months of one another still haunted her.

The major's lip curled and half his mouth disappeared under his bushy mustache. "Another Tillman?"

Shit! In her haste to explain the unexplainable without telling more lies, she'd inadvertently used her real father's name. The first Selena Tillman carried Ben's name, despite being illegitimate, but as far as Selena knew, she'd never had a stepfather. If she had, it wasn't likely he would have had the same last name unless Selena's mother married Ben's brother, and the colonel was Ben's only brother. But she could have married Ben and the colonel's cousin. It wasn't unheard of in the 1800's for a man to marry his brother's widow or even his own cousin—so why not his cousin's former lover?

She forced a smile and bluffed like hell."Thomas and Ben were second cousins."

Major Davis folded his arms across his chest and arched his brows. "I don't recollect the colonel mentioning a cousin either."

Dylan had never believed she was who she claimed to be, but the major had. Now, he seemed to question her identity, and she didn't think it was because of her medical knowledge. It was most likely, guilt by association. She trusted Dylan. He didn't, and now, he didn't seem to trust her either.

She held his gaze and faked a calm she didn't feel."Why would a colonel talk about a distant cousin with a subordinate? He was your commanding officer before he died, wasn't he?"

Rage darkened the major's eyes, but he didn't retaliate because Dylan stepped in front of her and challenged him. "Are you calling her a liar?"

Color drained from his face before he flushed a beet red and met Dylan's challenge with a threat. "I could have you court-martialed for speaking to a superior officer in that tone."

"Dylan, please," Selena said, her voice pleading. "Don't do anything stupid."

Did he not see the irony? He'd implied she was lying on

more than one occasion, but apparently, no one else could, especially not the major. She didn't know whether that please her or frightened her. She wanted to stop his murder, not get him arrested and thrown into jail.

Doc Adams placed a hand on Dylan's shoulder. "Captain, I'm sure no one would fault you for defending the lady's honor, but I'm equally sure the major meant no disrespect." He turned those soulful green eyes on Major Davis. "Did you sir?"

Davis puffed out his chest. "Certainly not. I'm just trying to get some answers."

He seemed convinced Dylan killed Mary, but that wasn't the root of his hatred. Something deeper fueled his rage.

The doctor nodded and stepped back. "Good. So let's all calm down and rejoin the festivities. Shall we?"

Selena nervously twisted her hands together while Dylan and Davis continued to glare at one another.

"I think the horse races are about to start," the doctor said when no one moved to follow. "You coming, major?"

"Not just yet, Doc. I have a few more questions for Miss Tillman." He looked away from Dylan and trained his suspicious gaze on her. "Why are you inserting yourself into this investigation?"

Her pulse jumped, and her palms sweat. She wiped them on her skirt. "Because Mary wasn't murdered."

"And you honestly think a tornado killed her?" He snorted his disbelief. "You have no proof. In fact, there's not a shred of evidence to support your ridiculous claim."

Aside from having been the victim of a tornado herself and an eyewitness to Mary's demise, she didn't have proof. She didn't even have a body. But there was evidence to support her claim.

She held up her index finger and began listing the facts she could prove. "A tornado hit Canyon Creek the day Mary disappeared. If you'd checked the storm cellar like I suggested, you would have seen that one of the doors is missing, and it wasn't missing prior to the tornado. If you don't believe me, ask Anita or Alberto."

She held up a second finger. "The doors latch shut with a double sliding bolt that's not easy to slide, so it's highly unlikely the wind blew them open. That means someone slid back the bolts and tried to get into the cellar, and Alberto and Anita were in town that day."

She held up a third finger. "Since you didn't find Mary inside the cellar and both she and a door are missing, it's reasonable to assume she didn't escape."

"Mary wasn't killed by a tornado," the Major snapped.

"Well, she wasn't murdered." His stubborn refusal to consider an alternate theory to murder flustered her.

"You could be right," the major agreed. Then he cast a withering glance in Dylan's direction. "But that doesn't clear Casey. You see, he's not just a breed, he's friends with the Comanche. They call him Long Blade, and I think he gave Mary to those dirty savages when she spurned his advances."

Selena gaped. "What are you smoking?"

She'd researched Mary's disappearance for years, and Indian abduction had never been a consideration. But Major Davis wanted to see Dylan hang, with or without evidence.

Would he also consider murder?

Dylan stiffened but said nothing. Davis dropped his hand to his sidearm and glared with open hostility. "Casey has a history of violence and deceptive behavior. I served with him in the war, and he never told anyone he was a half-breed. He posed as a white man. He even courted your cousin behind her father's back. When she came to her senses and got engaged to her own kind, Casey took her and gave her to those thieving, murderous Comanche."

Dylan took a menacing step forward, but Dr. Adams once more restrained him with a touch of his hand. "Easy, Captain. Don't give him a reason to arrest you. That's just what he wants."

Fear pulsed through Selena's veins. She stepped in front of Dylan and took his hand in hers. "You're innocent. Don't let this bigoted ass goad you into doing something you'll regret."

His fingers tensed around hers. She wasn't sure if he was reassuring her or if anger tightened his hand into a fist because he wouldn't meet her gaze. He was looking at Major Davis with an expression of pain and anger that nearly broke her heart.

He released her hand and stepped back. "We haven't been friends for a long time, Andy, but you don't want to make me your enemy."

Selena turned to the major, hoping to appeal to whatever

common sense he might possess. "If you think the Comanche have my cousin, then you should gather your troops and go look for her. Take a week or two, but find her."

He ground his teeth. "I can't do that without proof. It could start a war, and Colonel Harper would never allow it."

"Then search the storm cellar," she pleaded. "Find proof she isn't dead."

She wanted to grab Dylan's hand and beg him to run away with her. She might actually have done it if Mayor Huddleson hadn't stepped into the alley.

He nodded to Doc Adams and Dylan before stepping forward to clasp her hands. With his voice still raspy from his brush with death, he said, "You saved my life tonight, and I can never repay you, but after talking with the sheriff, we agreed to investigate your tornado theory. I'll talk to Colonel Harper over at the fort today."

Selena almost cried. "Thank you," she whispered. "Thank you so much."

Chapter 9

After the mayor's promise, Dylan sent Selena home with Anita and Alberto. Mentally and physically exhausted, she'd gone straight to bed, but thoughts tumbled around in her brain like a hamster on a wheel until she finally got up and lit a lamp. Then she pulled the blanket from the bed and headed outside to sit on the porch step.

Exhaling slowly, she lifted her face to the night sky. In this time, there were no planes or satellites circling the earth, just a dark inverted bowl studded with stars that sparkled like diamonds. There was no traffic and no echoing rumble of a diesel engine coming from the interstate to disturb the peaceful silence. There was only nature's quiet symphony of croaking frogs, chirping crickets, and the occasional screech of an owl or the lonely cry of a coyote serenading the darkness.

As the moon rose higher and the peaceful solitude soothed her nerves, Selena moved to one of the rocking chairs on the porch and drifted off to sleep. When she awoke a short time later, the kerosene lamp in her room had gone out, and the window behind her was dark, but the sky was no longer black.

She stepped off the porch and looked toward the east as the first pink rays of sunlight stretched toward the horizon, painting the sky in the most beautiful shades of mauve, blue, lavender, and orange. Stiff from having slept in a rocking chair all night, she arched her back and stretched.

A twig snap behind the house, and her muscles tensed. She paused to listen but heard nothing more than the constant ripple from the creek. Yet the hair on her neck stood on end. Someone was out there. Watching. Waiting.

Determined not to let her fears immobilize her, she entered the house and retrieved a small pistol she'd found in Colonel Tillman's bedroom earlier that week. She checked the chamber to ensure it was loaded and then slipped out the back door.

She briefly considered waking Alberto, but if she woke the man and his sleeping wife because a deer was grazing in the back yard, she'd feel like the helpless female they believed her to be. But she wasn't helpless—at least not in her time. She'd lived alone in Richmond, and she could handle a gun. She'd also taken self-defense classes while attending the radiologic technology program in Danville, Virginia. But this wasn't her time and here, she couldn't call the cavalry by dialing 911. She was alone, and she needed to stop relying so heavily on Anita and Alberto and learn to take care of herself in *this* time.

Taking a deep breath to still her nerves, she moved to the side of the house. *God, please let it be a deer.*

With the gun held close to her side, barrel pointed downward, she walked toward the creek. The blanket slipped from her shoulders and fell to the ground. She ignored the chill and carefully picked her way through the field of broom straw to the creek.

Before she reached the water's edge, a man dressed in full Indian regalia appeared before her as if he'd sprung up from the earth. She stifled a scream and jumped back. Her heart slammed against her ribs and stole what was left of her breath.

"Shit!" She fumbled the gun and nearly dropped it before she could raise it.

The warrior's mouth twitched, relieving some of her fears but not all. He stood bare-chested, gripping a rifle in one hand while the other hovered over a knife strapped to his thigh. He looked as if he'd just walked off the set of a television western.

A hint of laughter flashed in his eyes, but his mouth firmed. He hadn't made a move against her, nor had he actually threatened her, but that didn't mean he wasn't dangerous. Still, she lowered the gun, despite the trembling in her chest.

"Good morning." She forced the words from a mouth gone dry, hoping she wasn't making the biggest mistake of her life. Not that it mattered. He had a rifle. She had a pistol. And the only thing she'd ever shot was a cardboard target.

The Native's brows drew together, but he didn't respond. Then again, maybe he didn't understand her. "Do you speak English?"

She focused all her attention on the silent warrior until

movement in the tall grass on the other side of the bank distracted her. She looked to her left, her heart slamming against her ribs when a second warrior came over the ridge. The sun had barely crested the horizon and it shone behind his back, casting his face in shadows.

Ignoring her fear, ignoring the man in the field, she concentrated on the nearest of the two. He was an immediate threat.

She raised her gun again, pointing the barrel upward rather than at the warrior's chest. "I know how to use this, but I won't shoot unless you're a threat."

If he was, then she was dead already—or worse. Thinking of what worse entailed made her stomach clench and bile rise in the back of her throat.

His eyes narrowed, but he still didn't speak. From the corner of her eye, she caught sight of his companion, now heading in her direction at a fast clip. Her heart beat even faster. If she couldn't shoot them, she'd have to try to outrun them, but she couldn't outrun a bullet, and she probably couldn't scream loud enough for Alberto to hear. She stiffened her spine. False bravery could get her killed, but standing there waiting to be a victim wasn't smart either.

She aimed the gun at the Native American's chest. His eyes widened, but he still didn't speak. Fear cinched her chest, making speech difficult. "I know you understand me, I see it in your eyes."

Amusement lit his face. "Too stupid to be afraid?"

Startled by his fluent English and the humor in his voice, she took a step back but didn't lower the gun. "I'm terrified, but I'll shoot if I have to."

He smiled. "I won't shoot if you don't."

She swallowed her fear and lowered her gun. In a shaky voice, she said, "I'm Selena Tillman, and you're on my property. May I ask why?"

Instead of answering, he called out to his friend in his own language. The second man was taller than the one standing in front of her, and though his hair was much shorter, they were dressed in a similar fashion. Both were shirtless, but where the first man's chest was hairless, the second man had a narrow ribbon of hair trailing from his navel to the low-slung waistband of his buckskin britches. The tantalizing sight of his hard, muscled chest made Selena gasp, not only in recognition of this second noble warrior, but with a desire so sharp it made her knees weak.

Dylan had always been handsome, but Dylan dressed in his native attire was sexy as hell.

Her gaze lingered over his broad, bronzed shoulders and tight washboard abs as he moved toward her. Then she looked up and noticed the narrowing of his beautiful blue eyes and the thinning of his lips.

"What the hell do you think you're doing traipsing around in your night clothes and socializing with savages?" He stared at her chest, and embarrassed heat warmed her cheeks.

Squirming under his hot gaze, she said, "I'd hardly call this a social visit. You're lucky I didn't shoot."

Dylan snagged her hand, causing the other man to choke with laughter. Ignoring his friend's mirth, he pulled her full-length against his naked chest.

Selena gasped, and her gun fell to the ground. With only her nightgown separating them, she became embarrassingly aroused. Her nipples pebbled beneath the thin material, and as close as Dylan was, he no doubt felt the tight buds pressing against his naked chest. If the other man hadn't been there, she would have done what she'd wanted to do since the day Dylan kissed her in the parlor. She'd say to hell with getting to know him better and jump his bones.

His eyes briefly widened, as if recognizing her arousal. Then his brows snapped down over his eyes, and he pulled her close enough to feel his erection. Clenching his teeth, he said, "Get your gun and take your pretty little ass back to the house. If you were too stupid to be afraid before, you'd best be afraid now."

She looked into the same beautiful eyes she'd been seeing in her dreams since she was ten and gave him an answer designed to fan the flames of his desire. "Nothing you do would make me afraid of you, Dylan. Nothing."

#

Selena's taunting reply caused Dylan's manhood to become even harder. It took a great deal of willpower to stifle a growl and not pull her into his arms. Had White Deer not been standing so close with that damn smirk on his face, he would have done just that. Instead, he made himself a mental promise. He would take Selena Tillman before nightfall.

"White Deer," he said in English before switching to Comanche. "Go. I'll catch up to you."

White Deer nodded to Selena and spoke in English, "Good bye, Woman with No Fear. We will meet again."

"A friend of yours?" she asked when Dylan bent to retrieve the gun she'd dropped.

He snatched it up and shoved it into his waistband. "This is not a damned social call, and White Deer is not a guest."

"You're right. A guest would have knocked on the door."

"You're supposed to be his enemy, you damn fool. Or didn't you know decent white women don't run around half-naked making polite conversation with savages?"

"What was I supposed to do? Shoot first and ask questions later?" she countered to his stunned disbelief.

"No. You were supposed to be in bed asleep," he said with a sigh. Then he attempted to take her arm, but she stepped out of reach and pinned him with eyes as dark as storm clouds.

"What are the two of you doing out here at the butt crack of dawn?"

He hadn't wanted to say anything in case he failed, but she was like a dog with a bone. If he didn't answer, she'd just keep prying, and he'd never get her back in the house.

"After Anita and Alberto brought you home, Colonel Harper gave me permission to track the tornado. White Deer is the best tracker I know, so I rode out to his village to ask for his help. We slept on the trail and got an early start this morning." He shrugged. "We traced the tornado's path through Canyon Creek and found where it touched down again behind the creek. And as soon as you go back inside, we'll follow it to wherever it takes us."

"It jumped the house and then briefly touched down near the storm cellar before heading that way," she said, pointing toward the windmill.

Dylan stared into her eyes. "And how would you know?"

She lowered her gaze, a sure sign the next words out of her mouth were going to be lies. "I already told you about the storm cellar door, and the house is still standing, so…"

It was a logical assumption, but it wasn't the truth. Sighing, he took her arm and led her toward the house, but she stopped in front of the outhouse and pulled her arm free.

"Oh for God's sake," he muttered when she dashed inside and left him standing outside the door. "Do you have to do this now? You couldn't wait until I was gone?"

What woman would stop to take a piss when she was with a man? Most women pretended they didn't even have bodily functions.

"I just woke up," she said as she stepped out of the privy and let the door slam shut. "We're here, and I had to go. What was I supposed to do? Pretend I didn't have to pee because you're standing here? Please."

Selena was unlike any female he'd ever met, white or Indian. Shaking his head, he dragged her to the kitchen door. "Just go inside and put some clothes on."

As much as he hated becoming involved with another white woman, he had no choice. He was harder than he'd ever been in his life, and she was the only woman who could assuage his burning desire.

"Dylan," she said as he turned to leave.

When he turned back around, she placed her palms on his bare chest and rose up on tiptoes to touch her mouth to his. The gentle caress of her satiny lips set off a firestorm of need he could no longer ignore. He pulled her close, sweeping his tongue inside her mouth, deepening the kiss she started.

Selena melted against him and snaked her arms around his neck. Her hands tunneled through his hair before sliding down his neck to trace the contours of his body as if he were clay and she the sculptor.

He reached for her hips and gripped the tight, round globes of her bottom. Pulling her hard against his arousal, he kneaded her soft flesh through the thin material of her nightgown. His blood turned to liquid fire, burning through his body and setting him aflame.

Selena gasped, her soft breath a whisper against his lips. He expected her to pull away in shocked outrage over his lusty behavior, but she molded herself more firmly against him and answered his desire with a burning need of her own. Gasping for breath, he finally pulled away.

He cupped her face in his hands, searching her eyes for some sign of shock or disgust at what she'd allowed him to do. What he saw in the depths of those beautiful gray eyes was a longing that matched his own.

And it scared the hell out of him.

"*Adawehi*," he whispered as he gently rubbed his thumb over her lower lip. "We will finish this tonight."

"This will never be finished between us. It has no beginning and no end," she whispered, turning her face into his palm.

"You talk like the *Yunwiya*," he said, bringing her hands to his mouth to kiss her knuckles.

"What does that mean?"

"Real people. It's Cherokee."

She pulled back, looking up to meet his gaze. "You're Cherokee? I always thought you were Comanche."

"*Tetsalagi*. I'm Cherokee." He studied her face. For some reason, he felt as though she meant "always" literally, but that was ridiculous. She hardly knew him.

Her muscles tensed and her cheeks flushed before she lowered her chin and her gaze. "I guess I always assumed you were Comanche because you lived in Texas and when I think of the Cherokee, I think of the Eastern Band living in North Carolina."

"Do you think of the Cherokee often?" She wasn't lying, but she *was* being deceptive. It just didn't make any damn sense, any more than her referring to him in the past tense.

She kept her head lowered and shrugged. "You know what I mean."

No. He didn't. Her words and mannerisms were strange. She was definitely hiding something.

He held her at arm's length. "You're the most confusing woman I've ever met."

She dropped her gaze. "I don't mean to be. I just assumed you were Comanche."

"My father is white. His people emigrated from Ireland in the 1700's. My mother's people are Cherokee. They owned plantations in Georgia and were just as civilized as the whites. When the whites wanted more land, the government evicted the

Cherokee and herded them west—like cattle. The *Nunna Daul Tsuny* was The Trail Where They Cried. Your people called it The Trail of Tears."

When she quietly laid her head on his shoulder, he continued. "My mother's people marched that trail. Other Cherokees fled and hid out in the mountains of North Carolina. The government allowed a few families to stay, but they forced them to hunt those who'd fled or risk forfeiting their own lives. They later executed some of those captured. They evicted the rest.

"Nearly twenty thousand Cherokee left Georgia. Over four thousand died before they ever reached the Cherokee Strip. My grandfather and mother were lucky. They survived. My grandmother and two aunts didn't."

Selena snuggled against him. When he said no more, she raised her head and met his gaze. The understanding he saw in her eyes was almost his undoing. He cleared his throat and set her apart. "Thanks to the mayor and Colonel Harper, I've been granted a week to look for Mary's body, so I can't waste daylight, but I'll be back before dark. If you don't want me in your bed, don't answer the door."

Without saying another word, he walked away. His heart was still pounding like an Apache war drum when he caught up with White Deer.

Chapter 10

Selena paced. It had been hours since she'd kissed Dylan goodbye, and waiting to hear from him was tearing up her nerves. In her own time, she could have picked up the phone or texted him. Here, she couldn't even get in the car to look for him. So, she headed for the study to look for a book or a deck of cards to occupy her time.

She pulled back the heavy drapes, opened a window, and sat behind the colonel's desk, rummaging through the drawers until she found a deck of cards. She didn't know how long she played solitaire before anxiety turned to fatigue, and she laid her head on the desk and dozed. When movement in the hall startled her awake, she jolted upright.

A shadow fell across the desk. She raised her head and saw Dylan's tall, broad-shouldered silhouette filling the doorway. A tremor started in her chest and spread to her knees. She slowly rose to her feet, and came around the desk.

"We found her," he said quietly.

Selena's feet faltered. She stumbled but caught herself on the edge of the desk, her pulse pounding so hard she could barely catch her breath. "What?"

Dylan rushed forward and wrapped an arm around her waist to steady her. "Breathe. That's it. Just breathe."

The comforting weight of his arm and his compassionate gaze helped calm her racing heart and keep her from hyperventilating. "I'm okay. Really."

He pulled her closer. "Let's go somewhere more comfortable to talk."

Once they were seated in the parlor, he took her cold hands in his, warming her flesh as well as her soul. She looked at their joined hands, too afraid to meet his gaze.

"I don't understand." How could he find Mary's body if she'd never been found? "Where was she?"

"About five miles west of here. She was lying out on the open prairie. There wasn't much left—coyotes." He took a deep breath and let it out slowly, as if trying to steady his own riotous emotions. "The cellar door was lying just a few feet away. Her arm had been ripped from her body and her hand—or what was left of it—still clutched the handle."

He'd found a body, but that didn't mean he could identify Mary's remains or prove she wasn't murdered. "Are you sure it's Mary?"

He reached into his shirt pocket and held out a necklace. "This was tangled in the bones of her neck."

Cold slithered down Selena's spine. It was her locket—the one she'd worn since she was ten. "No. It's not possible."

She started to reach for it but quickly pulled back her hand. No one had lit the lamps in the parlor, just the ones in the hall, so Dylan's face was shadowed, but she could still see the worry in his eyes.

"Do you recognize it?" he asked.

She nodded, unable to speak. Mary dying with the necklace explained how her spirit attached to it, but if her body had never been found, then Uncle Robbie couldn't have inherited it—unless her body had been found and never reported.

Selena's heart slammed against her sternum. Someone had not only wanted Dylan dead, they hadn't wanted him to clear his name.

His fingers tightened around the chain. "When did you see it?"

"It was mine. I lost it." Her hand shook as she reached for it again. To her surprise, Dylan released it.

The silver was tarnished from exposure to the elements, but the delicate design engraved on the front wasn't worn smooth yet.

She pried it open with trembling fingers, revealing a somewhat faded picture of Mary, only now, Dylan's picture was on the opposite side—a pictured she'd never seen. She'd only known what he looked like because of the dreams.

The necklace slipped from her hand and hit the floor with a metallic chink.

Dylan balled his fists on his thighs. "How could you recognize a necklace I gave Mary just a few months before she died?"

"You gave it to her?" Jeff had been right. Mary's spirit was attached to the necklace, and because it bound her to Dylan in life, it had bound them in death. "I wore it next to my heart, dreaming of you, and I never knew."

He rose to his feet and stared down at her "How could you know?"

Her mind raced. There had to be an explanation for Mary's necklace being in her uncle's possession in the future. "Who else knows you found her?"

If he was killed because he'd found Mary's body, then that meant someone else knew he'd found her—someone who would do anything to stop him from clearing his name.

Dylan sat back down beside her. "Why does it matter?"

Even if she could explain, she didn't have time. Because of her interference, he'd found Mary's remains a week earlier, which meant she no longer had a week to save him. "It just does. So, who else knows, and have you reported it to the authorities?"

Her pulse raced as fast as her mind. Dylan removed the necklace from Mary's body. He'd have been better off leaving it. The nineteenth century didn't keep dental records, and DNA analysis was an unknown science.

"Just White Deer. I haven't had time to report it. Now tell me when you saw Mary's necklace."

Ignoring him, she rose to her feet and paced. It was possible Dylan had found the body all those years ago, removed the necklace, and was murdered before he could report it. Since White Deer knew about Dylan's discovery, whoever murdered Dylan had probably done the same to White Deer. Even if logic didn't play a big part in her life these days, her reasoning was sound. It just didn't explain how Uncle Robbie had come to own the necklace.

"Selena." Dylan stepped into her path and gripped her shoulders. "You couldn't have worn that necklace. What you're saying doesn't make sense." The suspicion in his eyes turned to worry when she shrugged him off and stepped out of reach.

Throwing up his hands in a gesture of defeat, he slumped in a chair and stretched out his long legs. The toe of his moccasin connected with the locket still on the floor and sent it sliding. The gold chain scraped across the hardwood as it disappeared beneath the sofa, the sound echoing in Selena's mind long after it came to rest against the baseboard.

Her vision blurred as a wave of dizziness swept over her. She gripped the back of a chair and closed her eyes. When she opened them, Mary stood before her, a hologram without substance.

"See," she whispered, and though her lips never moved, Selena heard the word clearly. Then in a blinding flash of white light, a mental image flashed in her mind, startling in its clarity and omnipotence.

He slumps in the chair and opens the locket. Grief shadows his face. He closes his eyes. The chain slips through his fingers and falls to the floor. He moves his leg. The locket slides beneath the sofa. He makes no effort to retrieve it. His shoulders sag, and he buries his face in his hands.

White Deer enters the room and speaks to him. Dylan raises his head and nods. Then White Deer leaves.

Dylan slowly stands. His fingers fist at his sides. For a moment, he doesn't move. When he does, his steps are hesitant. He glances over his shoulder one last time before opening the front door and stepping onto the porch.

There's only one horse tied to the hitching post and a trail of dust leading away from the house. White Deer is gone.

Something in the yard catches his attention. He turns. There's a puff of smoke. He clutches his chest, and blood blossoms on his shirt, seeping between his fingers.

He stumbles and goes down on one knee before collapsing onto his back. One leg is curled beneath him. His breathing is labored.

A man steps onto the porch, his entire body cast in shadows by the sun setting behind him. He reaches for Dylan's knife. Touching the blade almost reverently with his finger, he tests its

71

sharpness before taking the scalp of his enemy.
        The deed done, he drops the knife. It clatters
to the wooden planks as blood seeps from Dylan's
body, staining the porch forever.

As the vision faded, Mary whispered in Selena's ear. "Save him."

Selena gasped, and her eyes flew open. There was no one in the room but Dylan, and he was staring at her as if she had escaped from a mental hospital. Her grip on the back of the chair tightened. The metallic taste of fear clung to the back of her throat, hot and sour.

She breathed in through her mouth to keep from gagging.

"What the hell?" Dylan clasped her shoulders. "Talk to me."

She swayed against him. The image of him lying on the porch was one she'd seen often in her nightmares, but never with such clarity and never while awake.

Fear tightened her throat. "Did you hear anything? See anything?"

"Are you having the vapors?" He took her arm and guided her back to the sofa.

Concern shadowed his eyes, but she was honestly terrified. Dylan wasn't supposed to die until next week, but if the vision she'd just seen was correct, then he'd died after finding Mary's body. And he'd found it today—a week sooner than he was supposed to—because she had prodded him.

Tremors wracked her body, and she was unable to control them.

Dylan pulled her onto his lap and cradled her head on his shoulder. His hand stroked her back. His lips brushed her hair. "Talk to me, *Adawehi*."

"You shouldn't have taken the necklace." She drew strength from his embrace. "Without forensics and DNA to positively identify her remains, you can't prove it's Mary."

He pulled back enough for her to see his face, but he kept his arms loosely draped around her waist. "You speak strangely." Deep lines creased his brow. "I don't always understand your words, and I've spoken English all my life."

When she remained silent, he sighed. After a moment, he

said, "The authorities will know it's Mary's body. Her father's signet ring was still on her finger...or what remains of it. Once Sheriff Hobbs identifies her, her personal affects will go to your father—to Ben."

She was a direct descendent of Ben Tillman. His son, William, inherited the house and the necklace, but Dylan had left the ring with a body that was found and never reported.

"Why did you keep the necklace?" The lump in her throat made it difficult to speak.

A flush tinged his cheeks. "My reasons are personal."

"It doesn't matter." He could deny it all he wanted. He still had feelings for Mary. She may have betrayed him, but she'd obviously loved him. Her spirit had transcended death in a desperate attempt to save him and clear his name.

"Is White Deer here?" She'd seen him in her waking dream, so maybe he really was outside. "Have you sent him to town yet?"

Dylan narrowed his eyes. "How did you know he was here?"

She shrugged. "He was with you this morning, and if he's still here, you have to stop him from going to town to report the body."

He slid her off his lap and stood. "He's still outside. I wanted to talk to you before we went to the sheriff, but perhaps I should get Anita to stay with you when I leave."

"Don't go." She grabbed his hand and pulled him back down. She couldn't let him leave the house, and she couldn't let White Deer ride into Canyon Creek alone. She didn't know if she could save their lives or even change the sequence of events now that they'd been set into motion, but she had to try.

He pulled his hand from her death-like grip and touched her shoulder, giving her the side-eye as if she were a stray dog he didn't quite trust not to bite. "I know you've had a shock, but there's something else wrong, and I can't help if I don't know what it is. Talk to me."

Unable to meet his gaze, she laid her head on his broad shoulder. He'd put on a shirt before coming into the house, but it smelled faintly of sweat and horse. She wrinkled her nose. "I'm afraid, and I don't know what to do."

"Hush, *Adawehi*," he whispered, taking her into his arms once more. "Don't cry. You're safe. *Oea-Yah*. I swear by God."

Did he think she was afraid a tornado would get her too? Like that hadn't already happened.

He stood and pulled her to her feet. Then he led her into the bedroom and washed her face with cool water from the washbowl. His touch was soothing, but her heart ached. If she couldn't save him, he would die a week sooner than expected.

"Better?" He draped an arm over her shoulder. She silently nodded, and he guided her into the dining room.

Anita greeted them at the door and hugged Selena to her ample bosom. *Señor* Dylan told us he found Mary." She pulled away and swiped a tear from her eye. "She was like a daughter to me."

Alberto patted Selena's shoulder and said something in Spanish. She didn't understand the words, but compassion was universal. She hugged his waist and after a brief hesitation, he hugged her back.

She closed her eyes, fighting tears. The image she'd seen in her mind was not one she could easily dismiss, and the implications were clear. She no longer had a week to save Dylan's life. Somewhere outside, a killer waited. She shivered, and Alberto hugged her tighter. Then he stepped back, and after saying something to his wife, he slipped out the back door.

"Sit." Anita finished setting the table in the dining room, and without being asked, she'd set the table for two, a silent invitation for Dylan to stay for supper. He nodded his thanks and pulled out Selena's chair.

As she sat down, she looked over her shoulder at Anita. "Thank you. But would you mind setting another place? I'd like to invite Dylan's friend inside to eat with us."

Anita's eyes widened, and she made the sign of the cross over her chest. She didn't seem afraid of Dylan, but White Deer obviously frightened her. Selena wasn't sure if it was because he was a Comanche or because he was dressed like a warrior. Dylan, on the other hand, had put on a shirt and removed the rawhide strip from his forehead.

"Don't worry." Selena smiled, hoping to put Anita at ease. "He's civilized."

Anita didn't look reassured, but she nodded and left. The moment she was out of the room, Dylan leaned over to push in her chair and spoke harshly in her ear. "What do you think you're doing?"

His breath was warm on her neck, but his proximity sent a shiver down her spine. She was falling in love with him, but there was more to the spike in her pulse rate. She was terrified to let him out of her sight.

She shrugged. "He helped you find Mary, and he's probably hungry. There's enough food here, so why wouldn't I invite him to eat with us?"

Dylan blew out an exasperated breath and walked around the table to sit across from her. "White Deer is a Comanche Warrior. He won't eat under your roof."

She toyed with her napkin. The past should have rewritten itself the moment she met Dylan. Parts of it had. She'd certainly changed Mayor Huddleson's destiny. He wasn't dead, and he should have been. She raised her eyes from her plate, and a sudden sense of *déjà vu* sent a shiver down her spine.

Everything about this house and Dylan's murder seemed familiar, and it was more than just her dreams. She gripped the underside of the table to keep from swaying.

Time travel was not only possible, it had happened—quite possibly, multiple times before. Her life could be a continuous loop. The past was her future as well as her past, and her dreams had been memories from a time before she was born—a time when she lived in the past and died in the past—only to be born again in the future—and die again in the past.

Her head reeled trying to sort it all out and still have it make sense in her mind.

The sound of Alberto's voice in the kitchen pulled her thoughts from the crazy train, if only for a moment. It sounded as if he was issuing some kind of warning to someone, but Selena didn't speak Spanish.

She met Dylan's gaze across the table. He slammed his napkin down and stormed into the kitchen. A minute later, White Deer entered the room and Dylan followed, cursing fluently in Comanche, Cherokee, or possibly even both languages. Alberto set a plate, glass, and utensils on the table to Selena's left and backed out of the room.

Selena raised her eyes to White Deer and offered a shaky smile. "Please join us."

He nodded and sat down.

"Damned infernal, interfering bastard," Dylan mumbled as he sat across from his friend and began shoveling mouthfuls of baked chicken into his mouth. Selena shot him an annoyed look before serving White Deer's plate. He took a whiff, grunted, and started eating—with his hands. When Dylan stabbed his meat with a fork and shoved it into his mouth, White Deer picked up his fork and did the same.

"Mm. Good," he said before shoveling the food in at an astonishing rate. Selena's appetite was non-existent, so she moved her food around on the plate, barely touching it as she watched Dylan eat heartily, despite his black scowl.

White Deer cleaned his plate and then reached across the table to slide hers over so he could help himself to her leftovers. Meeting her gaze, he said, "Many starve on the plains. Food is never rejected when offered."

"Yeah, and if it's not offered, you just take it," Dylan mumbled, casting a murderous glare in White Deer's direction. White Deer raised his brows. "Who takes from who? The white soldiers corral us up like cattle. They tell us we cannot hunt buffalo. They feed us bad meat and moldy grain. I do not steal from Woman with No Fear. She offer. I take."

"Is Woman with No Fear my Indian name or something?" Selena asked, trying to get her mind off the morose thoughts swirling around in her head.

White Deer nodded. "It is a good name. Strong. Do you like it?"

"I'm flattered, but I'm not brave or fearless. I'm terrified." And she was no longer sure if it was Dylan's fate or her own surreal circumstances that sent fear coursing through her blood. It was quite possible she was stark, raving mad.

"Yeah, and it's about damn time you told me what you're afraid of," Dylan said as he lowered his fork and glared. "I've got a lot of questions for you, woman, and you haven't answered any of them truthfully. So no more bullshit, Selena, I want the truth."

She laughed as an old Tom Cruise movie came to mind, but

it lacked even a trace of humor. "You can't handle the truth."

His expression shifted from anger to concern. "Just talk to me. Honestly for a change. No more evasive answers or half-truths."

The hour of reckoning had arrived, but she was no longer sure of the truth herself. If she just stated the physical facts, maybe he could figure it out and explain it to her. "Fine. What do you want to know?"

Chapter 11

Dylan looked at Selena. From the beginning, he wasn't sure she was who she said she was. No one had ever found the horse she'd claimed threw her, she hadn't taken the stage, and her trunks had never arrived from Pecos. So, how had she gotten to Canyon Creek? And how the hell had he gotten so deeply involved? He could no longer deny he wanted her, but he still didn't trust her.

Tension filled the room. White Deer stared at Selena, and she kept her head lowered. Was that a tear rolling over her cheek?

"Why did you say you'd worn that necklace before when we both know it's not possible?" he asked, breaking the strained silence.

She raised her head. Her eyes were damp but for once, she didn't avert her gaze. "Because it's the truth."

"That's not an answer. It's another evasion—another lie."

White Deer reached across the table and gripped his arm, "Long Blade, does she lie, or do you ask the wrong questions?"

"Stay out of this, White Deer." He didn't need Comanche wisdom or mysticism at the moment. He just wanted to hear the truth from Selena's lips.

"But she is the one, my friend. She is the woman in Dream Speaker's vision."

Selena leaned on her elbows, giving White Deer her undivided attention. "Who is Dream Speaker?"

Did she think changing the subject would stop him from getting to the truth? "*Numunu*," White Deer said. "He's a wise and respected Comanche medicine man who interprets dreams and sees visions," Dylan said, and because he was tired of her evading his questions, he childishly added, "Unlike your visions about Custer and the buffalo, his are real."

White Deer cast a disapproving glare in his direction before turning his attention back to Selena. "He had a vision about Long Blade and a white woman who would change his fate. Long Blade doubts these visions. I do not."

"I respect the Shaman's abilities, but visions are like dreams. They can be misinterpreted." And he didn't always agree with Dream Speaker's interpretations.

Selena had alluded to a vision of Custer and the buffalo at the spring gala, but that had been nothing more than a diversionary tactic. He doubted she really believed in such things. Most white people saw the plains Indians as a superstitious bunch of heathens because they believed in magic and supernatural powers.

In reality, the plains tribes just had a different understanding of the creator. They were spiritual people who believed mans' continued existence depended on maintaining a relationship with the world around him. They placed great stock in visions, rituals, and ceremonies they believed would bring them closer to the powers of the universe.

"How did Dream Speaker say this woman would change Dylan's—um—Long Blade's destiny?" Selena asked, as if she might actually believe in visions.

Dylan snorted. At least she didn't claim to *be* the woman in Dream Speaker's dreams. If she had, he would have walked out the house and never looked back.

"The visions are not always clear," White Dear explained. "Dream Speaker wished to meet this woman and learn her secrets before Long Blade joined his life with hers."

"What the hell?" Dylan glared at the crazy Comanche. He'd gone off the reservation if he thought he'd join his life with a white woman. His dalliance with Mary proved that could never happen.

"Dream Speaker's vision foretold her arrival."

Dylan ground his teeth. "I think we should discuss this later, White Deer. Now is not the time. We've got more important things to talk about." He turned his attention to Selena. "Like the necklace."

She lowered her head and sighed. "I told you the truth. You just weren't listening. Or you thought I was lying, but the necklace *was* mine. My uncle gave it to me when I was ten. It had Mary's picture in it but not yours, and I lost it the day I got here."

His fingers curled into fists on the table. "You and I both know that's not possible."

"Maybe not, but it's the truth. I'm not sure I understand it myself. I know I can't explain it, but maybe this shaman can." She looked up, and there was a hint of desperation in her eyes. "I want to meet him. I don't have the answers, but maybe he does."

"Are you out of your mind?" Dylan pushed to his feet, nearly knocking over his chair. "Your people are at war with us, or don't you read the papers? You can't ride into a Comanche Village as if you were going to Sunday tea. You're white, or have you forgotten?"

"You're white too," she said quietly, "or at least as white as you are Indian. So why do you deny part of your heritage? Which parent are you ashamed of?"

His heart slammed against his ribs. Fury burned in his blood. "I don't deny anything, and I'm not ashamed of either parent. This isn't about me, you little fool."

She jumped when he raised his voice, but she didn't shy away or cry. She actually glared. As White Deer's new name implied, she wasn't afraid of him. And she damn sure should be. He was furious.

He slapped both palms on the table. Bending his elbows, he leaned forward until his face was so close to hers, he could see tiny gold flecks in her gray eyes. "You're a woman, and you're white. And I'm an Indian whether you chose to recognize that fact or not. In the white man's world it doesn't matter if one of my parents is white. What matters is that one of them is Indian. To a white man, that makes me a dirty half-breed. Most Indians, on the other hand, accept me as their *diganeli*, their brother. As long as I do not betray them, I'm welcome in their camp."

His rant was met with round eyes and an owlish blink. His fury spent, he dropped into his chair and leaned his head back to stare at the ceiling. Taking a deep breath, he closed his eyes and exhaled slowly to release the anger that had become his constant companion of late. "You're not going to see Dream Speaker, and that's final."

"Take me to see him," she insisted. "I need answers, and I can't find them here."

"No." He pinched the bridge of his nose. What in hell was the matter with her? He couldn't take her into Indian Territory. He'd damaged her reputation enough at the spring gala, not to mention the fact he'd been inside her home more than once. He wouldn't damage it further. "It's a three-day journey across the plains into Indian Territory, and whether you want to believe it or not, there is a war going on. I'll not have you traipsing off in the middle of it."

He raised his head and met her gaze. She stood, clasping her hands prayer-like in front of her as she came around the table and knelt before him. Placing her palms on his knees, she raised pleading eyes to his. He looked away, angry that she could still make him hard.

Mumbling an expletive beneath his breath, he shoved back his chair and stood. It only took a second to realize his mistake. With him standing while she remained kneeling, she was in the perfect position to give him the carnal relief he so desired.

Her face was mere inches from his painfully hard erection.

"Get up," he snapped, lifting her to her feet. Embarrassed and more than a little angry, he ignored the hot tears flowing freely from her eyes.

"Don't take me then. Just promise you'll go. Leave out the back door and take White Deer with you."

"You've had a vision," White Deer said, rising from his chair. Dylan had all but forgotten his presence, damn Selena's eyes.

"I'm no psychic," she protested, "but you're both in danger."

White Deer apparently believed her. He turned to Dylan and glared. "I will take her to Dream Speaker if you do not."

"Over my dead body!" Selena was white. Not even White Deer could guarantee her safety if the chief thought her a threat.

"Our shaman has foreseen the coming of a white woman who knows the fate of the Indian nation. I believe Woman with No Fear is that woman."

Dylan raked a hand through his hair. "Have you two forgotten about Mary? Her body is still lying out on the open prairie. Don't you think it's been exposed to the elements long enough? I need someone other than myself to identify the body so we can lay her to rest, and it would be nice if someone in authority could declare her true cause of death as something other than murder. Frankly, I'm damn tired of being under suspicion."

Then looking at White Deer, he added, "Are you going with me to town or not?"

"Don't go." Selena grabbed his arm, forcing him to face her. "Send Alberto. He's not in danger. You are."

She wrapped her arms around his waist and cried against his chest. He didn't hesitate. He just pulled her closer as tears flowed from her red-rimmed eyes and dampened his shirt.

"Why are you so afraid I'm going to die?" He touched her cheek, feeling her tremble. Her fear was real. It was a tangible thing radiating out from her body to encompass them both.

"Because I've seen you die over and over in my dreams," she whispered, turning her face into his palm.

"You've known me less than month." It was getting harder to dismiss her fears. He just wasn't sure they were rational.

"And I've dreamed of you most of my life," she added, quickening his pulse.

"Dream visions are powerful," White Deer said. "You must heed their warnings."

Selena stepped out of Dylan's arms and turned to look at White Deer. "I'm trying." Then she turned her gaze back to Dylan. "I thought Major Davis hated you enough to kill you, but at the spring gala, you said he used to be your friend, and he said you betrayed him. So, maybe his hatred is tempered by regret."

He'd like to think so. They'd once been as close as brothers. He'd hate to think Andy never had a kind thought about the past. "Andy wants me arrested. Not dead."

"But if that never happened, would he take the law into his own hands? Would he execute you without the benefit of a trial?"

Andy wasn't a murderer. He'd proved that during the war. He never once executed a prisoner. "No. He's an ass, and he'd see me hang if I were convicted of Mary's death, but it would be for justice, not vengeance."

"Then it has to be the surveyor," she said, sending a chill down his spine.

He pulled away and held her at arms' length. "What do you know about Tommy Walters?"

"He worked at the fort, and he was engaged to Mary, but she was in love with you and Tommy knew it. Didn't he?" Her eyes widened as if she suddenly had a thought. "He hated you enough to kill you."

Icy fingers snaked down Dylan's spine, and the hairs on the back of his neck stood on end. She was talking about him in the past tense again.

"Tell me what you know, or what you think you know," he demanded, cupping her chin in his hand. He turned her face up so he could see into her eyes. He'd know if she lied.

"You have to leave here. Don't ask me why. Just go."

She hadn't answered his question, but her fears were real. She genuinely cared, and that caused an ache in the center of his chest.

He frowned, not liking the way she made him feel. For no matter how much she protested otherwise, a white woman would always be ashamed of his Cherokee blood. Yet even as he thought it, a tiny seed of hope took root in his heart.

"Once you take this path, there's no turning back," he said, surprising himself.

"I couldn't turn back if I wanted to. It's my destiny."

Her gaze was so honest and direct it scared the hell out of him.

Chapter 12

Dylan drew a detailed map pinpointing the location of Mary's body for Alberto to take to Sheriff Hobbs in the morning. While the men discussed the map, Selena slipped on her blue jeans and threw a change of clothes into a saddlebag along with a brush and a few essentials.

Around midnight, she and Dylan slipped out the back door and met White Deer in the barn. Once they'd saddled the horses, they left the Tillman farm by way of the creek, completely avoiding the front drive and the road leading into town. Neither Dylan nor White Deer understood the need for such stealth, but Selena wanted to get Dylan out of Canyon Creek in one piece. Unfortunately, the trip proved more difficult than she would have imagined.

None of them had had any sleep, and it had been years since Selena had ridden a horse any further than the half hour it had taken to get to Canyon Creek the day of her arrival. As the sun climbed higher in the midday sky, she shifted in the saddle, trying to get comfortable. Her butt ached, and she was so tired she could barely hold open her eyes.

She glanced at White Deer, who rode beside her while Dylan scouted the trail ahead. Both of them worried about an Apache attack, but White Deer was worried about the cavalry as well. He didn't want some overzealous soldier mistaking him for a hostile who'd kidnapped a white woman.

No wonder Dylan was irritated. She'd been so naïve, thinking she knew something about life in this century. Worrying about the Apache was bad enough without having to worry about the "good-guys" killing them. How many other dangers would they face that she'd failed to consider before insisting on this trip?

Stupid. Stupid. Stupid!

In an effort to distract herself from morbid thoughts, she studied the slowly passing scenery as they traveled ever closer to

Indian Territory. She'd driven through this area in her own time. The constant wind hadn't changed, but in the future, the dust would be much worse because of soil erosion from over development. In the future, The Great Plains still existed, but seeing it now, Selena realized just how vast this part of the country was. Devoid of civilization, the miles and miles of amber grain waving in the wind looked like a vast, alien ocean.

Trees were scarce along the plains but grew in abundance along the river valleys and streams. Most were scrubby but still provided a modicum of privacy when they stopped for the noon meal. As she was coming out from behind a tree she'd used as her restroom, she nearly collided with Dylan. He nodded, and the two of them walked back to the creek where they'd left the horses to graze.

Dylan patted his horse on the rump and reached into his saddlebag for a canvas sack. The biscuit he handed her was dry, and the greasy meat-like substance looked like a glistening, homemade slab of beef jerky. She sniffed. "It stinks. What is it?"

"Pemmican. An Indian staple made from dried buffalo, berries, bone marrow, and melted fat. It's not exactly what you're used to, but it'll keep you from starving."

"Well, I'll try anything once." She took a hesitant bite and shuddered. It was slick and chewy, but not as nasty as she'd expected. "Not too bad," she added before taking another bite. "The taste kind of lingers—even after you swallow—but it tastes better than it smells."

Dylan's mouth hitched up on one side. It was the first smile to cross his face since they'd shared a laugh at the spring gala. Then the smile faded. "How you holdin' up?"

Pulling her eyes away from his sexy mouth, she rubbed her backside. "I'll be a little sore in the morning, but I think I can make it."

He smiled, showing a single dimple in the left corner of his mouth, and her pulse tripped into overdrive. Then he wiggled his dark brows up and down in a comically lascivious manner. "Want me to kiss it and make it better?"

"Yes." He could kiss her anywhere he wanted.

Her cocky response left him visibly affected. The evidence of his desire standing at attention in those tight military pants was—well—evident. When her gaze drifted back up to meet his, he self-consciously tugged on his left pant leg to make room for his increased size.

Selena snatched the canteen from his hand and took a large swallow of water before replying, "You're a dangerously tempting man Dylan Casey."

With a low growl, he pulled her to his chest. The canteen caught between their two overheated bodies as he leaned forward and whispered seductively. "Maybe I should see just how tempting you think I am."

He lowered his hands to the curve of her buttocks and pulled her flush against his erection. "You're a real flirt, aren't you? So tell me, Selena, how many lovers have you taken to your bed?"

Ice water couldn't have curbed her appetite any faster. Fury mixed with pain warmed her cheeks. She ground her teeth but didn't attempt to pull away. "Don't try to turn this into something ugly. Just because I know about the birds and the bees, doesn't mean I'm a whore. I can count the number of men in my life on two fingers. Can you say the same?"

A flush stained his cheeks, but his mouth quirked upward on one side. "No. I've never been with a man."

She rolled her eyes. "You know what I mean."

He dropped his gaze. "I'm an ass. I don't care if you're not a virgin, and I shouldn't have insulted you. But White Deer is less than fifty yards away, and as savage as you think I am, I don't take women with an audience."

She ground her teeth, trying to control her rising anger. "I've never called you a savage, and I didn't say I wanted you to *take* me now."

He smiled. "But we both know you want it. I feel it every time I touch you."

She made a point of looking down at his crotch. "Yeah? I feel something too. But I'm not stupid."

#

Selena's bold comment sent Dylan's blood racing, but the second half of her statement doused his desire like a bucket of ice water.

So, she wasn't stupid enough to bed a dirty half-breed. She

86

could bed a couple of white men without the benefit of marriage, but she wouldn't lie down with a half-breed no matter how desirable she found him. Her rejection hurt, more than Mary's ever had, but he would not let the pain cripple him.

Embracing the anger, he fanned the flames, and his tender caress became a punishing grip. He balled his fist in her hair and tilted her head back while his other hand pressed against her spine. "So, you can get your appetite from a half-breed but you'll eat elsewhere. Is that it?"

He expected her to cry or struggle, but she turned her body toward the hand holding her hair and twisted her hips, breaking his hold. The moment she was free, she raised her knee into his groin.

Pain shot up from his genitals to his abdomen. His eyes watered and his stomach heaved as he dropped to his knees, clutching his throbbing manhood. *Jisa*, woman," he squeaked in a higher voice than normal. "Where in hell did you learn that maneuver?"

White Deer howled with laughter from his perch in the saddle. He'd already remounted and had ridden close enough to witness Dylan's humiliation, which only made Dylan angrier. He'd kill the nosey bastard—just as soon as he could stand.

"What the hell did you expect?" Selena ground her teeth, balling her fists at her sides as if she were planning to pummel him into an apology—which he owed her, considering how badly he'd treated her.

Shame flushed his cheeks. His mama had raised him better.

"Where the hell do you come by such fast reflexes, woman?" he gasped through the pain. Damned if she hadn't nearly unmanned him.

"Stop acting like a baby," she said as he struggled to his feet. "I didn't do any permanent damage. It should still work as well as it ever did."

The coughing fit that plagued him after that comment was more painful than the initial shock of her kneeing him in the balls. He was now beyond shock and humiliation. To make matters worse, White Deer was laughing his damned fool head off.

Trying to move without throwing up, he snatched the discarded canteen and hobbled to the creek to refill it. When he got back to the horses, he looked at Selena. She stood stiff and proud, and he'd never felt more ashamed.

"Mount up." He would have helped her onto the saddle, but he didn't think it possible. He'd be lucky if he could pull up himself. His balls were still throbbing.

For the remainder of the day White Deer scouted ahead while he and Selena rode behind. Thanks to her swift reflexes, they set a considerably slower pace than before and with every dip in the road, he clenched his teeth. He wanted to apologize—he needed to apologize. He just didn't know where to begin without admitting her rejection hurt, and he'd overreacted. He just hoped she'd find some satisfaction in knowing their slower pace had nothing to do with her sore backside.

"I'm sorry I kneed you in the groin, but you were a real asshole," she said after several miles of stony silence.

Her apology made him feel even more like an ass. He owed her one, not the other way around. But damn if the woman didn't keep him off balance. "Forget it."

"I can't. I'm not normally a violent person, but you really pissed me off, and I reacted instinctively. I don't normally attack the people I care about."

"Lady, you don't know me well enough to care," he replied, though his heart was pounding more rapidly than normal in his chest.

"I care. A lot." She pulled on the reins and brought her mount to a stop.

He turned his horse around until they were facing one another, but he still didn't speak. It seemed every time he opened his mouth, he just made matters worse.

Her gaze sought his. "I know you don't trust me, but I've been as honest as I can be, and I swear I'd never betray you."

He flicked the reins and turned his mount. He wanted to ride on and just not say a word, but he couldn't. And he couldn't allow himself to hope that she might be different.

"Your cousin made that same promise," he tossed over his shoulder. "Look how well that turned out."

#

Close to dark, they dismounted and made camp. Earlier in the day, Dylan had killed a rabbit, and he was now cooking it on a spit over the fire while White Deer saw to the horses. Selena sat on the ground and leaned against a bedroll looking exhausted.

He looked away, trying to ignore the tender feelings she stirred in him. No matter how much she claimed to care, his heritage would always come between them. Hadn't Selena admitted as much?

"Yeah? I feel something too. But I'm not stupid."

She'd admitted to having feelings for him. Then in the same breath, she'd admitted she wasn't stupid enough to act on those feelings. He should be so smart. It took every ounce of willpower he possessed not to walk over there, pull her in his arms, and beg her forgiveness.

Instead, he poured a cup of coffee and carried it to her. "Here."

She peered over the rim and frowned. "Thanks, but no thanks. I can't drink this black goo you call coffee without cream and sugar, and I doubt you packed either in your saddlebags. So if you don't mind, I'll just stick to water."

"Suit yourself." She wouldn't even accept his peace offering, but that didn't stop him from bringing her water.

When the rabbit was done, he handed her a plate and they ate in silence. After a while, she finally looked at him. "When will White Deer eat?"

"Why?" Guilt warmed his cheeks. "Are you afraid to be alone with me now?"

"No." She blew out a breath and stood. "I'm tired. It's been a long day, and your attitude has made it seem even longer. I don't want to fight, but you seem to be looking for one. I know you don't believe me, but I do care for you. More than you know."

He couldn't allow himself to believe that. He slung his coffee grounds in the fire and looked up. "I find that damned hard to believe because that's exactly what your cousin said."

"Yeah? Well, I'm not Mary. Not even close. So stop comparing us." Without a backward glance, she turned and walk toward the bedroll she'd unwound earlier.

Dylan jumped to his feet and ate up the distance between them. Grabbing her from behind, he swung her around to face him. "Stop taunting me with promises we know you can't keep. You're white. I'm not. So let's just keep our distance until this journey is done. Then we can go our separate ways in peace."

"I'm not taunting you. I feel as if I've known you forever. I just can't explain it." She glanced from the hands holding her prisoner to his face. "And at the moment, I can't explain why I care for you either, because you're acting like an ignorant jackass. So, kindly let go."

Dylan's grip tightened briefly as he searched her eyes for the truth, but it was as elusive as ever. So he let her go, dropping his arms to his sides. Then holding her head high, she walked toward her bedroll and dropped to the ground. With a tired sigh, she curled onto her side, turned her back to him, and put an end to any further conversation.

He took a deep, frustrated breath and released it through tightly clenched teeth before taking off his shirt and stretching out on a bedroll on the other side of the campfire. Stacking his hands behind his head, he stared blindly at the night sky.

Guilt and anger consumed him. He hadn't meant to hurt her but damn it, he couldn't take a chance on another spoiled white woman. Mary had caused him enough heartache. He didn't think he could survive a rejection from Selena. Despite what he'd said to her, she was nothing like her cousin. But she was still just as white.

In the beginning, Mary had claimed his heritage didn't matter either. They were lovers for months before the colonel found out and all because of that damned locket he'd given her for her birthday. The next week, they'd met at the spring gala. They stood together to watch the parade, holding hands behind her skirt, slipping away as often as possible to find a secluded area so they could be alone. Later that evening, they met at the photographer's booth, careful not to stand too close to one another. And when they were alone, Mary placed the tintypes inside the locket.

Despite the secret rendezvous and the care they took to make their meetings seem accidental, people talked, and it didn't take long for rumors to reach the colonel. When he saw Dylan's picture inside the locket, it confirmed his suspicions.

The colonel responded with bribes and threats. When Dylan refused the bribes and ignored the threats, Colonel Tillman sent him out on patrol. He was gone for three months, and when he returned, Mary was engaged to Tommy Walters.

He'd been hurt by her betrayal, but after the colonel's death, he couldn't stay away any longer. He still remembered the look of hurt, followed by pure rage that washed over Walters' face as he stood in the shadows listening to every word Mary said. Yet despite that, Dylan had done nothing to protect Mary from Walter's wrath. Before finding her body yesterday, Dylan had thought Walters killed Mary just as everyone else believed he'd done the foul deed. If not for Selena, he would have believed until his dying day that Tommy Walters murdered Mary Tillman—and he would never have known peace. But Walters didn't kill Mary. A tornado had.

Maybe now, he could let go of the guilt.

Chapter 13

Instinct awakened Dylan from a restless sleep. Rolling to his feet, he gazed across the glowing embers of the dying campfire to the slim form huddled beneath the bedroll, and his chest cramped with longing. He'd drifted to sleep thinking of Mary, but he'd dreamt of Selena.

He shook his head to clear remnants of the erotic dream from his mind and stretched his arms over his head. White Deer's silent approach had nearly caught him off guard.

"My watch." Dylan glanced up to check the moon's position in the sky. It was less than three hours until daybreak.

White Deer chuckled. "Woman with No Fear makes you slow like old man. I make more noise than buffalo before you wake up," he said in his native tongue.

Heat burned Dylan's cheeks. Damn that Comanche.

"Shut up, White Deer," he responded in English before snatching up his rifle and heading toward the creek. White Deer's laughter followed him to the water, darkening his mood even more.

With a good three hours of night watch ahead of him, he had little to do but sort through his confusing thoughts. He was fond of Selena and liked her a hell of a lot more than he should. She was Mary's cousin, and she'd lied about her arrival in Canyon Creek.

Suspicious from the start, he'd checked into her story the day after her arrival, and he discovered a lot of inconsistency. For starters, she claimed to have taken the stage from Fort Worth to Pecos, but there was no record of her doing so. Though it was possible she'd used another name, he couldn't find any evidence of her buying a horse in Pecos either.

Wanting answers and knowing he wouldn't get them from her, he'd contacted his old friend and Texas Ranger, Jed Hoskins. Through his contacts back East, Jed had learned that a young woman named Selena Tillman had taken the train from Richmond sometime in late November. She arrived in Louisville on schedule, but the trail ended. No one by the name Selena Tillman had ever boarded the train to Fort Worth, nor had she taken a stage. Four months later, Selena showed up in Canyon Creek claiming to have ridden a horse from Pecos, but no one had ever seen this mysterious horse and Selena hadn't mentioned it again after claiming it threw her and ran off.

Trying to understand how she'd arrived in Canyon Creek was hard enough, but what he found harder to understand was her unusual speech and the strange remarks she often made about the future. Unlike White Deer, he didn't think she was a psychic or a woman who had visions, but she was definitely strange.

Her behavior following the discovery of Mary's body was anything but rational, yet her fear seemed real. What he couldn't understand was why she thought he was in danger or why she was worried about Tommy Walters. He wasn't. The man may have been furious over what he viewed as Mary's betrayal, and Dylan may have suspected him of killing Mary before he discovered her body, but Walters had never given Dylan any indication he carried a grudge against him. If anything, Walters had been unnecessarily polite the one time he'd run into him after Mary's disappearance. After all, Mary had betrayed them both.

So what made Selena view Walters as a threat? In the absence of any reasonable explanation, he *would* seek the advice of Dream Speaker.

Six months ago, he'd asked the shaman how to find Mary. Dream Speaker had told him he'd need the help of a white woman who came from far away. He also said this woman would change his destiny and foretell the fate of the Indian nations. Dylan doubted Selena could foretell anything. Even if she could, he couldn't trust her. She'd lied to him from day one.

A twig snapped. Dylan crouched and reached for the knife sheathed at his side. As if conjured up by his innermost desires, Selena emerged from the moonlit shadows of the cottonwoods. Her tangled hair had escaped a fancy braid and her eyes were puffy from sleep. She wore the same long-sleeved blue shirt she'd worn earlier in the day, but now the sleeves were rolled up, half the buttons were undone, and she'd knotted it at the waist. She wore no shoes or pants, just her bloomers.

Lilly Gayle

Desire speared him, quickening his pulse.

"What the hell are you up to?' he growled, once he finally found his voice.

Unperturbed by his gruff manner, Selena yawned and scratched at the back of her head, loosening more silky strands from her braid. Then she stretched, pressing her breasts more firmly against the fabric of her partially buttoned shirt. The sight of her nearly sent him to his knees.

"My butt hurts and my legs ache. I couldn't sleep, so I thought I'd sit in the creek for a while. I'm hoping the cool water might relieve my stiff muscles," she said, brushing passed him to sit in the shallow water, and Dylan's anger mounted.

He knew she wasn't use to sitting all day in the saddle, and she was probably hurting in places she'd never known existed, but she knew he stood guard. Earlier, he'd warned her not to tempt him if she didn't want him in her bed, and by God, he meant it. If she were going to flaunt herself, then she'd damn well better be prepared to face the consequences.

Blood racing, he splashed into the creek after her. He lifted her up by the shoulders and pulled her back against his chest to drag her from the water before swinging her around to face him. His eyes roamed every inch of her body from the gentle swell of her breasts visible above the V of her partially unbuttoned shirt, beyond the indention of her navel beneath the knot at her waist, to the long expanse of bare, wet legs.

Raising his eyes to the shadow of her sex, now visible through the wet fabric of her bloomers, he grew painfully erect. He ground his teeth, trying to rein in his burning desire. "Where are your clothes?"

"Hanging on a tree branch. Right over there," she said, nodding her head as Dylan's grip tightened on her biceps. "Now let go. You're hurting me."

"You're lucky I haven't done more than threaten to shake some sense into you," he snapped, still holding her arms. "Don't you know better than to parade around in front of strange men half-naked?"

"I'm not half-naked and you're not strange. Well, not too strange, anyway. Besides, what did you expect me to do—sit in the creek fully dressed? Get real."

94

"Get dressed," he demanded, gripping her arms harder. "Or by God I will take what you so carelessly offer."

Without waiting for a reply, he pulled her roughly against his solid frame to capture her lips in a brutal kiss. His tongue swept deep into her mouth, hard and demanding as he ground his lips against hers. Unable to resist his unbridled lust, Selena gave in without a struggle, and her weak acceptance tore at his conscience. Never in his life had he taken a woman against her will, and he wasn't about to start now.

Abruptly ending the kiss, he tore his mouth free and held her at arms' length. His gaze traveled the length of her body before coming to rest on her passion bruised lips.

"Keep your distance or I swear, you'll find yourself beneath a half-breed," he stated in a voice trembling with need.

She stood on her tiptoes and planted a tender kiss on the corner of his mouth. Then gently touching the side of his face, she whispered, "I've dreamed of you all my life, and there's no other place I'd rather be."

The tender confession tore at Dylan's heart. Before he could change his mind or argue himself out of it, he pulled her into his arms and lowered his mouth to hers. The eagerness of her response amazed him. She clung to him, her warm tongue mating with his as she matched his passion, stroke for need-filled stroke, and like a man dying of thirst, he greedily drank from her eager lips.

Aching for what he'd wanted for so long, he slid his hands beneath the wet fabric of her drawers and over her damp body to grip the cool globes of her bottom. As he pulled her more firmly against his hardened arousal, she stepped out of her bloomers.

The sounds she made in the back of her throat as he lowered her to the sandy bank nearly sent him up in flames. She was no virgin, and he wouldn't have taken what she offered if she were. Mary hadn't been innocent either, but that never bothered him. Thinking of Selena's previous lovers did.

Dark jealousy threatened to dampen his ardor. He refused to allow it. Groaning with need, he pushed aside her half-buttoned shirt and concentrated on the way her pink-tipped breasts fit perfectly in the palms of his hands.

Her nipples tautened as he brushed his callused thumbs

over the sensitive flesh before lowering his mouth to taste her. He suckled first one breast and then the other. Selena moaned, arching her back and pushing her hands into his hair to hold him closer. Drinking his fill, he slowly lifted his mouth to taste hers.

He held himself up on his left arm while his right hand glided over her breasts, before sliding lower to curve over her hips. When his fingers splayed over her abdomen, she shuddered. Another quiver shook her as he brushed his hand over the golden curls at the apex of her thighs. And when he finally dipped his finger inside, she whimpered her need and pulled him closer.

A groan escaped before Dylan sealed his lips to hers, quieting her vocal response. She moved against him, her back arching, her thighs tensing in a desperate quest for release, making him harder than he'd ever been in his life.

Unable to restrain himself further, he raised up enough to push his buckskins to his knees, freeing his engorged sex while keeping his lips sealed to Selena's. Aching with a need that bordered on painful, he raised himself up over her supine body.

The tip of his shaft pushed eagerly against her slick passage, and Selena wrapped her legs around the back of his thighs, pulling him closer as he thrust inside.

"*Jisa!*" he swore, unable to control the violent shiver that shook him, pushing him to ride her hard and fast until he was spent.

He'd never before taken a woman so roughly or so selfishly.

He pulled out, barely comprehending what had just happened. How could he have lost control so easily? Her frantic urgings had pushed him beyond his endurance, and he'd selfishly sought his own release without a thought to her pleasure.

"Who are you?"

"Excuse me?"

"You're no virgin."

Her blond brows grazed her hairline. "I never claimed to be, and um, neither are you, Bucko, so don't be casting stones in my direction."

He wasn't casting stones. Men were expected to sow their wild oats before settling down, but Selena was a woman—a white woman—and decent white women didn't sow oats, wild or otherwise. Even Mary had expected romance and gentle caresses, but he'd rutted over Selena like a dog in heat, and she wasn't even complaining. Perhaps, she was used to men abusing her. He just didn't know. He didn't know a damn thing when it came to Selena.

He started to rise.

"Don't go," she whispered, reaching out to him. "I knew it was going to be rough the first time with you. But you'll be gentle this time. I know it."

"Ah hell," he swore as he lay down beside her on the sandy bank.

Pulling her close to his side, he tried to slow his erratic breathing. He was throbbing painfully, needing to be inside of her, taking his sweet time—needing to see the pleasure on her face as he brought her to a quivering climax. He just couldn't understand how he'd lost control the first time or how long he should wait before taking her again.

His whole body went rigid when she lightly grazed his manhood. At his sharp intake of breath, she began to stroke him until he ached. Then he pulled her across his body until she straddled his thigh. "Damn woman, but you would tempt a saint."

#

Dylan's thigh pressed so intimately against Selena, she ached to have him inside her again. He'd been a bit rough the first time, but she could no more have slowed him down than she could have stopped a speeding train. And she hadn't wanted to. He'd brought her to the brink. Now, she wanted to plunge headfirst over the edge.

Needing to feel every inch of his hard body, she ran her hands down his arms. His rock hard biceps bunched in response. Aroused by his body, she ran her hands from his flat, muscular belly to his hard, sleek chest. She followed her hands with her lips, scraping her fingers along the tightly corded column of his neck to the edge of his strong jaw. Then she ran her fingers through his thick hair and lowered her lips to his.

As he dipped his tongue into her mouth, she rode his bare thigh. The harder he kissed her, the more frantic her movements. She rocked against him until a tightening sensation began to build between her legs. Gasping for breath, she rose above him and impaled herself.

"Oh God!" She straddled his hips, riding him hard, rocking against him until the tension became unbearable.

She pushed harder, hovering over the edge, unable to reach a climax. The building tension became almost unbearable—until Dylan rolled her onto her back and pressed so deeply inside her she reached the summit. Heaven was now within reach.

He pumped harder until the urgent need inside her became a physical force, exploding outward like a champagne cork released under pressure. Crying his name, she clung to him as heat flowed like liquid fire from the center of her body, and the tremors finally subsided.

She had never been more satisfied, not even in her dreams.

Chapter 14

Selena was sore the next morning, and the feel of the saddle between her legs was a teasing reminder of the night before. Making love to Dylan was the most wonderful experience of her life, but once he'd brought her to an earth-shattering climax, he'd pulled away from her as if she had syphilis.

Really? She'd just had unprotected sex for the first time in her life, and he was worried?

His obvious regret over what she considered the single most important event of her life was more than a little disheartening. She hadn't expected him to profess his undying love, but cold brooding silence sucked. After White Deer gave him a knowing look at dawn, Dylan had ridden ahead, a very unhappy camper.

They'd set a grueling pace since dawn, and she wasn't used to such strenuous riding. Spoiled by the twentieth century, her lack of stamina and endurance took its toll. Shortly before noon, Dylan pulled his mount alongside hers and shouted her name, interrupting a dream. Her head snapped up and she almost fell off the horse.

Dylan spoke to White Deer in one Native dialect or another before taking her reins and heading west. In less than twenty minutes, they were riding into a grove of stunted live oaks bordering a shallow creek.

"Why didn't you tell me you needed a break," Dylan asked as he helped her dismount.

"I was too tired to shout, and you were riding too far ahead to hear me if I did." She could barely hold her eyes open, and her muscles burned. She wasn't even sure her legs would support her weight if Dylan released her arm.

"Next time, say something. I don't need you falling out of the saddle and breaking your damn fool neck."

"Gee, thanks for caring." Tears welled behind her eyes, burning her throat. She swallowed them, refusing to cry.

Muttering under his breath, he led her to a shady area beneath the trees while White Deer led the horses to the creek. Dylan handed her a hard biscuit and dried meat. Then he turned without further comment and joined White Deer by the water. Tired and disappointed, Selena barely tasted the biscuit as she washed it down with water from her canteen.

Too exhausted to chew the dried meat, she put the remains in her shirt pocket after just two bites. Then she stretched out on the grass in the partial shade and fell asleep before her eyes fully closed. She would have liked nothing better than to spend the afternoon napping in the shade, but all too soon Dylan was nudging her awake.

"Come on. It's time to go."

"Five more minutes," she grumbled, rolling away from him.

"*Kam!*" He hunkered down and shook her shoulder.

"Hmm?"

"Now," he translated. "Come on. Get up. You're the one who wanted to go on this trip. Remember? So you've got no right to complain about it now."

Brushing the hair from her eyes as she struggled to sit up, she focused on Dylan's face as he squatted on his haunches. As usual, those piercing blue eyes gave away nothing.

"Come on," he said gently, breaking eye contact as he helped her stand.

After Dylan lifted her into the saddle, he and White Deer mounted up, and White Deer took the lead, leaving Dylan to bring up the rear. By mid-day, Selena was again having trouble staying awake in the saddle, and by late afternoon, she'd had enough. She pulled her horse to a stop and waited for Dylan to catch up. That's when she noticed an unusual rock formation springing up from the prairie like some sort of monument.

Fist-sized rocks arranged in a circle around several larger rocks encircled the bleached-out skull of a Texas long horn. Another rock painted with unusual markings topped the skeleton head.

"What is it?" she asked when Dylan rode up beside her.

"Medicine-sign. It draws the buffalo to the hunt. We're in Indian territory now so you better stay close."

#

Dylan remained alert as Selena followed behind on her slower mount. Although they were still traveling south of the region assigned to the Comanche at the Treaty of Medicine Lodge, there was every indication a hunting party was nearby despite government restrictions on tribal movement.

White Deer rode ahead to intercept the warriors who'd strayed far from tribal lands in search of the buffalo. With any luck, the hunting party belonged to Chief Dog Ears' Wichita band of Comanche. Of course, he had no way of knowing for sure until they caught up with the group, but if they had just stumbled upon Dog Ears' band, it was possible they'd find Dream Speaker as well. The old Comanche often accompanied the warriors on hunting trips and raids, as his visions often proved beneficial.

He hoped Dream Speaker was with them because the Wichita's usual summer camp was only a half-day's ride from his father's ranch. If he had to travel into Bexar County to find the medicine man, his father would eventually hear about it, and he didn't need the added guilt of being so close to home without visiting.

It had been over a year since his last visit, but he didn't think things were likely to have changed between him and his mother. He could well imagine her reaction when she learned of the trouble Mary had caused, especially since he was now involved with Mary's cousin.

Damned if she wouldn't have plenty to say on the subject. *Jisa*! If only he could get through one visit without his mother's lamenting about the past, and she would raise holy hell if she found out he was traveling with an unmarried woman who lacked proper chaperone. Melody Smith Casey might be Cherokee, but she'd been born in Georgia, and southern gentility was as ingrained in her as in any gently bred southern lady.

If she were to meet Selena and discover he'd slept with her—and she would figure it out—she'd see to it he did the honorable thing—even if Selena didn't want to marry him. It wouldn't bother his mother that Selena was white. After all, she was happily married to a white man, and she'd rather see him married to a white woman than a Comanche.

His mother hated the Comanche and had done so without

101

remorse since the government took most of the Cherokee's land and gave it to the plains tribes in retribution for the Cherokee's southern sympathies during the war. In her opinion, the plains tribes were the antitheses of everything in which she believed. They were wild and untamable, and she considered them a bad influence on the young Cherokee, her son included. His mother was still under the misguided impression the government would leave the Indians in peace if they acclimated themselves to the white man's world.

It hadn't worked in Georgia, and it wouldn't work in the west. The white man wasn't interested in living peaceably with the Indians. He should know. He'd spent most of his life trying to fit into the white man's world without success. The fact he was part white himself, didn't make a difference. In the eyes of the white man, he would always be an Indian or worse, a dirty half-breed.

Cursing under his breath, Dylan pulled back on the reins, bringing Ishtabe to a halt. The animal danced beneath him, and though he had yet to hear the warning thunder, he felt the ground tremble beneath him.

"What's wrong?" Selena halted her mount beside his. She'd yet to feel the ominous rumbling of the earth or hear the thunderous warning of their approach, but he didn't take time to explain his haste. He snatched her reins from her grasp and pulled her along beside him as he spurred their mounts forward.

#

Selena felt the ground tremble beneath her only seconds before she heard the distant roar of thunder, but Dylan was racing to the top of a hill, dragging her and her horse behind him. When they reached the summit, she glanced back over her shoulder and gasped. Less than a mile away, a living mass moved rapidly across the plains in the midst of a thick cloud of dust. The roaring thunder increased as the mass moved closer, and her heart rose into her throat. Had Dylan not acted so quickly, the stampeding buffalo would have overtaken them.

As the bison topped the ridge in a choking cloud of dust, tears stung her eyes, but the awesome sight below held her spellbound. Then Dylan pulled her from the saddle and settled her in front of him. She glanced over her shoulder. A red bandanna covered the lower half of Dylan's face. Behind the mask, his eyes smiled as he tied a second bandanna over her mouth and nose. Then he secured the reins of her Appaloosa to his saddle horn and used nothing more than the firm pressure of his knees to control the large chestnut gelding beneath them. With both hands now free, he wrapped his arms tightly around her waist and held her firmly against his chest as the buffalo thundered passed.

Impressed with his skills and his thoughtfulness, she shifted on his lap so she could better see his face.

"Thank you," she shouted above the thunderous din of the trampling beasts.

As their eyes locked and held above their masks, his burned like twin blue flames, sending an electrically charged current of awareness pulsating through her body. The air between them sizzled and for several seconds, everything around them ceased to exist.

When a shrill cry rent the air and brought the world back into focus, a lean, bare-chested warrior rode bareback into the stampeding herd. As he thundered passed at an astonishing speed, he dropped low to the side of his mount's right flank. Hanging by nothing more than his ankles, he released a rapid-fire volley of arrows over his horse's back, bringing down two buffalo at once. The warrior's cry of victory sent chills racing down Selena's spine.

"That was amazing!" Better than anything, she'd ever seen on the big screen.

"No one's better on a horse than the Comanche," Dylan said in her ear. "But don't get too excited. Black Fox already has a wife. Of course, that shouldn't be a problem. The Comanche practice bigamy."

"Very funny," she said over her shoulder as White Deer galloped passed to join the hunt. His presence among the tribe reassured her they were in no imminent danger from a hostile band or renegades.

Sitting with her back against Dylan's chest, she watched as more than a dozen warriors chased after the flying herd. Marveling at the spectacle before her, she watched one warrior let loose a blood-curdling war cry as he brought down a large bull with a single arrow. Then, he jumped from his still moving horse and landed on the back of the heaving beast as it lay dying. As the buffalo took its last shuddering breath, the warrior raised his bow high above his head and gave a shrill victory cry.

Selena's skin prickled with gooseflesh.

The buffalo was a central part of the nomadic tribes' lives, and their passion for the hunt was obvious. Given this strange opportunity to witness history firsthand, Selena realized hunting was as much a sporting event as a means of survival. Unlike the white man who slaughtered the buffalo by the thousands for their hides alone, the plains Indians wasted nothing.

The carcasses provided fresh meat for now and a stockpile of dried meat for winter. They used the hides for blankets, moccasins, tepees, and clothing, and turned the sinew into thread and bowstrings, but in a few short years, there wouldn't be enough buffalo left to hunt or any free Indians to do the hunting. She couldn't remember when it would happen, but congress would pass a bill that would end tribal life and force the Indians to bend to the white man's will. Then they'd open Oklahoma territory to white homesteaders and strip the last of the Indians of their land and freedom, giving Native Americans two choices. Give up their tribal allegiance or live out their lives within the boundaries of a reservation. Once the government destroyed the Indian's way of life, their indomitable spirit would finally be broken.

She didn't know Dylan's age, but if he was still alive to witness the government's destruction of his people, it would destroy him. She twisted in the saddle and aligned her body so she could see his eyes over his bandanna. "How old are you?"

He grunted and redistributed her weight. Her wiggling must have aroused him because his erection poked at her bottom. She couldn't help smiling.

He grunted. "Thirty. Why?"

"I just wondered." She couldn't share her dark thoughts. They were too depressing. And he'd never believe her.

His gaze held hers. "How old are you?"

She immediately sensed a change in his attitude. His arms tighten imperceptibly around her waist, and his reaction seemed to hinge on how she answered his question. With only the slightest hesitation, she answered honestly. "Twenty-five."

Dylan's arms became rigid, locking around her like steel bands as he lifted her off his lap and onto the Appaloosa's back. Both Selena and the horse were taken by surprise. The Appaloosa nervously pranced in reaction.

"Stay put," he demanded, pointing an accusing finger in her face before riding off at a gallop.

Unable to determine the cause of this new anger, she watched him ride into the melee below. He spoke briefly with White Deer before returning to snatch the reins from her grasp. Without a word, he turned the horses around and set off at a quick pace, pulling her along behind him as if she were a prisoner bent on escape.

"What's wrong?"

The black scowl he cast over his shoulder as he lowered his bandanna told her without words. He had no intention of answering.

Chapter 15

As they approached the Comanche Village, Dylan halted the horses and held a finger to his lips, silently warning her not to speak. Then he called out a greeting to two heavily armed sentries. After a brief exchange, they waved them through without incident, but a half dozen other young men watched from behind rocks and hills.

Common sense told Selena to be afraid, but believing she was visiting a Hollywood movie set was easier than accepting this twisted new reality. At least fifty tepees circled a centralized camp along the banks of a wide creek. Outside the four-sided conical structures, women worked while half-naked children ran around in breechcloths playing games with sticks or listening to old men tell stories outside their lodges.

Selena's stomach clenched. She'd wanted to talk to the shaman, but she sure as hell didn't want to ride through a Comanche village. She was the enemy.

As Dylan led her horse through the camp, children took note of their arrival and ran alongside them. Some just stared but others brandished miniature bows and arrows. Children didn't normally frighten Selena, but these kids looked well-armed and possibly dangerous.

One particularly vocal child seemed to be giving her a piece of his mind in some guttural tongue she couldn't understand. Then Dylan's horse suddenly stopped, and her Appaloosa had to sidestep to keep from walking into the rear end of his larger mount.

He narrowed his eyes and spoke in clipped tones. "You're in the enemy camp now. So, don't speak unless I tell you to."

As if she could get a word out around the lump of fear cramping her throat.

She nodded and swallowed bile. By now, the Comanche women had taken notice of their arrival, and they looked less friendly than the children did—and a lot more dangerous. One by one, they stopped what they were doing to stare. A few brandished sticks and shouted until a young woman stepped forward and silenced them with a single hand gesture. Then the woman turned to Dylan and addressed him in her own language.

Though he smiled when he answered, his words were apparently not the ones she wanted to hear. She stamped her foot and pointed an accusing finger at Selena, speaking harshly, using choppy hand gestures Dylan seemed to find amusing. With one last lethal glance in Selena's direction, she stomped off in a snit, looking very much like an angry lover.

Selena's heart twisted. Dylan obviously knew the beautiful woman, and from her reaction, Selena guessed the two had been intimate in the not so distant past.

"Good girl," Dylan said as he dismounted. "Now keep quiet just a little longer."

He helped her to the ground and handed the horses' reins to a young man who gave Selena the stink eye. Then Dylan pulled her to his side. "If you don't want to lose your scalp or wind up servicing the entire Comanche Nation, I suggest you do exactly as I say, without question. Do-you-understand?"

She nodded, and her heart slammed against her ribs.

I'm not in Kansas anymore. She wasn't even in the twenty-first century.

Dylan grunted his approval and then led her to a large, brightly painted tepee and planted her outside the flapped entrance. "Don't. Move."

She couldn't if she wanted to. Fear rooted her to the spot.

After calling out a greeting in a native dialect, he disappeared inside the darkened interior, leaving her alone in an alien environment.

Cold sluiced through her, leaving her chilled despite the heat. Dylan's presence by her side had isolated her from reality. Now that he was gone, she remembered the Comanche believed in torture, and she nearly peed her pants when the young Comanche woman sauntered over and made a threatening gesture with her hands, mimicking a knife cutting off a nose. Then White Deer rode into camp, and Selena nearly cried when he dismounted and headed in her direction.

He held her gaze, his eyes warning her to keep quiet. Then

he turned to the Comanche woman who was still glaring at Selena. After a brief exchange in their native tongue, the woman left, but not before saying something to Selena that didn't sound like a compliment.

White Deer turned back around and met Selena's gaze. "I see you met Yellow Rose."

Selena shook. Her teeth chattered. "Yeah, she's my new BFF."

Shaking his head at her strange words, he spoke in English again. "Better for Long Blade if he were Comanche. Then he could have Yellow Rose and Woman With No Fear. It would cost him many ponies, but it would save him much trouble."

Selena wasn't amused, but at that moment, Dylan stepped back outside. He'd taken off his shirt and had replaced his cavalry hat with a wide strip of rawhide around his forehead. After speaking to White Deer in a language she didn't understand, he turned to her. "The chief has granted permission for you to enter and speak. So stay calm, *adawehi*, and don't say anything until I tell you to."

She swallowed a lump of fear. "Okay, but before we go in, can you tell me what *a-da-we-hi* means."

"It's not important." Taking her arm, he tried leading her into the tepee, but she held back.

Her heart raced. "Please tell me. I need to know."

"Angel. Happy? Now let's get this over with."

Warmed by the endearment despite his irritation, she followed him into the darkened lodge. The air inside was hot and thick, smelling of damp earth and wood smoke. Breathing deeply to quell the nervous flutter in her stomach, she followed Dylan as he led her around the periphery of the tepee. As her eyes adjusted to the darkened interior, she studied what would surely have been an anthropologist's wet dream.

The lodge was a good fifteen feet high with an opening at the top to let smoke out and sunlight in. The circumference of the hide-covered floor was larger than she'd expected, and on one wall, there were four elevated sleeping mats on two-foot high bedsteads made of wood and sinew. They looked like fur-covered army cots.

Near the cooking circle, metal utensils—evidence of the

white man's influence—were stored alongside gourd ladles and wooden bowels. Lances, coup sticks, bows, and arrows, were stacked against another side of the hide walls. Selena was no expert in Indian culture, but this didn't look like a medicine man's lodge.

Dylan's next words confirmed her suspicions when he introduced the old man seated before her as Chief Dog Ears. Looking into the man's homely face, she could see how he'd gotten his name.

The Comanche chief's ears stuck out from the sides of his square head and the fleshy, unattached lobes dangled when he made any sudden movements. His hair was long and black, liberally sprinkled with silver, and a single eagle feather dangled from his scalp lock. With his small mouth and meaty jowls, he looked like a basset hound—a potentially dangerous basset hound.

Glaring from beneath bushy brows, he raised one hand and said, "*Maruawe Numuukahni.*"

Selena nearly lost it. For a brief moment, she'd thought he was going to say, "How."

Regaining control of her emotions, she nodded respectfully and sat down when Dylan did.

"Chief Dog Ears welcomes you to his lodge," Dylan said, translating.

"T—tell him, thank-you." Terror squeezed her throat, making speech difficult.

The old man gave her an assessing look before speaking again to Dylan, who translated. "The chief says the white eyes are his enemy, but the Wichita do not kill anyone who asks for hospitality. Not even the white eyes. You are safe for as long as you remain in his camp."

The caveat being, he would not guarantee her safety when she left.

Her blood turned to ice. She looked at Dylan, and he held her gaze, a silent promise to keep her safe as he translated the chief's next words. "The *parabio*, the chief, wants to know if you trust his word, the word of your enemy."

At her nod of acceptance, pride shone in Dylan's eyes, but all he said was, "The chief asks why?"

Looking at the chief who seemed to see beyond her eyes

109

and into her very soul, she spoke as Dylan interpreted. "Because Dylan, the man you call Long Blade, trusts you. If he says you're honorable and will keep your word, I have no reason to doubt you."

The chief seemed to study his fingernails a moment as he watched her from beneath his thick brows. Then he raised his eyes and furiously gesticulated with his hands, and Dylan repeated the words in English.

"The Great White Father in Washington cannot be trusted. He sends his council chiefs to make honey-talk with the *Nermenuh*, the People. He tells us not to raid, and the blue coats will leave us in peace. We get presents. The white eyes get our land and kill the buffalo. We cannot feed our children. We raid. The white eyes take more land. The blue coats make war. We make war. People die.

"It is your wish to see the shaman, to ask for his help interpreting your visions. Dream Speaker believes you can see the fate of our people, but I need no vision to tell me what I know to be true. My People will not let the white man pen us up like cattle. We will fight. We will not surrender. There can be no peace. *Suvate*. That is all."

As Dylan completed the translation, the chief folded his arms, rattling the bone bib he wore over his bare chest. The ominous clatter sent chills dancing along Selena's suddenly cool skin. She swallowed her fear and met the chief's angry, obsidian gaze. "Eventually, even Quanah Parker of the *Nocona* will surrender."

Thankfully, she'd recently read a novel about the life of the chief's mother, Cynthia Parker, who was kidnapped as a child and raised by the Comanche. Cynthia Parker married a Comanche chief, Nocona, and Quanah, her son, was the last free chief of the Comanche Nation. If Selena remembered correctly, Quanah Parker didn't surrender until 1876.

"In the end, when the buffalo are gone and your children are starving, you won't have a choice. There are fewer Indians in the world than white men, and they will not give up until they rule this land from ocean to ocean."

Dog Ears sat up, pride shining in his eyes as Dylan continued to translate his angry words. "We are *Wichita*. We are not so strong now but the *Naconi* and the *Pentanka*, our *Tah-mahs*, our brothers, will never surrender. They will not listen to the honey-talk. They will not give up their lands. There will be war, and we will again rule the plains."

Dylan looked as if he didn't liked hearing the truth any more than Dog Ears. Then again, Dylan didn't believe she spoke the truth. He thought she was crazy, and maybe she was. She was sitting in a Comanche chief's tent discussing ancient politics.

How sane is that?

She shook her head, casting off her fear and dark thoughts. If this were real, she had a chance to change history. If it wasn't she'd never know.

"There will be war, but it will not go well for your people," she said, struggling to overcome her near-paralyzing fear. "You'll win a couple of battles but in a few years, you'll either be dead, living among the whites, or living on a reservation. The best thing you can do for your people now is to remember how you have lived and pass those memories down to your children."

#

As Dylan translated, goose flesh pimpled his arms. Selena painted a bleak picture of The People's future, but she was no damned psychic. She couldn't be. She'd probably researched the facts and had come to sound, logical conclusion regarding the fate of the Indian Nation. It didn't take a fortuneteller to realize the Plains Indians were doomed. The white man had outgunned and outmaneuvered them for years.

When the flapped entrance to the lodge opened, White Deer entered, followed by the old and stooped figure of Dream Speaker. Dylan inhaled deeply and looked at Selena. She tensed and fear widened her eyes as they darted between Dog Ears and the ancient shaman. Sitting cross-legged on the floor, she leaned forward and gripped her knees while worrying her bottom lip with her teeth. As Dream Speaker shuffled forward, her trembling breath came in short, rapid spurts.

Dylan ached for her, but he did nothing to ease her fears. He couldn't—not without risking both their lives.

Once the shaman took his place beside the chief, Dog Ears reached for the long, white ceremonial pipe. After lighting the pipe, he offered the first puff to the Great Spirit before taking another long drag. Exhaling slowly, he blew smoke in the direction of the four winds before passing the pipe to Dylan. He repeated the process and handed the pipe to White Deer.

Selena watched White Deer and then Dream Speaker draw the acrid smoke into their lungs before the shaman handed the pipe back to the chief. She didn't say a word, but her fear was palpable. When Dream Speaker stood and shuffled forward, her face paled. Despite the possible danger, Dylan reached for her hand. Then the Shaman knelt before her and lifted her chin with a gnarled finger. Selena squeezed Dylan's hand so hard he winced.

"You cannot see visions, but you have seen the future," the old man said in a gravelly voice as he spoke in halting English. "This, I do not understand."

Confusion shadowed his eyes before he stood and turned his dark gaze on Dylan. Pointing a crooked finger, he spoke in Cherokee. "*Neetah Intahah.*"

Spoken in a raspy whisper, the words wrapped themselves around Dylan's heart like a cold fist, squeezing until he thought his chest would explode. The words themselves weren't ominous and yet, he felt somehow threatened by them. Trying to control the racing of his pulse, he waited for the old man to continue.

"For you, it is changed," the shaman added, nodding his head emphatically. Then without another word, he turned and left the tepee.

"Dylan?" Selena spoke in a strangled whisper as she stood and touched his arm. Until then, he'd not been aware of having released her hand, nor did he recall standing. He looked into Selena's troubled eyes, seeing his own anguished reflection in their stormy depths.

Her grip tightened. "What did he say to you? What does it mean?"

His continued silence frightened her, but he didn't know what to say. He had no explanation for the irrational fear the shaman's words evoked. The old man had spoken no great truths nor answered any questions. His words were nothing more than gibberish meant for superstitious old women.

"Dylan," she repeated, her voice rising. "Talk to me. What did that old man say to you?"

"*Neetah Intahah,*" he said absently, looking from White

Deer to the silent Comanche war chief.

"It's a Cherokee proverb," White Deer said when Dylan remained silent.

Selena's face turned chalk white. "But what does it mean?"

Dylan inhaled deeply, trying to overcome his unnamed fears. "The days appointed to a man. The Cherokee believe there is a fixed time and place where all men must die and that it cannot be change."

White Deer laid a hand on his shoulder. "But Dream Speaker said it changed for you, Long Blade."

"Yeah, I know. But who the hell knows what that means?" He shook his head. If only he could just as easily shake off the sudden chill snaking down his spine.

"Oh God," Selena whispered, drawing both men's attention. "I was right. That was when it was supposed to have happened. If we hadn't left Canyon Creek when we did, you'd be dead. He would have shot you and then scalped you with your own knife. That was your destiny, Dylan. According to history, you shouldn't even be here. You should be dead. You should be dead because he killed you."

"Who?" Dylan asked, but Selena didn't answer. Covering her mouth with both hands, she fled the lodge in tears.

"Woman with No Fear needs you, my friend. Shouldn't you go after her?" White Deer asked as the three men stared after her retreating figure.

Angered by unwanted emotions, Dylan spoke harshly. "No one dare harm her while she's under the chief's protection."

"You do not want to lose her, my friend. If she were harmed, your heart would burst with sorrow. Trust me, *diganeli*. I know." Without another word, White Deer stepped into the late afternoon sun leaving Dylan alone with the old chief.

Turning to face his elder, he watched as Dog Ears stood on spindly legs. He pointed in the direction Selena had run. "Go after your woman, Long Blade. Dream Speaker has gone to the sweat lodge to pray. He can tell you nothing more without a vision from the Great Spirit."

With a stiff nod, Dylan turned on his heel and sprinted after Selena. He caught up with her when she reached a field of blue flowers at the foot of the canyon wall and dropped to the ground as if her legs would no longer support her. Then she wrapped her arms around her upraised knees and lowered her chin. Her shoulders shook with silent sobs. Dylan wanted to take her in his arms and tell her everything would be fine, but his heart still raced from the impact of the shaman's words.

Had Selena changed his destiny?

Walking toward her, he knew the moment she became aware of him. Though she gave no outward sign, he was conscious of an almost preternatural attraction between them as he lowered himself to the ground beside her. He draped one arm over a bent knee and slid his other hand into hers, entwining their fingers.

"The flowers are beautiful." She spoke softly without looking at him.

"They're bluebonnets."

She picked a single blossom and inhaled its clean, fresh scent. She tugged her hand from his and idly twirled the stem between her palms as she stared absently across the field. The silence grew but it wasn't uncomfortable. He waited patiently, praying she would finally tell him the truth.

Anticipation quickened his pulse. From the moment Selena confessed her age, he'd known she was an impostor. Mary's cousin was only twenty. So, Selena couldn't be Ben Tillman's daughter. He just prayed she had a damn good reason for pretending she was.

Chapter 16

Taking a deep breath, Selena looked sideways at Dylan as he sat with his elbows propped on bent knees and his hands dangling between his legs. He seemed lost in thought, but he was probably waiting for her to speak. His patience had worn thin, and it was her last chance to come clean. But the truth was stranger than fiction.

"I know you think I'm a liar but I'm not, not really. I just can't explain everything. I don't know how," she said looking away when he turned his head toward her.

His silence encouraged her to continue. "The first time I stepped onto my porch in Canyon Creek, I knew you would die there." She stared across the field of bluebonnets, unable to meet his probing gaze. "It wasn't a vision, but when I closed my eyes, I could almost see you bleeding to death on the porch. I didn't know who killed you, but I suspected it was the surveyor until I met Major Davis. But then I ruled him out after the spring gala. That left the surveyor. He blamed you for Mary's death, you know."

When he still remained silent, she faltered, but she still couldn't meet his gaze. She wasn't lying, but she hadn't told the entire truth either. She couldn't. It defied explanation.

The bluebonnets wavered before her watery gaze. "The other night when you showed me Mary's necklace, I knew you were supposed to die that night. Don't ask me how I knew, I just did. Okay?"

Bracing herself for his rejection, she finally turned to face him. She'd expected some anger—confusion even—but the fury in his gaze staggered her. His sharply chiseled features were as hard and unyielding as granite, and he'd drawn his brows together over sharply narrowed eyes that nearly scalded her with the intensity of their furious glare.

Fear quickened her pulse. She'd lost him.

A muscle jumped in his clenched jaw as he wrapped his

fingers around her shoulders in a talon-like grip and pulled her to her knees. "Don't!" he growled. "Not another lie or by God, I won't be responsible for what I do to you."

She choked on a hiccupping cry. Tears gathered in the corners of her eyes and slid slowly down her cheeks as she tried to stifle the sobs that rose from a bottomless pit of despair. Half-truths would never be enough, and the whole truth was unimaginable. Yet even if she could think of enough words to explain her existence in a time before her birth, Dylan would never believe her.

"Say something, damn you!" he shouted before releasing her shoulders and surging to his feet.

"What's left to say?" she asked in halting gulps as she tried to control her hiccupping sobs. "I told you everything I can, and it's still not enough."

"I guess that's it then," he said harshly, glaring down on her with such loathing, she couldn't bare it. She lowered her chin and closed her eyes.

"In the morning, I'm taking you back to Canyon Creek," he said, his voice devoid of emotion. "After that, I don't ever want to see you again."

Selena never looked up. She couldn't. Seeing him walk away would have destroyed her.

Left alone, she lay on her side and curled into a tight ball while gut-wrenching sobs wracked her body. Trapped in a nightmare from which there was no escape, she wept until she had no tears left. Eventually, the trembling subsided and she drifted off to sleep.

When she awoke a few hours later, it was dark. Though she hadn't eaten in hours, food was the farthest thing from her mind. She was too upset to eat, and the thought of stumbling through a Comanche Village alone at night was terrifying. She wished Dylan were with her, but he'd probably sought solace in the arms of Yellow Rose.

Losing him was hard enough, but imagining him in the arms of another woman felt like a knife wound to her heart. She rolled onto her stomach and propped her chin in her hands.

She lacked the energy and motivation needed to stand, so she stayed where she was. Her tears had tried, and as her vision started to clear, a silhouette took shape in the darkness. It moved toward her. Too despondent to care, Selena watched as the hunched figure of Dream Speaker drew nearer. Raising stick-like arms to the moon, he chanted in a singsong cadence that sent a shiver dancing down her spine. Then the smell of his unwashed body reached her, and she gagged.

She'd noticed a pungent aroma emanating from many of the Comanche, especially the women, but the shaman's rancid breath and body odor nauseated her. When he dropped down beside her like a sack of wet cement, she had to breathe through her mouth to keep from retching.

In a scratchy voice that chilled her blood, he said, "What visions do you see?"

"I see no visions," she replied, trying not to inhale. If he were a real psychic, he wouldn't have to ask.

"You come from another place."

"No shit, Sherlock," she said under her breath. Speaking aloud, she replied, "I'm from Virginia."

"You have seen the future of my people."

"I don't see visions." She wanted him to go away. He couldn't help her. No one could.

"You know things." Dream Speaker studied her, his eyes disappearing under the wrinkled folds of his brow. "You have changed Long Blade's destiny."

The hairs on the back of her neck stood on end. The old man wasn't such a fool after all. He did see things. But could he see she came from the future?

"You say I've changed Long Blade's destiny, but have I saved his life?" Her breathing hitched. She needed her life to make sense, but if she couldn't save Dylan, then there was no reasonable explanation for her time travel. And there had to be a reason. She needed one to preserve her sanity.

Dream Speaker tilted his head. "Can you not see his future now?"

If only she could...

"No, but I don't see visions. I know about the future because it's my past. For me, Long Blade's death happened a long time ago, and what happens to your people is history."

"What is my people's history?"

117

She should have paid more attention in history class, but most of her historical knowledge came from long talks with her grandmother and genealogy research, which was probably more accurate than what she'd gleaned reading historical romance novels and watching western movies with her father.

"In less than twenty years, all the land now known as Indian Territory will belong to the white man. In a few years, the Comanche Nation will surrender, and the People's way of life will cease to exist. The white man will win the war, but the memory of your culture will not die. Your people, and how they lived, will be remembered."

She wanted to tell the old man more, but it wouldn't do any good. She couldn't change the destiny of an entire race of people. She wasn't even sure she could change Dylan's destiny.

Her throat burned. She hadn't felt this useless since her first code blue when the doctor pronounced time of death before her image even came up on the portable x-ray unit's digital screen.

When Dream Speaker reached for her hands, she didn't flinch, but she almost hurled. As his dirty, twisted fingers rubbed the lines of her palms and traced the veins on the backs of her hands, he chanted in hushed tones. Then he dropped her hands and stared into her eyes. "Your future lies in the past. There is no going back. Change what you can. Accept what you cannot. *Suvate*. It is done."

The skin between Selena's shoulder blades tingled, but it was from more than just the shaman's words.

She quickly glanced over her shoulder. Dylan stood just few feet away. She didn't know how long he'd been there or how much he'd heard, but at least he no longer looked pissed.

Without another word, Dream Speaker rose to his feet and ambled off, chanting in a whispered monotone as he went. Selena took a deep breath and stood on shaky legs to face Dylan and whatever remained of her future.

"I brought you something to eat." He handed her a piece of charred meat.

"Thanks." She sniffed, praying it wasn't something she'd never knowingly eat—like a dog or rat. A hesitant bite relieved her fears. It tasted like chicken. It could have been anything, but she didn't want to know. It was gone in a few bites.

She smiled, but it felt wobbly. "Any chance I could get a bath?"

"Come on," he said with a grunt. He took her by the elbow and led her to a clump of trees along the edge of the creek that were thick enough to ensure a modicum of privacy.

He released her arm and turned his back. "Don't take too long. I'll be right here, standing guard."

She had no towel, no soap, and no washcloth, but the water looked inviting. She stripped out of her clothes and stepped in. Mud squished between her toes. It wasn't exactly a spa mud bath, but it was better than nothing. So she hunkered down and scooped it up with her hands. It glistened like sparkling wet sand in the moonlight and felt like gritty clay, possibly limestone.

She rubbed it over her skin and scrubbed her scalp before ducking under the water to rinse off. She didn't exactly smell like lilacs. She smelled like a fishpond. But it was better than the lingering aroma of Dream Speaker's unwashed body.

Once she'd bathed as best she could, she waded out to the middle of the creek. The water was waist high, and she couldn't resist a quick swim to ease some of her tension. There wasn't a strong current so she pushed off from the sandy bottom and set out for the opposite bank about thirty feet away. When she reached the other side, she swam back to the middle of the creek and floated on her back while staring at the diamond-studded sky overhead.

"What in hell do you think you're doing?" Dylan growled, shattering her peaceful solitude as he splashed toward her.

She sputtered and tried to regain her footing. Once she did, she hurriedly lowered her exposed breasts beneath the water's surface and stared mutely. Dylan was furious and for the life of her, she couldn't understand what she'd done to piss him off this time.

"I brought you here to bathe, not frolic in the water like some damned mermaid." He stood in the waist deep water wearing nothing but a breechcloth, staring at the tops of her exposed breasts.

Her mouth went dry, her pulse quickening as she stared at the water beading on his bronzed, muscled chest. Desire speared her. Last night, he'd made her forget her fears, and she wanted to forget again.

119

She stood. Water rolled over her skin like a lover's caress, bringing her nipples to tight, aching points. Goosebumps shivered over her skin as she stepped forward until she was close enough to touch him. Taking a deep breath to bolster her courage, she wrapped her arms around his neck and pressed her naked body against him.

A low growl rumbled from his chest before he swept her up into his arms, and headed for shore. It wasn't until her bottom hit the ground that she realized he was angry. His keen eyes had taken in every inch of her body—even the faint tan lines she still sported from her last visit to Virginia Beach.

"What in hell kind of clothes do you wear? You have sun on your entire body except for those tiny white strips," he said, leaning closer to point an accusing finger at her breasts.

"Dylan, I . . ." What could she say? The bikini hadn't been invented yet. In his time, few women swam. The ones who did wore more clothes than she wore to church in the spring.

"Why would you dress like a whore if you aren't one?" He ground his teeth. A muscle in his jaw jumped. "Do you think stealing an inheritance is more honorable than selling yourself for money?"

She scooted away from his fury and sat up to cover her nakedness. She felt like Eve in The Garden of Eden. Shame burned her cheeks. "I didn't steal, and I'm not a whore."

But she wasn't Ben Tillman's daughter either. She was his descendent—one who conveniently shared the same name as his deceased daughter.

He leaned over her. A vein throbbed in his forehead. "Stop lying. You can't cover the truth burned into your skin. You pleasure men for money—and you do so in broad daylight, wearing practically nothing."

She slapped his face. He flinched and straightened.

"You arrogant son-of-a-bitch!" She scooted away from him on her bare bottom. His leather breechcloth was all that stood between her and his aroused manhood.

He gripped her arms and hauled her up against his chest. They knelt facing one another. "Do you charge half-breeds more than your white customers? How much do I owe you for the last time?"

Chapter 17

Selena stiffened, and her face flamed. He froze.

What the hell am I doing? He'd never taken a woman by force, and he'd never treated anyone as shamefully as he'd treated Selena. Damned if he wasn't a bastard—a damned half-breed, savage bastard.

"I'm sorry." He raised his hand to touch her face. She flinched as if he were about to deliver a blow. He'd never felt so ashamed in his life.

"I'm sorry," he said again. He reared back on his heels. "I thought...It doesn't matter what I thought. You didn't deserve that."

She bit her lip to catch a sob. Her hands covered her breasts. She looked so utterly lost and victimized; he'd never outlive the guilt. With a sigh, he prepared himself for tears or angry words. He wasn't prepared for the spitfire who sat up and punched him in the nose.

"Your words hurt far more than the back of your hand ever would," she said through her tears as she rubbed her knuckles.

Then she jumped to her feet and marched off, leaving him sitting on the ground leaning on the palm of his left hand. The little hellcat had bloodied his nose.

Shaking his head to clear it, he lightly touched his nose with his right hand. It wasn't broken but it hurt like hell—not that he didn't deserve it.

He watched her walk back to the trees and slip into her clothes. After giving him a look that would have melted butter, she turned back toward the camp and bravely marched up the hill. Dylan rose to follow.

When she reached camp, she stopped, looking lost and confused. Before Dylan could approach her to explain their sleeping arrangements, Yellow Rose slipped out of a nearby lodge wearing nothing but a buffalo robe.

"Go back to the meadow White Eyes. Tonight I am Long Blade's woman," she said in Comanche.

Selena couldn't understand the words but she obviously comprehended the meaning. Female competition was the same in any language and women, especially Comanche women, could be vicious when they felt threatened.

Earlier in the evening, he'd made it clear to Yellow Rose he would not be sharing her lodge, but she was tenacious when she wanted something, and despite the language barrier, Selena seemed to understand.

"You can have him," she said. Then she turned to walk away and slammed into Dylan's chest. His arms banded around her.

"Where do you think you're going?" Damned if he wasn't proud of her. Even if she were a liar and probably a whole lot worse, she had guts.

"I was looking for White Deer. I want to leave. Now."

He pointed to the guest lodge Dog Ears had offered them for the night. "Go inside the lodge, Selena. It's late, and you're sleeping with me."

She arched a brow. "I don't do threesomes."

With a snort of disgust, she brushed by him and marched back to the meadow.

Dylan dashed inside the guest lodge to grab a buffalo hide and then ran after her. She was still under the chief's protection, but he'd told Dog Ears Selena was his woman. If she wandered off, some warrior might decide she was fair game, and he'd have to fight to keep her.

Fear pushed him, and he ran faster.

#

Selena sat in the middle of the bluebonnets and cried herself to sleep. Sometime before dawn, she awoke to the realization she wasn't alone. When she slowly opened her eyes, Dylan's face was only inches away.

"Forgive me," he whispered. Then he lowered his head and using his lips and body, conveyed an apology words never could.

His lovemaking was slow and sweet and when he finally brought her to the edge, it was like a wine cork slowly slipping from the neck of a bottle. It was so unlike the climatic explosion of

122

their first encounter. That first time had been unimaginably passionate. This time was heartbreakingly tender, and with her climax, came tears.

"I'll never disrespect you again, Selena. *Oea-Yeh*. I swear by God."

"You better mean that. I won't forgive you again," she stated firmly, meaning every word.

"*Ansa Kai-e-koh-ga*. I do not lie. I have a temper, but I swear I'll never call you names again. Believe this, if you believe nothing else."

He held her in his arms, her head cradled on his shoulder as they drifted to sleep on their bed of earth and buffalo hide. They dozed for half an hour before he led her up the hill to the guest lodge where she promptly fell back to sleep. She would have been content to sleep the morning away in his arms, but Dylan woke her up a few hours later, and he was obviously still obsessing over her tan lines.

A frown marred his handsome face as he ran a finger along the pale bathing suit line. "Will you explain these now? Please."

She avoided his gaze. "They're tan lines."

"I know what the hell they are." His fingers clenched into a fist on her belly. "I want to know how you got them."

"The sun?"

His eyes narrowed and his nostrils flared. He wasn't laughing.

She rolled to her back and stared at the top of the tepee. "When I swim, I wear a bathing suit. It's a small, fitted garment that allows freedom of movement. If I wore those swimming dresses with the billowing skirts and bloomers, I'd drown."

"So," he said slowly as he blew out his breath, "you're telling me you wear a small strip of cloth tied around your breasts and a breechcloth to avoid swimming naked?"

"I guess it is a bit like a breechcloth, but that's my story, and I'm sticking to it."

Dylan's scowl deepened. "You want me to believe you can't bring yourself to swim naked, but you can parade around in the sun with nothing more than two thin strips of cloth tied around you?"

"What I want you to believe," she said rolling onto her side

123

and taking his face in her hands, "is that I'm not a whore, and I've never deliberately lied."

"You're far from innocent," he said with a sigh. "You've lied to keep the house, and you're afraid of getting caught. I understand that. But I won't marry you just to give you a home if that's what you're after."

Her heart stilled in her chest. "I'm not after anything."

"Why else would you sleep with a half-breed in a Comanche camp?" He smiled. It didn't reach his eyes. "We both enjoyed last night and this morning. It was great sex, but I can't marry a white woman."

His words were cold, but his eyes were sad.

Her breathing hitched. She felt as if he'd stabbed her in the heart. Again. Whenever she thought he was starting to feel something for her, he made a point of cutting her to the quick. How could he make such passionate love to her one-minute and carelessly discard her the next?

"I never claimed to be innocent, and I'm not interested in marriage. So don't worry Dylan," she said as she rolled from his arms and pulled a buffalo robe around her naked shoulders. "I won't nag you about it. But if you think so little of me, then why did you tell Chief Dog Ears I was your woman?"

He blanched, but his eyes hardened. "I didn't think being raped by half the Comanche nation would appeal to you. If I hadn't told them you were my woman, you'd of been fair game. With you being white, I can promise it wouldn't have been nearly as enjoyable as it was with me."

"Egotistical prick," she said under her breath as she turned her back on him.

Without another word, Dylan dressed and slipped out of the tepee. Where he was going or what he expected her to do next, she hadn't a clue. Her shoulders slumped. Dylan would never trust her. The lies of her life would always come between them and soon, she would have no choice but to tell him the truth. It wouldn't make any difference; he wouldn't believe her anyway.

She'd hoped Dream Speaker could give her the answers she sought, but she'd learned nothing from the old man she didn't already know, though he had told her she'd changed Dylan's destiny. But for how long? In time, everyone died. She only hoped

Dylan's time would come much later.

After dressing, she stepped outside the tepee and saw Dylan saddling their horses. Her heart sank when she realized he meant what he'd said last night. He was returning her to Canyon Creek, despite the intimacy they'd shared.

When she approached, he handed her the canteens. "Fill them at the river."

"Boy, did you wake up on the wrong side of the hide or what?" she mumbled as she stomped off to do his bidding.

As she walked to the river, fear pebbled her skin. The Indian village was abuzz with morning activities as Comanche women prepared meals, hauled firewood, and cared for small children. Some cast curious glances her way while others stared with obvious loathing. No one bothered her as she made her way back to camp, but that didn't make her feel any safer.

The warriors hadn't returned from the hunt, and Selena assumed they would dress the animals before bringing them back to camp. The young braves and older warriors who'd stayed behind to protect the women and children sat outside their tents chanting their morning songs. Others sleepily stumbled from their beds to relieve themselves or bathe in the creek. The women, it seemed, had put in a half-day's work before the men could finish taking a leak.

"You seem to have adjusted to life in a Comanche camp without too much trouble," Dylan said as she handed him the filled canteen, and he handed her a hollow gourd containing food. She shrugged.

"Sorry it's not what you're used to," he added when she said nothing. "I know you're used to the finer things in life, but all we have is Indian bread cooked on hot rocks and honey. So I guess you'll just have to forgo your usual luxuries a little longer."

"My usual luxuries?" She must have punched him harder than she'd realized. "I'm used to luxuries you can't even imagine, and I've done pretty damn good to get this far without them."

Then without another word, she turned and carried her food back inside the tepee.

Chapter 18

Before riding out of the Comanche camp, Dylan thanked the chief. As he was walking back toward the horses where he'd left Selena with White Deer, Dream Speaker approached, and Selena paled. Dylan came up behind her as the shaman was speaking.

In a raspy tone that sent chills racing down Dylan's spine, he said. "Woman with No Fear has ridden the winds of time, giving Long Blade a future once more. You are dead to your people, my child, and your life now reaches out in two directions. Your future is your past, and your past is your future. You can never go back. *Suvate*, that is all."

Selena's breathing hitched, and she leaned against White Deer. Dylan glared at Dream Speaker. "What the hell does that mean?" he asked, but the medicine man said nothing more. When he walked away, chanting his medicine song, White Deer turned to Dylan.

"Listen to the wind. It talks, and change is coming. For you, it has already happened. For the people, it is yet to come. I can no longer stand with Chief Dog Ears, clinging to the old ways. I will listen to the wind, and so should you, my friend." White Deer steadied Selena and then stepped away from her to extend a hand to Dylan.

They grasped one another's forearms at the elbow. Then White Deer turned back to Selena and said, "We borrow this land from our children. So I will learn to read and write the white man's words so I can write down the stories of our people, and I will paint pictures of the old ways so when the last days of Our People come, there will be something to show the People of tomorrow what it was like to live free today."

Selena cried as she hugged him goodbye, and tears still shimmered in her eyes when Dylan helped her onto her horse. As they rode away from the camp, she kept glancing back over her shoulder until White Deer was out of sight. Dylan kept glancing back at Selena, unable to get her earlier comment out of his head.

Luxuries he couldn't imagine.

Just how uncivilized did she think he was? He knew more about luxuries than White Deer, and unlike his friend, he hadn't grown up in a teepee. He'd told Selena his grandparents had owned a plantation in Georgia. He'd even gone to school back East before the war. Just because he was a half-breed didn't mean he knew nothing about luxury.

"I'm not a savage," he said as he dropped back to ride alongside her Appaloosa.

Selena barely looked at him. "I never said you were."

"I've seen gaslights and indoor plumbing. I even used a mechanized bathroom when I was in a hotel in Dallas. I pulled a chain and hot water poured from a spigot over my head like a warm waterfall. It was a luxury hotel with every imaginable amenity, but the manager kicked me out when he realized I was a half-breed and not an Irishman like my father."

"Then he was an ass." Selena met his gaze and glared. "And you're a bigot *and* an ass for thinking all white people are the same."

"Other than my father, every white person I ever met thought they were better than me, even the ones I considered friends. And that's something you'll never understand."

"Experience shapes us all, but it doesn't have to define us." She looked so sad and defeated, he wanted to take the words back, no matter that they were true.

"White people define me as a half-breed. It doesn't matter that I'm half Cherokee and not Apache or Comanche, but white people think all Indians are the same."

"But I'm not all white people," she said with a snide smile. "Can you see the irony there?"

He snorted and said nothing. Some things could not be changed.

The Cherokee had been assimilating themselves into the white man's world since before the Revolution, but the whites still considered them savages. Even after the government herded the Cherokee west, they'd rebuilt another Nation to rival the one they'd left behind in the East. They'd established a democratic government, churches, businesses, and a better public education system than the whites, but it didn't change anything. Neither had the white man's war.

Dylan joined the Confederacy against his mother's wishes, but he didn't do it to support slavery or states' rights. His Uncle Quinn and cousins supported Stand Watie, and he couldn't have fired upon an enemy who might have been his uncle or one of his cousins. Dylan had also believed in the Confederate promise to reinstate Cherokee lands if the South won.

They lost, and since Stand Watie was the last Confederate general to surrender, the Union punished the Cherokee by giving much of their land to the Plains Tribes. What little remained in Cherokee hands was located near the new capital of Tahlequah, and Dylan's parents lived in nearby Cheeratahge.

Cheeratahge was close to the Comanche war trails and not located on reservation land. It was also prosperous, so the chances of the government allowing it to survive were slim. The last thing a white government wanted was organized, intelligent tribes governing themselves in a democratic society. His mother disagreed, but that was nothing new. She never agreed with Dylan, and she'd never forgiven him for fighting on the losing side of the war, which shouldn't have surprised him. She'd never forgiven her brother for not walking The Trail, but she was his mother, and he was overdue for a visit. He just hadn't told Selena that's where they were going.

"Why are we headed north?" Selena asked, drawing his attention. She glanced at the sun and then back at him. "Isn't Canyon Creek south of here?"

"Yeah, but where we're going isn't." His reasons for going to Cheeratahge were complicated. No way in hell would he try explaining them to Selena.

She blew out an audible breath. "So do I have to beat it out of you, or are you going to tell me where we're going and why?"

"The Edwards Plateau in Bexar County is only a two-day ride from here. Now quit your jawing and try to keep up." Spurring his horse into a faster gait, he left a considerable distance between them, preventing any further conversation.

#

Thank you, God, Selena silently prayed. She might not

know where Dylan was taking her or why, but at least he wasn't dropping her in Canyon Creek and riding off into the sunset alone. For now, that was all that mattered.

For the rest of the day, Dylan spoke very little, but at night, he pulled her close. They didn't make love again, but she wasn't disappointed because he spent the time telling her about his past. He told of his strained relationship with his mother and about the time he spent back East before the war. He also spoke of meeting his Uncle Quinn for the first time and how the meeting had caused the first rift in his relationship with his mother.

He talked a lot about the war and though he tried to remain detached in his narrative, the pain he'd suffered was unmistakable.

Most half-breeds—God how she detested that word—served under Stand Watie during the war while most full-blooded Cherokee sided with John Ross, dividing the Cherokee Nation further. In 1862, John Ross switched his allegiance to the South, causing more dissension amongst The People.

"Before then," Dylan said as they stared up at the stars, "I served with the Cherokee Special Services. Later, I was reassigned to the Special Forces of the Confederate army. That's when I met Andy—Major Davis."

As he talked, it became evident the major's later betrayal and prejudice hurt him deeply. She saw it in his eyes every time he mentioned his former friend. He tried to remain impassive as he described the agony of having to choose sides in a war that not only divided the country, but the whole of the Cherokee Nation, but he wasn't as tough as he pretended. Lying nestled in his arms, she heard the strain in his voice and felt the tension in his muscles. The woman he'd loved and his best friend had both betrayed him because of his heritage, and the government mistreated all Native Americans.

From his perspective, white people were bigots.

"Whites aren't the only ones who judge half-breeds," he continued. "When Stand Watie was elected chief, he captured the Cherokee capital at Tahlequah and ordered John Ross' home in Park Hill burned to the ground. There was a lot of hatred among my People between the full bloods and mixed races. Farms were burned, innocents were killed, and many Cherokee fled to Kansas. Eventually, more Cherokee lived in Kansas than the Indian

Territory could house or feed. Many starved. Others froze. They called it Bleeding Kansas for more reasons than one. Many Cherokee bled there as well."

"I knew the war was bad, but the reality is so much worse than anything I ever read or saw on—I'm sorry you had to live through something like that," she whispered, placing her hand over his heart. She felt him stiffen before he relaxed and placed his hand over hers.

"War makes people do things they wouldn't normally do, Selena. So does desperation. Whatever you've done, whatever you're hiding, you can tell me. Believe me, after everything I witnessed during the war, there's nothing you could say that would surprise me." He squeezed her hand. "I can accept anything but more lies."

"Trust me, Dylan," she replied with a sad smile. "Fiction is sometimes easier to believe than the truth."

"Try me."

Instead, she spoke of inconsequential things about her life, giving no details that might lead him to suspect the truth. Not that it was a real possibility. Who in their right mind would suspect a person of time travel?

Just to be on the safe side, she shared family memories that could be from any family in any time. She talked about her cousins, Jeff, Lance, and Larry, teaching her to ride a horse and about the time she spent with both her parents before her mother's death from breast cancer. The pain of losing her mother and then her father six months later still grieved her.

"After Mama died, Daddy was inconsolable. He left his medical practice and refused get help, shutting everyone out of his life, including me." She sniffed back tears. "Six months later, he died. The doctors said it was a heart attack, but it was really a broken heart. My father couldn't live without my mother."

Dylan's arms tightened around her. "He loved you too, and I'm sure you did what you could to console him."

She pulled back just a bit, just enough to meet his gaze. "I should have tried harder to get him the help he needed, but he needed to grieve, and I thought we'd have more time. We didn't. My family is gone, Dylan, and I'll never see them again."

Within two years, she'd lost everyone she ever cared

about—first her parents—and then everyone else the day of the tornado. She swallowed her sorrow and swiped a tear from her eye. "Life is short, Dylan, and we never have as much time as we think. You might want to remember that the next time you see your mother."

He grunted. "My mother's not going to change. She's a very controlling woman, and I refuse to be controlled."

"You sound just like her," Selena said, smiling in the dark when he grunted again.

He quit trying to pry information from her, but they continued to talk as they lay by the campfire, and the threads of their relationship grew stronger. Perhaps one day, those threads would be strong enough to withstand the truth.

Until then, all she could do was hope.

Chapter 19

The next morning, Selena awoke when Dylan squatted next to her and kissed her forehead. "Don't get up, and don't leave camp if you do. I'm going hunting for fresh meat, but I'll keep close. Holler if you need me."

She stared into his eyes, and her heart did somersaults. When she was younger, her mother told her a kiss on the lips could be sweet or passionate, a kiss on the cheek implied friendship or compassion, but a kiss on the forehead was a kiss from the heart. Her cheeks warmed. "Okay, but I wish you could hunt up some bacon and eggs."

Laughing, he stood. "I was thinking more along the lines of a squirrel or rabbit."

The sun was barely above the horizon, but Selena couldn't get back to sleep. She was awake and restless, and she wasn't helpless. She could hear water, and if she could hear it flowing, it wasn't that far from camp, and the canteens needed filling. So, she gathered them up and then pulled the colonel's gun and a change of clothes from her saddlebag. If she just happened to sneak in a quick bath, Dylan didn't have to know.

They hadn't seen a soul since leaving the Comanche village, so it shouldn't be a big deal. The lightweight skirt she'd packed wouldn't be as comfortable to ride in as her jeans, but her pants were starting to stink. She could wash them in the creek and then hang them from the saddle horn to dry and wear them again tomorrow.

When she reached the edge of a wide creek, she looked around to make sure the area was as deserted as it seemed. There wasn't a soul in sight, not even a prairie dog. So, she stripped out of her clothes and washed them as best she could. Then she tossed them on the bank and quickly scrubbed her hair and skin with limestone before rinsing off and rushing back up the bank.

Once she was dressed, she slipped the gun in her skirt

pocket and filled the canteens. Then she gathered her wet clothes and the canteens, and headed back to camp. She'd just cleared the trees when she heard a twig snap behind her. "Well, well, well. If you ain't a tasty little morsel."

Selena dropped the canteens and her clothes and spun around, her hand automatically dropping to the pocket where she'd put her gun. It wasn't there.

A scraggly looking man smiled, showing rotten stubs where his teeth should have been. His dark, greasy hair was matted to his scalp, and Selena could smell his unwashed body from five feet away.

Trying not to panic, she looked down, hoping to see her gun—hoping she could get to it before he attacked.

"Looking for this?" He waved her gun in front of her. "You done dropped it back by the river where you was bathing.

Her heart squeezed. "What do you want?"

She should have listened to Dylan. This wasn't her time. It was his, and he'd known what could happen to a woman alone.

"Why, I want me a piece of ass. I ain't had none since I deserted the army, and I can't remember the last time I had me a white woman."

For the first time since his intrusion, Selena noticed his uniform. He was a private, and even if he was a deserter, maybe his regiment was nearby. "You take one step closer, and I'll scream."

"Go ahead. I left my regiment two days ago. They ain't nowhere near here."

The army might not be nearby, but Dylan was. She backed away, drawing air into her lungs. He stepped closer. She screamed and turned to run back toward camp.

Her skirt tangled around her legs. She stumbled and righted herself, but her attacker gained the advantage. He grabbed the back of her shirt and roughly pulled her against his chest. She screamed again and tried kicking backward into his groin, but the skirt wrapped around her legs.

"Cut that out." The soldier grabbed a fist full of hair and jerked her head back against his shoulder. Selena's struggles ceased. One twist and he'd snap her neck.

"Don't fight me, and I won't kill you." His hand snaked

around her waist and groped between her legs, but she wasn't about to give in without a fight.

When he relaxed the pressure on her throat, she released all the air from her lungs and elbowed him just below his rib cage. Then she stomped the top of his foot. When he howled and let go, she spun around and brought her palm up under his nose.

Bone crunch and blood spurted, but when she tried to complete the self-defense maneuver by kneeing him in the groin, the skirt tangled around her feet again, and she fell. He roared and came down on top of her.

"Bitch!" He tried shoving up her skirt, but she clawed his face and scrambled out from beneath him. Cursing, he grabbed her ankles and pulled her legs out from under her.

When he rolled her to her back, she brought up her fist to connect with his jaw but punched his shoulder instead, sending a sharp pain racing up her arm. She screamed again, and he came down on top of her, forcing all the air from her lungs.

"Stop fighting me, or I'll snap your neck and take your corpse."

She stilled, the pulse in her ears pounding so hard she could hear nothing else. Closing her eyes, she counted the heartbeats in her head, willing her pulse to slow, trying to catch her breath so she could renew her struggles.

The man's fetid breath fanned her cheek. "That's better."

He moved above her, struggling to free himself while keeping her pinned to the ground. She kept her eyes squeezed shut and held still, hoping to give him a false sense of security. At some point, he would have to rise up off her to lift her skirt, and when he did, she'd kick him in the groin. As long as she had a working plan, she could keep the panic at bay.

Please God.

If she couldn't escape, she prayed she could survive the rape. The blood roaring in her ears drowned out everything else. Then the pressure on her chest was suddenly gone.

Too afraid to open her eyes, she held still and waited for the world to stop spinning. Then she opened her eyes and turned her head toward the sound of hollow thumps and heavy breathing. Less than fifty feet away, Dylan crouched over the soldier's unmoving body and raised his knife. His fingers curled in the man's hair as he lifted his head.

Selena cried, and Dylan turned his savage face in her direction. Gone was the man she loved. In his place was a heartless warrior.

She turned her head and retched. She couldn't watch Dylan take a scalp. It appeared as if he'd already beaten the man nearly to death, and for the crime he'd been about to commit, he deserved it, but no man deserved the punishment Dylan had in mind. Then without warning, strong arms banded around her as Dylan pulled her close.

"*Ts(ga)toli*," he whispered, kissing her hair. "Your eyes. Open them, *adawehi*."

She shook her head. She didn't want to see the blood on his hands. She just wanted to feel his strength and know that whatever he'd done, he'd done to protect her.

"I didn't do it," he said, gently lifting her chin. "It was just a threat, but I didn't scalp him. Selena, look." He turned her head so she could see the man's limp form as he twitched and groaned. "The bastard's still alive."

Selena leaned into him and sobbed harder. No words would come, only tears, as Dylan lifted her into his arms and carried her back to camp.

"You're safe now." He lowered her to the blankets still spread out on the ground where they'd slept. Then he dropped down beside her and pulled her into his arms.

"Why did you wander off?" he asked when her trembling subsided.

She swallowed bile. "I wanted to rinse off, wash my clothes, and fill the canteens."

"You can't wander off like that. We're not as far from civilization as you might think, but we're far enough away that the law no longer applies. Besides rogue Indians, outlaws and deserters roam the area, and it's not safe for you to be alone."

"But you left me to go hunting, so I thought…"

"Shh." He pulled her closer. "I told you I would stay close, but when you wandered off, it took me that much longer to reach you when you screamed."

He set her away from him and searched her eyes. "How badly are you hurt?"

Her neck felt stiff, her head ached, and her throat was raw, but she was relatively unscathed. Other than the emotional trauma, she'd done more damage to the bastard who attacked her than he'd done to her. "He didn't...I'm okay."

Dylan gently kissed the top of her head and set her away from him. "Don't move. I mean it."

She couldn't if she wanted to. Her legs were still shaking.

After rising to his feet, he looked at her once more, nodded as if satisfied she wouldn't get up, and then he walked back toward the river. He returned a few minutes later with her wet clothes and the canteens.

He hung her clothes from the saddle horn and then handed her one of the canteens. "Drink. Then if you're feeling up to it, we need to get out of here. I don't want to be around when that deserter wakes up, because either he'll kill me or I'll have to kill him."

Selena bit back a fresh wave of tears and nodded. Then she took a swallow from the canteen and sucked it up. She was the reason they needed to hasten their departure and why they wouldn't get breakfast. Even if Dylan had killed fresh game, he'd obviously dropped it when he rushed to her rescue.

While she caught her breath, he packed up their gear and saddled the horses. Then he handed her a dried piece of meat and helped her to her feet.

"I'm sorry we're not eating fresh game," she said as he helped her mount the Appaloosa she'd named, Dalmatian.

"We weren't likely to have meat anyway. I didn't want to wander too far from camp, and the only meat I saw was rattlesnake, and I didn't think you'd eat it."

"It's good on pizza, but I've never eaten it plain."

Dylan paused as he was mounting Ishtabe and looked over his shoulder. "Pizza?"

"It's Italian."

#

They didn't talk much that second night. Selena washed all their clothes in a creek and hung them up to dry. Then the two of them wrapped up in blankets and curled next to the fire. She'd hoped Dylan would make love to her and make her forget what had very nearly happened, but he treated her as if she were made of

136

glass, and she soon fell asleep.

They arrived in Cheeratahge before noon the next day.

Although Dylan said the Cherokee built the town, it looked nothing like the Indian villages she'd seen on television westerns, and it looked nothing like Dog Ears' hunting camp. Cheeratahge looked like the streets of Dodge City in a Gunsmoke rerun— without all the white people.

As they rode passed a church, Dylan pointed to the parsonage. "Ralph Raintree is a Christian. So are most of the other residents."

Selena nodded but didn't admit how surprising she found that bit of news. Then a half-hour east of town, they came upon a good-sized ranch house situated amongst rolling green pastures and freshly plowed fields.

Dylan had mentioned his parents lived in a sod house, so she wasn't expecting to see a brick one. It took her a moment to realize the bricks were made of sod, a combination of clay and tough roots of buffalo grass, sun dried into blocks and layered with limestone and clay.

As they rode into the yard, a tall, lean man stepped onto the porch, shading his eyes with his hand. Silver-streaked dark hair curled around his collar, but Selena couldn't see his face. Then he lowered his hand, and stepped off the porch..

"By God, son, it's good to see you," he said in a slight Irish brogue.

Dylan climbed down from his horse and embraced him. "Hello, Da."

Selena slid to the ground and slipped up beside them, quietly waiting for an introduction.

"Aye, and who might this lovely young lass be?" The older man smiled, but concern overshadowed the curiosity in his gaze.

Selena shifted her feet and looked at the ground. She wore jeans and an old cotton shirt, and she was dirty and disheveled after hours on the trail. Besides the masculine way in which she was dressed, his father had to know she'd spent time on the trail with Dylan without a chaperone.

It may not be a big deal in her time, but here—in this time—it was.

Dylan pulled her to his side. "Selena, this is my father,

Sean Casey. Da, this is Selena Tillman."

An awkward silence followed, but before Dylan could say more, a harsh voice boomed across the yard. "More than a year without a word and now you show up with a woman. What in God's name have you done now?"

A short whirlwind of a woman posed the question as she stepped off the porch and marched up to Dylan as if she were going to box his ears. She stood only as high as his chest, and as she arched her back to look up at him, he visibly cringed.

Dressed in a brown silk dress like the ones worn by the women in Canyon Creek, she could have passed for any other Victorian lady had it not been for the copper hue of her skin and the long, dark braid hanging down her back.

Dylan took Selena's elbow and pulled her closer. "This is Selena Tillman, mother. She's a friend, and she's white. That should make you happy."

His mother's face fell, but she didn't cry. She just notched up her chin and turned to Selena. "Well, you've obviously traveled a good distance without a chaperone. So unless you're my son's wife, which I seriously doubt, I want to know what he is to you."

Dylan flinched, and Selena's heart thumped against her ribs. Without time to think of a better answer, she blurted out the truth. "My future."

"Damn it, Selena." Dylan tightened his grip and swung her around to face him.

"There now," Sean said, lightly touching Dylan's arm, "Is there something you need to tell your mother and me, or do you need a few minutes alone with your eh, lady friend?"

"Oh, I need a hell of a lot more than just a few minutes." Dylan scowled down at her with fire in his eyes. "So, if you'll excuse us, there are a few things we need to get straight."

Tightening his grip, he muttered what could only be a profanity in one dialect or another and pulled her toward the barn while dragging their horses behind him. Sighing heavily, Selena trotted along without protest, dragging her feet every step of the way.

#

Dylan released Selena's arm so he could lead the horses into separate stalls before turning to glare at her again. Her storm gray eyes shone with a mixture of humiliation and anger.

Damn, if he hadn't broken his promise and manhandled her again, but by God, he was angry too. He was beyond angry. He was damn furious.

Her future, indeed. She was a proven liar and yet, his heart had begun to pound the moment she'd spoken those words.

Cursing himself for even hoping such a lie was true, he chose to vent rather than nurture even the tiniest seed of hope. "You can lie to me, Selena, but don't you dare lie to my folks. I won't stand for it."

"I didn't lie." She ground her teeth but kept her chin lowered.

Her inability to look him in the eye angered him even further. More lies. Damned if he could stand much more. He raked a hand through his hair, dislodging the thong he'd tied around his head. It fell silently to the ground. "Damn it, Selena. I've told you things about myself, things I've never told another living soul, and still you lie to me."

She crossed her arms over her chest. "I've never lied about the things that matter."

He believed her parents were dead. Her emotions had been too honest not to believe, but she had to know she couldn't keep Mary's house. Once the attorney in Canyon Creek discovered she wasn't Ben Tillman's daughter, he'd have her removed from the property, and she'd have to find somewhere else to live. She might not love him, but living with a half-breed was better than living on the streets—or worse. And he'd accused her of worse.

His stomach knotted. She was alone and desperate, and he'd taken advantage of her. Now, he was going to pay the price.

"Damn it, Selena, if marriage is what you want, then fine. I'll marry you. I owe you that much."

Her chin shot up. "You owe me?"

"I do. You gave yourself to me with expectations. So, we'll get married."

"Expectations?"

Now she just sounded like a damn echo. "Isn't that the real reason you took me to your bed—to secure a marriage proposal?"

Her eyes blazed. He ignored her fury and continued. "But before you tie the noose around my neck, give me a straight answer. *Gado dejado?* What's your name?"

"You know my name!"

The incredulity in her voice angered him. He clenched his fists and ground his teeth. "I know what you said your name was, but we both know that's a lie. There's no way in hell you can be Ben Tillman's daughter. She's only twenty, and you told me yourself you're twenty-five."

Color leached from her face. "Oh shit."

On the verge of losing what little self-control he still possessed, he ground his teeth until his jaw ached. He couldn't stand more lies. "For God's sake, tell me your name. If you'll just tell me your real name, I'll marry you before a minister, a rabbi, a Comanche shaman, or the damned pope if that's what you want. Just tell me your name."

She took a shuddering breath and reached up to place her hands on either side of his face. "I swear by God, the moon and the stars, by the life of my unborn children and their children's children that my name is Selena Loraine Tillman, and I am twenty-five years old."

"Who's your father?" He held her gaze. He wouldn't let her lie to him again.

"Thomas Tillman. That wasn't a lie either," she said quietly, dropping her hands to her sides.

"Where's Ben Tillman's daughter—his real daughter?"

"Dead. She died of scarlet fever somewhere between Louisville and Fort Worth. Her family doesn't know. I really am related to Ben through my father, and since I have the same name as her and knew she wouldn't need the house, I claimed it. I didn't have anywhere else to go. I didn't lie about that either. My father died two years ago, six months after my mother, and my last remaining grandparent died when I was eighteen. Except for two uncles, their wives, and three cousins—who are way beyond my reach—I have no one."

She was still hiding something, and he didn't fully trust her, but for whatever reason, he still wanted to marry her. So where did that leave them?

Accepting what few answers she'd given as truth, he pulled her to his chest and murmured softly in Cherokee. He couldn't voice his thoughts in words she could understand, but he needed to say it. He wanted to marry her because he couldn't stand losing her.

Chapter 20

Selena sat on a bale of hay and watched as Dylan rubbed down the horses and unpacked their gear. He avoided eye contact, but he didn't suggest she go to the house. When there was nothing left to do, and he could no longer postpone the inevitable discussion with his parents, he dusted off his pants and offered her his hand. *"Mea-dro."*

"What?"

"Let's go." He pulled her to her feet, and led her to the house.

Selena worried her lip. They'd spent so much time in the barn, his parents had gone about their business, but they would be waiting inside to see what Dylan had decided. Granted, he'd asked her to marry him, but she hadn't said yes, and she had no idea what he'd tell his parents.

Her stomach fluttered as she followed him into the house, but his parents weren't in the front room, and they didn't answer when Dylan called out to them. The house itself reminded Selena of a rustic mountain lodge, only there wasn't a wide screen television over the mantel. The living room was a mix of Victorian era styling and hand carved tables, with a flagstone fireplace opened on both sides that allowed her to see into the kitchen. His parents didn't seem to be in that room either, but when she followed Dylan into the kitchen, the table had been set for two.

Dylan pulled out a chair. Once she was seated, he filled two plates with bacon, beans, and a biscuit. He smiled. "Mother and Da must have already eaten, but you finally get your bacon."

Selena picked up a crispy strip, but she didn't feel much like eating. Even if Dylan had planned on them spending the night, she would never sleep with him under his parents' roof, but his mother hadn't even offered her a guest room. She wanted Dylan to take her to a hotel.

After taking another bite of bacon, Selena swallowed

around a lump in her throat. "So, where do you think they went?"

Dylan shrugged. Then he ravenously put away food. Selena nibbled on bacon and a biscuit, studying the kitchen while she ate. Besides the table and chairs, there was a cupboard and a Hoosier hutch. The sink had an indoor hand pump, and in addition to the fireplace, there was a large Dutch oven but no woodstove. "Is there an outdoor kitchen or summerhouse?"

He stopped eating. "Didn't you see the clay, conical-shaped building behind the house when we were coming from the barn? It's designed like the summer kitchens on southern plantations."

As if she ever lived on a plantation. "Oh." She couldn't think of anything else to say. She was used to electric appliances.

After they ate and did the dishes, Dylan opened a door off the kitchen. Standing back, he looked at her with a smug expression. "Look inside the water closet."

"O-kay." She peeped inside. A strange contraption next to a copper tub looked like a fancy antique dressing table. "Okay, so there's a dresser next to the tub."

He smirked. "I thought you were so used to luxuries I couldn't even imagine."

"Don't be a smart-ass Dylan. Just tell me what it is and why I need to see it."

"Watch your mouth," he absently mumbled. "It's a Sheraton Dressing table. While you're here, you can enjoy real luxuries. You won't have to use an outhouse or a chamber pot. My parents are civilized."

He didn't have a clue. But she allowed him to show her the fabulous Sheraton Dressing Table. She really didn't want to use an outhouse the way she did in Canyon Creek. And she was tired of using trees as she'd had to do on the trail.

The top center cabinet of the black walnut cabinetry housed a porcelain pitcher located above the washbowl. Shelves along the side contained several bottles of oils and lotions surrounding an oval mirror. A shaving mug, razor, and razor strop sat on a shelf on top of the washstand. Underneath the washbowl were several smaller drawers and one very large drawer in the center that flipped down instead of pulled. When Dylan opened it, he exposed a porcelain pan that looked like a bedpan.

"Seriously?" Would she have to dump her own poop?

"I told you they were civilized," he said, mistaking her sarcasm for disbelief. "The Sheraton Dressing Table is the most modern thing in the world next to mechanized plumbing in cities with municipal water systems. When you pull this lever, the pan empties automatically."

She leaned closer and noticed the opening of a pipe hidden under the wooden "seat." When Dylan pulled the lever, a metal disc covering the pipe slid open to empty the waste. It wasn't exactly a flushing toilet, but at least she wouldn't have to dump a bedpan. She'd done enough of that working in radiology.

"My parents also have a tub," he continued, as if she didn't know what the big copper thing next to the dressing table was. "Like the kitchen sink, it has a hand pump. Whenever there's a fire in the fireplace, hot water can be pumped directly into the tub without having to light a side furnace or heat water over the stove. It comes in hot and drains right out the bottom of the tub."

Dylan extended his hand toward the copper tub as though offering her a glimpse of paradise. She smiled, unable to resist goading him. "And where does one bathe in warm weather when there is no fire in the fireplace?"

#

Dylan got the uneasy feeling Selena was making fun of him. He liked it less than he understood it. His parents' house was more luxurious than her house in Canyon Creek, yet she seemed more amused than impressed. He just couldn't understand why. She didn't have a hot waterline at the Tillman farm or a fancy bathroom. All she had was a chamber pot and an outhouse.

She had an indoor bathtub, but taking a bath in the copper tub in her water closet was a time-consuming endeavor. He remembered from when Mary lived there. His parents' bath facilities were better than what she had in Canyon Creek, unless she'd had something better in Virginia. Still, he couldn't believe she'd ever seen anything more modern.

Taking her by the hand, he led her outside to the summerhouse. He opened a wooden stall-like door beside the kitchen. Inside was a large metal tub. A window separating the bathroom from the summer kitchen was above it. He lifted the leather flap covering the window, reached inside, and turned a lever on the kitchen pump.

"As long as there are hot coals in the stove, you can take a hot bath. All you have to do is pump."

"If you tell me I can have a hot bath right now, I'll be forever at your mercy."

Selena at his mercy conjured up erotic images that sent heat pooling in his groin. He nearly groaned aloud. "I'm going to hold you to that," he said, his voice tight.

When he pumped warm water into the tub, she squealed with delight. "Can I really take a bath? Now?"

He smiled. "Yes."

She threw her arms around his neck. Then she stepped back and began peeling issuing orders for a towel, soap, and clean clothes. Dylan stood slack-jawed for a moment as he watched her rapidly shed her clothes and climb into the tub with a contented sigh. Then he rushed to do her bidding. When he returned, she was scrubbing her hair with a sliver of soap and singing in a sultry voice that conjured up all sorts of sexual images in his mind.

"What are you singing?" he asked as he laid her things out on a plank bench beside the tub. Selena jumped and splashed water over the sides.

"Jeez, don't sneak up on me like that," she said, sliding back beneath the water's surface. "I thought maybe your parents had returned."

"The wagon's gone, so I think they went into town for supplies. They'll be gone for a while." Looking at Selena's glistening, wet body, he hoped it would be a good, long while.

She laid her head against the back of the tub and closed her eyes. "Thanks for letting me take a bath. It's the best one I've had since leaving home."

"Canyon Creek, home?" he asked as he admired her body beneath the water's surface. She was a beautiful woman. Strange—but beautiful.

"No. Virginia, home," she said lifting one eyelid to peek at him.

He quickly turned his back so she wouldn't catch him staring. "I take it that's where you experienced all your so-called luxuries."

"Yep, the ultimate in indoor plumbing," she said without elaborating.

He arched a brow. "I suppose Richmond has a municipal water system that would allow those sort of luxuries, but don't expect to find anything like that around here."

"I'm not a diva. I took a bath in the river when I was on the trail and didn't complain once," she added, standing up to reach for her towel. He couldn't get it to her fast enough. "I really am used to a lot more, but I'm very adaptable. I can acclimate myself to just about any situation, and you'd be surprised at some of the situations I'm talking about."

When he merely raised his eyebrows, she turned her back on him and started dressing. Dylan quickly divested himself of his clothes and climbed into the tub before she noticed his arousal. While she sat on the bench brushing her hair, he bathed, feeling domestic as hell. He could get use to this. And that scared the hell out of him.

When he stepped out of the tub a short while later, Selena didn't turn away. She even smiled when she noticed his erection. "If I wasn't afraid your parents would come home…"

He stepped into his pants and pulled her into his arms without fastening them. "My mother does all the cooking and cleaning, and the ranch hands seldom come up to the house. So, we're alone."

He kissed her hard and deep, hoping to persuade her to take off the clothes she'd just donned. His hands skated down her back to cup her luscious bottom. Selena groaned but didn't comply. Yet. But he'd convince her. She wanted him as much as he wanted her.

She lowered her head to nuzzle his neck. "No siblings?"

He almost had her. He just needed to convince her they wouldn't get caught in a compromising position.

"No," he breathed into her hair as his hand covered one breast beneath the soft cotton of her shirtwaist. "My mother had a difficult time with my birth, but no doctor would travel into Indian Territory for a squaw. A Cherokee midwife cut me from her womb. She nearly bled to death."

He shrugged as if it was of no consequence, but his sense of guilt had never lessened. "There was a lot of damage, and I was a big baby, so no brother or sister is going to walk in on us either."

Selena sighed and dropped a kiss on his chest. "She was lucky she survived."

He ducked his chin to taste her lips, but Selena suddenly reared back, and her eyes widened. "We haven't used any protection. Not once. So, what if I'm pregnant?"

At the mention of children, he nearly jumped out of his skin. Instead, he stepped out of her arms. How in hell could he have been so stupid? Not once while making love to her had he considered what would happen if she became pregnant.

He fastened his pants and slipped on the clean shirt he'd brought out when he gathered the items for Selena's bath. Then he scooped up their wet towels and dirty clothes and walked back to the house without a word. Selena silently followed.

#

Selena rushed to keep up, but Dylan acted as if it were a race. By the time she entered the kitchen, he'd disappeared into the next room, leaving her alone to face his mother.

Damn, that was close. If Dylan's parents had come home any sooner, they would have caught one or both of them naked. It didn't matter that Selena and Dylan hadn't been screwing while they were gone. They were both damp from a bath, and his mother would assume the worst.

Selena cleared her throat and forced a smile. "Hi."

Mrs. Casey eyed her from head to toe, her face impassive. "Fix your hair. We're going into town, and I don't want to keep anyone waiting."

"Waiting for what?" Selena asked, but Mrs. Casey left the room without answering.

Dylan walked in a minute later. His hair was slicked back, but a stray lock slipped over his forehead. Selena was tempted to brush it from his face until she noticed the dark, brooding scowl.

"We're going to town." He laid a hairbrush and white ribbon on the table. "Braid your hair in that fancy braid you wear and come outside. I'm going to saddle Ishtabe."

"Aye, aye, Captain." She gave him a mock salute, to which he just grunted. Then he stomped out the back door.

When Selena stepped outside a few minutes later, Dylan's mother was already sitting in the front seat of a fancy buggy with a fringed top. Sean held the horse's reins. "Climb in lass. Dylan's decided to ride alongside us."

Selena smiled and climbed into the back of the buggy. The

seats were diamond-tufted leather and looked much fancier than the buggies she'd seen in Canyon Creek. She sat down and almost sighed. It was a lot more comfortable than the wooden spring seat on the buckboard wagon that'd belonged to Mary. It made the short ride into town seem almost as comfortable as a car would have been.

By the time they reached Cheeratahge, it was almost dark.

"I'm too damned tired to be squired about like the prodigal son," Dylan mumbled as he climbed from his horse's back.

"Stop whining," his mother said as Sean dismounted and tied the buggy to a hitching post outside of a dimly lit building. "While you were settling things in the barn, your father and I rode into town and had a talk with Ralph Raintree. We've already made the arrangements. If you agree, he'll marry the two of you tonight. If this isn't what you want, then you can take her somewhere else, but I'll not have you sleeping under my roof with a woman who is not your wife."

Selena felt the color drain from her face. She looked at Dylan. He didn't seem nearly as shocked as he should have. He looked as if he had known what his mother was up to and wasn't happy about it, but he wasn't protesting either.

Did he honestly expect her to go along with it?

"I wasn't planning to sleep with Dylan under your roof," Selena said, not attempting to mask her irritation. "I would never disrespect his family like that."

All eyes swung to Dylan, but he avoided looking at Selena and addressed his mother instead. "Are you giving me a choice?"

His mother didn't even glance in Selena's direction. "You're a grown man. You make your own choices, and I make mine. It's short notice, but it's either this or take her to a hotel. If you don't care enough about her to marry her, then I don't care enough to have her in my house."

Shock rendered Selena speechless. She'd felt helpless and lost since the tornado, but she was finally taking control of her life. She'd be damned if this short little control freak was going to make decisions for her. "Excuse me?"

Melody Casey addressed her son as if they were the only two people around. "It'll be a Christian ceremony, but Ralph won't forget the traditions of our ancestors and neither should you. You are a part of both worlds, son. Don't ever forget that."

"As if you'd let me," he said, sounding like a sullen little boy.

Selena couldn't believe he wasn't arguing. He sure as hell argued every time she opened her mouth. But he let his mother ride roughshod over him. Perhaps he was just being respectful. Or maybe he was a mama's boy.

God, don't let him be a mama's boy.

"Excuse me," she said again. "Did you say we were getting married tonight?"

"Do you have a problem with that?" Melody asked as she eyed Selena with a disapproving frown. "Do you love my son? You've obviously been with him in the biblical way. If the two of you care enough about one another to act married, I see no reason why you shouldn't make it legal."

"I can think of several." She'd been dreaming of Dylan for years and was already half in love with him before they met. But fantasy and reality were worlds apart, and just because fantasy had collided with reality, didn't mean she and Dylan should marry. "For starters, your son hasn't asked."

"I asked. You didn't answer," Dylan grumbled.

Selena swung her eyes on him, glaring. "That was not a proposal." He may have mentioned it in the barn, but he did not ask. When he dropped his gaze, she turned back to his mother. "Until he actually asks, it's a dead issue."

Melody Casey's eyes widened. Her husband's mouth gaped. Dylan stepped into her line of vision. His face was red, his eyes narrowed. "The arrangements are made, and we will get married."

"I won't marry a man for any reason other than love, and I certainly won't marry a man who's never asked." She'd be the voice of reason if it killed her. From the angry look on Dylan's face, it just might.

"You're not getting any younger," he said, as if that would change her mind.

Melody glared. "You slept with him; you'll marry him."

Selena crossed her arms over her chest. She would not let this little woman bully her. "Did you try to marry him off to the other women he's slept with over the years?" There, that ought to shut her up.

It didn't. With an indignant lift of her chin, she said, "He didn't bring the others home."

Why that grudging admission should make Selena's heart beat faster, she didn't know. It didn't mean anything.

"Mel, stop." Sean took his wife's arm. "We need to let these two talk without our interference. And you need to let Dylan make his own choices without your judgment."

She grumbled in her own language but allowed her husband to pull her away. When Selena turned to face Dylan, he scowled as though this insane marriage was her idea. She slung an arm out toward his parents. "Are you just going to stand there and let your mother plan your wedding?"

"It's *our* wedding, and I certainly wouldn't know how to go about planning one," he said, as if that made any sense.

This was more than just planning a wedding. His mother meant for them to get married right. Right now. And he didn't seem inclined to stop her.

Chapter 21

He'd never been so afraid of losing anyone in his life, and the fear galvanized him into action. He gripped Selena's shoulders and pulled her close. Earlier, he'd been afraid she would try to force him into marriage. Now, he was afraid she would refuse him. Although he couldn't begin to understand why he suddenly wanted to marry her, it was now exactly what he wanted.

"I said I'd marry you if you told me your real name, and a deal's a deal. So, what's it going to be? Are you going to marry me or not?" he asked, denying the fear he felt deep in his gut.

"How could a girl resist such a romantic proposal?" She pulled from his embrace and glared. "I don't need you or any man to take care of me. I'm doing just fine by myself, thank you very much."

He reached for her again and turned her to face him when she would have pulled away. Feeling as though he were treading water in quicksand, he held her shoulders as he carefully weighed each word before speaking. He was terrified of sinking deeper into the quagmire he'd made of his life. Since the moment he met Selena, he'd wanted her. Now, he had to decide if she was worth the risk to his heart.

"I can't tell you I love you, but I can honestly say I want you. Please Selena," he said as he gently brushed his knuckles across her cheek. "Would you do me the honor of becoming my wife?"

She sighed, sounding defeated and sad. It nearly broke his heart. "I think I've loved you nearly all my life. But I don't know you—not the real you. I don't even know how I came to be here— or how long I'll stay, no matter what Dream Speaker says."

His heart clinched. "If you marry me, you'll stay forever. Marriage is a commitment. If you agree, it will be forever. That's what I want. Forever. With you." There. He'd said it. It wasn't an admission of love, but it was a true statement.

151

A sad smile crossed her face. "If I say yes, I'd want forever too, but I may not have a choice."

"Everyone has a choice, Selena. If you choose to marry me, you will choose to stay with me—until death do us part."

"I don't know if I can make that promise."

His heart thumped in his chest. Did she still believe Tommy Walters was going to kill him? "I don't fear death, and neither should you. Just promise you'll marry me. We'll face the rest together."

"I don't fear death. Not anymore, and we were destined to meet," she said in that cryptic way she had that raised the fine hairs on the back of his neck. "Despite all odds, maybe we *are* destined to be together forever."

"Then you'll marry me?" he whispered, gently kissing her forehead.

"Yes." Her breathing hitched. "I'll marry you."

His heart jumped. Smiling his relief, he wrapped his arm around her shoulders and shouted to his parents. "Okay, she's accepted. What's next, Mother?"

#

As it happened, the minister, Ralph Raintree, looked nothing like Selena's expectations. He wore no feathers in his short, graying hair, and with his dark suit and string tie, he looked no different than any other nineteenth century man. As Selena walked up the aisle alone, Dylan held her gaze.

Walking by the mostly empty pews, she felt a lump rise in her throat as she thought of the family and friends she'd left behind in the future. With her parents and grandparents dead, she'd envisioned Uncle Robbie walking her down the aisle with her aunts, uncles, and cousin in attendance and her best friend, Kate, by her side. Now, only strangers looked on. And she wasn't even wearing a white dress.

Her heart clenched when she glanced down at the simple skirt and blouse she wore. This wasn't the wedding she'd envisioned as a child. Even when she used to daydream of one day meeting and marrying the handsome man from her dreams, it was a modern wedding in modern times. But she wasn't even carrying a bouquet. In what Melody said was a Cherokee tradition, Selena carried a decorative basket of corn that symbolized her promise to care for her husband.

When she reached the front of the church, Dylan presented her with meat wrapped in butcher's paper and tied with a velvet bow. In the Cherokee tradition, it was a symbolic gesture of his manhood and ability to provide for his family.

The entire ceremony was an odd mixture of Christian and Cherokee traditions, right down to the vows they exchanged. It wasn't the wedding she'd dreamed of, but she was marrying the man of her dreams. Literally.

After the ceremony, Sean led them to The Promised Land Hotel in the center of town. There, he introduced them to friends and neighbors and for the most part, Selena could see no difference in the way the people of Cheeratahge lived as compared with those in Canyon Creek. In both towns, the men and women dressed pretty much the same, but in Cheeratahge, race didn't seem to play a big part in the way a man was treated. Here, everyone was friendly to everyone else. Cheeratahge was a town ahead of its time, and the festive atmosphere helped soothe her anxiety.

Sean led his family to a table in the center of the hotel's restaurant and ordered a bottle of wine to toast the bride and groom. Then he nodded toward the people pouring into the hotel lobby. "Everyone is always willing to show up at The Promised Land whenever you holler. It's too bad we couldn't have gotten more folks out in time to see the wedding."

Dylan's father seemed happier about the marriage than his wife, even though she'd made all the arrangements. Melody had done nothing but frown since the ceremony, and her attitude was apparently contagious. Dylan was in a worse mood now than before the wedding.

"Cheer up, son," Sean said with a hearty slap on the back. "I've announced your wedding to the entire town and tonight, we celebrate."

Dylan grunted, and his lack of enthusiasm sent Selena's spirits into a downward spiral. No matter what she did, Dylan seemed determined to prove she would one day betray him as Mary had done. Life in this century was hard enough without having to constantly prove to the man she loved that the color of his skin didn't matter.

When everyone finished eating, the hotel staff cleared the

dishes, pushed the tables aside, and announced the musicians were ready to play. Sean dragged his wife onto the dance floor for a waltz while Dylan avoided eye contact.

Selena watched them dance. She could waltz. No biggy. It was just slow dancing using the box step, but when the musicians played a Virginia reel, she panicked. She'd never square danced in her life, and she was from Virginia, supposedly in a time when the dance was popular.

She needn't have worried, Dylan didn't ask her to dance.

"You weren't expecting a bunch of savages to know anything about civilized music. Were you?" he asked unexpectedly as he leaned across the table.

Was he seriously trying to pick a fight on their wedding night? He must not want to get lucky. She sighed, regret and heartache souring her mood further. "Stop trying to prove I give a rat's ass about the color of your skin. You're the one who seems bothered by it. Not me."

Shock registered on his face for the briefest of moments before he got up from the table without another word. After a brief exchange with one of the musicians, the band began playing a lively tune that reminded Selena of the music played in her favorite Mexican restaurant back home in the future. She smiled and tapped her foot to the beat, laughing aloud at Dylan's confused expression. He'd expected her to hate the exotic rhythms of Latino music, but he had a lot to learn about his white wife.

Before he could sit down, she jumped up and dragged him onto the dance floor.

Watching the other dancers, she mimicked their rhythmic moves and danced circles around her husband. Then she took the lead and tried to guide him through some modern dance steps she'd learned at her favorite club. His jaw dropped and his feet froze. He was so not ready to move like Jagger.

When the song ended, his face was the color of a hot pepper. He dropped her off at her seat and then walked around the table to speak to his father. Then the two of them walked up to the band and one of the musicians handed Dylan his guitar. Sean then pulled a harmonica from his pocket and held it to his mouth. On cue, they began playing an Irish ballad. When Dylan began to sing the haunting melody, Selena's heart melted.

Her sexy husband could play the guitar and sing. Ignoring her sulking mother-in-law, she kept her eyes on Dylan until the last dying note.

"You sing beautifully," she said when he returned to the table. Before he could respond, however, Sean claimed her hand for a waltz.

#

Dylan watched his wife dancing gracefully with his father. Who was this woman, who claimed to be a Tillman cousin? She seemed more like a chameleon than a woman, adapting herself to each new environment the way other women adapted their wardrobe to the weather. She was nothing like other white women of his acquaintance. Hell, she wasn't like any woman he'd ever met of any race.

"Dylan," his mother said, gaining his attention.

He dragged his eyes away from Selena and met his mother's frown.

"I noticed your wife enjoyed dancing to that Spanish music," she said, looking more stern than usual. "She seems a bit forward to me. I hope you can handle her."

"She's not a whore, if that's what you're getting at." Not that he was her first. Then again, he was no green kid himself.

Her frown deepened, and guilt burned his cheeks. His mother loved him, but he was no longer a child she needed to discipline.

"She's not what I would have chosen for you, but you made the choice when you brought her into my home. You knew my rules, and you brought her anyway." Her eyes narrowed, and she scrutinized him as if she could see the truth if she looked hard enough. "You manipulated me. You knew I'd force you to make a choice, and you didn't fight me on it. This was your plan all along. Wasn't it?"

Not consciously, but he'd known. He dropped his gaze and shrugged, feeling like he did the first time his mother caught him sneaking out to meet a girl when he was little more than a kid. "I had a good idea what to expect if I brought her home. I just didn't know we'd be getting married tonight. I thought Selena could stay with you and Da when I returned to the fort, and you'd have time to get to know her. Then we could have gotten married when I got back." He shrugged. "This way's better."

"I know we don't always agree," she said with a sigh that twisted his gut with guilt, "but believe it or not, all I've ever wanted was for you to be happy. Did I mistake your feelings for this woman?"

"No." He cared for Selena, but he wasn't sure if it was love or something Dream Speaker said that made him think they belonged together. "But I'm a half-breed trying to live in the white man's world. I don't know if happy is possible."

He was rubbing salt in an open wound, but he couldn't help it. He'd never fit in anywhere, but with Selena, he felt as if it might be possible. And that scared the hell out of him.

"We make our own happiness in this life, son," his mother said with tears in her eyes. "And I refuse to apologize for loving your father and giving him a son."

He felt like an ungrateful bastard. His mother didn't owe him an apology. She'd given him nothing but love. He took her hand. "I'm sorry, Mother. I was out of line, and I love you too. And I don't hate who I am, I just hate the way the white man treats our people."

She placed her right hand over their joined hands as his father returned to the table with Selena.

Dylan looked at his wife, and his chest cramped. He wanted to give her the life she deserved, but she was still keeping secrets, and he couldn't trust her if she wasn't honest, but he would protect her. She'd become his responsibility the moment they left Canyon Creek.

Even if he'd wanted to, he couldn't take her home now. The townspeople would eat her alive for riding off with a half-breed and an Indian. Besides, she didn't have a legal claim to the house. If Ben Tillman found out his daughter was dead, he could have Selena arrested. It was one of the reasons he'd married her. He didn't want to worry about her when he rode out in the morning to rejoin his regiment.

He'd said nothing to Selena about his plans and responsibilities because he hadn't known how this trip would end. Now that it had ended, it was high time he remembered those responsibilities. He still had a job to do for the United States government, and he needed to make sure he was no longer a suspect in Mary's death. He'd promised Colonel Harper he'd do some scouting in Sioux territory, and it was high time he got started.

Back in sixty-nine, a Sioux warrior agreed to let some professor dig for fossil bones on the reservation, and Chief Red Cloud reluctantly agreed. Now prospectors were snooping around in the Black Hills looking for gold, which wasn't part of the deal, and Rain in the Face wasn't going to allow it.

If Rain in the Face were to join forces with the Cheyenne chiefs, Crazy Horse and Sitting Bull, the whites would have hell to pay. If there was something Dylan could do to stop it, he would. But if he believed even half of what Selena told Chief Dog Ears, he was wasting his time. Still, he had to try. At the very least, he wanted to convince the warriors to keep to the Black Hills and stay out of Texas.

Shaking off such depressing thoughts, he stood and pulled Selena to her feet. Once on the dance floor, he took her in his arms and sang softly in her ear as they gently swayed to the music. The words were in Cherokee, and even though she didn't understand them, he knew his singing pleased her.

"You're gorgeous, sexy, and you can sing. If you hadn't already gotten me into bed, I wouldn't stand a chance now," she said as she snuggled against his chest.

"Actually," he said smiling, "we've never had sex in a bed. We've done it on the ground and in a tepee, but never in a bed."

"Well, not yet anyway," she whispered, pressing her body closer to his. Her hips met his groin, and he sucked air between his teeth.

"And just so you know," she added in response to his physical reaction to her nearness, "I'm not wearing any underpants."

"If you don't stop," he growled, "we may not make it to a bed tonight either."

"Then I suggest we hurry home before I get carried away and rip off all your clothes, right here on the dance floor."

Dylan couldn't get out of the hotel fast enough. Once outside, he pulled Selena in front of him on Ishtabe and rode back to his parents' house as fast as possible. They barely made it through his old bedroom door before he was tearing the clothes from her body.

As he fumbled with the buttons on her bodice, he nearly tore the fabric. With only half the buttons undone, he impatiently shoved it to her waist and bent his head to her breasts. Taking a taut nipple in his mouth, he sucked greedily as he released himself from his britches. Selena's hands reached for him before he was free, stroking him until he feared spilling his seed in her palm.

He quickly discarded the rest of their clothing and carried her to bed. Then he entered her as soon as their entwined bodies met the down filled mattress.

"I love you," Selena whispered.

The words scared the hell out of him, and although he wasn't ready to say them back—was unsure if he'd ever be ready—it didn't stop him from showing her with his body what he couldn't say aloud. "I'm going to take you slowly, and you're going to come with me."

It wasn't a promise of love, but it was the best he could do. Eyes locked onto hers, he took her on a slow ride that turned into a frantic coupling.

They reached the summit together.

"I love you," Selena cried again as she collapsed onto the pillows.

He didn't respond with words. He just pulled her to his side and held her close. He hated to spoil the afterglow of their loving, but they needed to talk. Tomorrow would be too late.

"I'm leaving early in the morning." God, he hated hurting her, but he didn't have a choice. Where he was going, she couldn't follow.

"How early do we have to get up?" she asked drowsily, stifling a yawn against his shoulder.

"You don't have to see me off," he said, but Selena interrupted him before he could explain.

She sat up in bed and stared down at him. "I know you're not fixin' to dump me off on your parents and ride off into the sunset like some bad spaghetti western."

Trying to ignore her beautiful heaving breasts, he contemplated her strange words. *Fixin' to dump? Spaghetti western?* What language did she speak? Even if he asked, she wouldn't give him a straight answer.

He took a deep breath and exhaled slowly. "I have to get back to work, and I can't just take you to Canyon Creek and leave you there. The color of my skin may not matter to you, but it does to those people."

"No, but you could take me to your house. You don't live here, and I don't think you live at the fort. There were no records of such, at any rate." She dropped her gaze and twisted a corner of the sheet in her fist.

"What records?" He seldom understood everything she said, but asking questions would only frustrate him more because she was still keeping secrets.

He sat up and dropped one leg to the floor, turning just enough to see her face. "I have my own place, but it's not this nice, and I wouldn't leave you there alone. If you stay here, I won't have to worry about your safety."

She looked up, finally meeting his gaze. "But your mother doesn't even like me."

"She will."

"Get real. Your mother isn't the issue here, and you know it," she snapped as she crawled out of bed and put on his shirt. "This is supposed to be our honeymoon, and your timing really sucks."

God, but she looked sexy wearing his shirt. She'd buttoned it no higher than her navel, and he found it hard to concentrate on what she was saying because he was thinking of their scents mingling in the cotton fabric. He also had trouble understanding her words. *His timing sucked? Get real?*

"I am real, Selena. Real serious. I have to get back to work. I have a job to do. I gave my word to Colonel Harper, and I won't break it. My ranch can wait. You can wait, but the situation with the Sioux can't. If I can divert any more bloodshed, I will. If I can't, then I have to take sides. Do you have any idea how damned hard that could be for me? I may not be Sioux, but I am Indian."

How in the hell had she pulled so much emotion from him? His throat had closed, and he was having difficulty swallowing. He'd never told anyone how much it hurt to be caught in the middle of two worlds at war. So why was he telling her? She'd never understand. Hell, he didn't understand it himself half the time.

"I'm so sorry, sweetheart." She sat beside him on the bed and kissed his forehead.

"I don't need your damn pity," he growled, pulling back as she gazed into his eyes.

"I don't pity you, you idiot. I love you. How many damn times do I have to tell you?" She grabbed a pillow and swatted the side of his head to emphasize her point.

"Hey! Watch it," he said as he steadied the bedside lamp. She'd very nearly knocked it over. "What are you trying to do, set the house on fire?"

"Sorry. I'm not used to kerosene lamps."

"Why not? I've seen them in your house. Don't you use them?"

"I . . . um, had gaslights in Virginia," she said, after a moment's hesitation.

He didn't care if she used beeswax candles and tallow. It was the lying he hated.

He sighed, refusing to ask more questions he knew she'd never answer.

"Let's just go to sleep. I have to get up early, and I'll be gone before you're even awake. It could take six weeks, six months, or six years. Just do me a favor," he added, unable to stop himself from lashing out and hurting her as much as her continued lies hurt him. "If you get tired of waiting, don't just walk away. Divorce me. I'm sure you'll have no trouble finding a lawyer who'll end your marriage to a half-breed."

He expected her to cry, or maybe tell him to go to hell since she wasn't like most women. She did neither. His beautiful, defiant wife stuck up her middle finger and mouthed a profanity he never imagined a woman would know, much less repeat. It was much worse than "go to hell" and all he could do was stare as she snatched up a handful of bedcovers and flung herself down on her side.

She kept her back to him the rest of the night.

Chapter 22

It was Selena's first morning as a new bride, and she was alone. Her husband of less than twenty-four hours had ridden out of her life while she still slept. The too soft mattress still held the impression of his body, and his scent still lingered on the sheets. She hugged her face to his pillow and cried.

She should never have gone to sleep angry, and as much as she wanted to blame him for ruining their wedding night, she had to accept some responsibility. She was still lying to him, and he knew it. Now she had to face the music—and his parents—alone.

But why couldn't he have woken her up to say goodbye?

Okay, so maybe he had a job to do. She understood responsibility, and his weighed heavily on his shoulders, but he was wasting his time playing diplomat. In less than a decade, the Indian Nation would no longer exist, and the army would dismiss the Native Americans who'd served, and strip them of their rank as if their sacrifice meant nothing. If Dylan planned to stay with the army until the end, he'd be no better rewarded for his loyalty.

With a frustrated sigh, Selena climbed out of bed and pulled up the covers. Then she washed off in the washbowl and redressed in the same clothes she'd worn the night before. Once she was dressed and her hair combed, she slipped on her boots and headed to the kitchen. Her mother-in-law was sitting at the table drinking coffee. Selena got the distinct impression the woman was waiting for her.

"Excuse me," she said as she hurried into the water closet to use the *fabulous* Sheraton Dressing Table. Her bladder was about to burst, and she didn't want to be waylaid by questions.

When she came out of the bathroom, she washed her hands at the kitchen pump and then dried them on a scratchy hand towel before turning to face Dylan's mother.

The older woman smiled, but it didn't reach her eyes. "Did you sleep well?"

Selena flushed. Last night was her wedding night. What did she expect her to say? After screwing your son's brains out, he told me he was leaving in the morning without me, so I had trouble sleeping.

Not hardly!

"I slept fine. Thanks for asking." She poured herself a cup of coffee from a blue speckled pot sitting on the stove and then paused. Without a refrigerator, she didn't know where to look for the cream. Anita had kept it in the cool pantry and had given it to Selena before she could even ask.

Mrs. Casey nodded to a small silver pitcher and matching bowl sitting on the table. "There's cream and sugar here on the table."

Selena mumbled her thanks and sat across from the woman. Tension knotted her stomach as she fixed her coffee the way she liked it and then took a sip. It went down about as smoothly as battery acid. She was so not ready for a confrontation with Dylan's mother.

When Selena looked up, Mrs. Casey was staring with blatant disapproval. Then she placed her coffee on the table and leaned forward. "My son left early this morning."

Selena exhaled, unable to hide her growing frustration. "I know."

The older woman narrowed her eyes. "You didn't get up to see him off."

"We said our good-byes last night." Her gut twisted. Dylan had slipped out of bed without waking her.

Her mother-in-law gave her another disapproving scowl. "As his wife, you should have been there for him. He was heartbroken by your callous treatment. How could you stay in bed sleeping while he was preparing to leave for God knows how long?"

Heartbroken? He was probably pissed, and it was all her fault. Selena bit her lip to keep from crying. Despite all the chances she'd had to tell the truth, she hadn't. She'd allowed him to believe she was a liar rather than risk him thinking her insane. Too late, she realized she should have given him the opportunity to decide for himself what he believed. Assuming he *wouldn't* believe her was no different than him assuming she'd never accept his

Cherokee heritage.

"Mrs. Casey," she started as she lowered her cup. Her hands were shaking so badly, she spilled half her coffee on the table.

"Melody," the woman stated, grudgingly.

"Fine. Melody, then." She avoided eye contact and drew her finger through the spilled coffee. It only took a second to realize her random doodles were letters, and she'd spelled Dylan's name.

Her pulse jumped, and her cheeks warmed. She raised her eyes to find her mother-in-law studying her with a sad expression in her eyes.

"So, you do care."

"Of course I care. I love him. He's just so . . . so...stubborn, and he . . ." Choking back tears, she was unable to continue.

Melody reached across the table and touched her hand. "I know he seems unfeeling at times, but he isn't. If anything, he feels too much. He just doesn't know how to show it."

Selena squeezed her hand. "I know. He's sensitive and caring, but he's got this overdeveloped sense of responsibility. He expects too much from himself and tries to fix things that are beyond his control." She took a deep breath to keep from crying. "He's also sweet and funny, when he forgets to be brooding and miserable. Sometimes, I think he gets so wrapped up in what other people think of him, he forgets who he is."

"I'm not sure my son knows *who* he is. He's too caught up in being white or being Indian to embrace either culture. So, he's never found his place in this world."

"We make a dysfunctional pair, don't we?" Selena said with a bitter laugh. "He can't find his place in the world, and I've lost mine. I use to know who I was and what I wanted out of life, but now everything's changed, and I don't know anything."

"Marriage is sometimes like that," Melody said, having no clue as to how much Selena's life *had* changed. "Especially when you've been forced into it, but I can't say I'm sorry. It seemed to be what you both wanted. Was I mistaken?"

"I can't answer for Dylan, but I'm not sorry I married your son. I love him. I just don't know what to do with myself now. I could cope when he was around, but now I'm not so sure. I miss him already," she added in a trembling voice.

"I know," Melody soothed. "But you have the heart and spirit of the *Yunwiya*. You'll do just fine until Dylan returns. Until then, Sean and I will take care of you. After all, you are now *hottuk oretoopah*, one of my beloved people."

#

She didn't make it. Selena wasn't even close to the washbowl when the contents of her stomach splashed onto the floor and splattered her bare feet.

"Melody!" She staggered back to bed and flung herself across the mattress. "Melody!"

Her mother-in-law rushed into the room but stopped short when she saw the vomit on the floor. Her face paled. "Did the roast not sit well on your stomach tonight? Are you sick?"

"I think I'm pregnant," she mumbled miserably as the room stopped spinning and her stomach settled down.

"Pregnant? Are you sure?"

"No. But I don't think I'm sick, and I just threw up."

"What's all the shouting about?" Sean came running but skidded to a halt just inside the door.

"But it's not morning. It can't be morning sickness," Melody said unreasonably.

"Well Junior here, can't tell time." Selena placed her palms over her stomach. "I've missed my period, I'm dizzy, and I just barfed on your floor. I don't know about you, but those sound like symptoms of pregnancy to me."

"Barfed?" Melody and Sean echoed together, looking from Selena to one another.

"Well then, me darlin'," Sean said, winking at his wife, "I guess one of us needs to be cleaning up the . . . um . . . barf, while the other gets a wee bit of Irish whisky to celebrate."

"Let me guess," Selena said with a fleeting smile. "Melody has barf detail."

Sean laughed and shook his head as he left to retrieve a tray of drinks for their impromptu celebration. Melody headed for the kitchen to get a cleaning bucket and rags while Selena closed her eyes, recounting the weeks since her wedding.

It had been eight weeks since Dylan rode out of her life and roughly ten weeks since her last period. She wasn't a doctor, but she could pretty much guess when the baby was due. Sometime in January, she'd be a mother and though the thought filled her with wonder, it brought a sense of urgency as well. She couldn't wait for Dylan's return, and she couldn't live in limbo any longer.

She was no longer wearing Mary's hand-me-downs. Melody had hired a woman in Cheeratahge to sew Selena an entire wardrobe. She was also learning how to cook on a woodstove. But soon, she was going to be a mother. She couldn't care for a child if she couldn't care for herself, and as long as she stayed with Dylan's parents, they'd insist on taking care of her.

Her mother-in-law did most of the cooking and cleaning, and a woman from town did the laundry. Sean had all the help he needed on the ranch, and with her lack of skills and knowledge of the times, she was as useless here as she'd been in Canyon Creek.

Then there was the endless boredom. Though the nights were the worst, she had trouble finding ways to pass the daylight hours as well. She'd tried reading a couple of dime novels she picked up in town. The romance and adventure stories were considered somewhat risqué in this time, but she found them to be extremely tame and predictable.

On Sundays, she attended church services with her in-laws. Though Native traditions weren't forgotten, most of the residents in Cheeratahge were Christians. The Casey's religious following was an odd mix of Sean's Protestant mother and Irish Catholic father and Melody's Cherokee heritage and Baptist teachings. Selena found it all quite interesting as well as the town picnics after the service. Unlike Canyon Creek, the people of Cheeratahge welcomed her with open arms.

She loved the town and her in-laws, but her place was with her husband. Since he didn't seem to know where he belonged, her place was on his ranch. For her own sanity and the welfare of her child, she needed to become more self-reliant, which meant moving out of her in-laws' home and into Dylan's. She just hated saying goodbye and starting over. Again.

#

Traveling to Canyon Creek in a wagon with Sean took a lot longer than traveling on horseback with Dylan and White Deer. Because of her condition, Sean wouldn't allow her to ride astride, so it took an extra day and a half to reach the Tillman farm. The trip was also a bit more awkward because she never knew what to say to Dylan's father, and his mother stayed behind, refusing to set foot in Canyon Creek again.

Years ago, Sean and Melody were turned away from the hotel in town because Melody wasn't white. They were also refused service in the hotel restaurant and the diner. Now that Selena had seen firsthand what Canyon Creek was like, she didn't much care for the historic version of the town her ancestors had called home.

As she and Sean rode through town on the way to the farm, the citizens of Canyon Creek made it quite clear they wanted her gone for good. When someone actually spat in their direction, Selena had to grab Sean's arm to keep him from stopping the wagon and going after the man. "It's not worth it, Da. Tomorrow, we'll go to the lawyer's office, and I'll sign the house over to my brother. Then we'll head to the ranch and kiss this place goodbye."

By giving the house to William, she hoped to set history back on a forward course. The Tillman house would eventually become a tenant farm, and once the railroad bypassed Canyon Creek, the town and the Tillman property would be abandoned. Knowing the town's fate made it a little easier for Selena to tolerate the hostile glares, but it was still a welcome relief when they reached the Tillman farm.

Upon their arrival, Alberto and Anita greeted her with a hug and warmly welcomed Sean.

"How long will *Señor* Casey be staying?" Anita asked as Sean unloaded the wagon and Alberto unhitched the horse.

"We'll both be leaving in a couple of weeks. I'm moving to Dylan's ranch, and as soon as I can make the arrangements, I'm giving this house to my half-brother, William."

At the crestfallen look on Anita's face, Selena quickly added, "Don't worry, I'm deeding the guest house and five acres of land to you and Alberto."

Tears sprang to Anita's eyes, and she wrapped her plump arms around Selena's waist. *"Gracias, Señora* Casey. We have lived here since *Señorita* Mary was born, and it is our home. We will take good care of your brother if he requires our services."

"I'm positive he'll hire you both."

166

"That would be nice," Anita said as the two women entered the house. Sean followed, carrying the suitcases.

"*Señor* Dylan is no longer a murder suspect," Anita added. "It was in the newspaper, but they still call him a half-breed."

"What's this about murder?" Sean asked, his voice rife with worry.

"It's a long story." But Selena gave him a condensed version of Mary's death and Dylan's troubles before they went to bed that night. The next morning, the two of them went into town.

When they entered the lawyer's office, the secretary treated her with such disrespect, Sean bristled, and Selena feared he'd actually punch the man in the face.

"It's okay, Da. Let it go. I don't want you getting into trouble on my account."

"I'll not have him treat you like river trash," he fumed under his breath when the secretary turned up his nose and stepped into the back room to get the lawyer.

"I don't care. These people and this town don't matter. In another fifty years, the town won't even exist. Now I know why. It was too full of hatred to survive."

"I'll grant you that, lass," he said with a concerned frown, "but you can't be sure that Canyon Creek won't be here long after we're gone. They expect the railroad to come through, you know."

Selena just smiled and patted his arm.

Mr. Dudley made them wait forty-five minutes before summoning them into his office. Then he didn't bother to stand when Selena entered the room.

"Good day, Mr. Dudley," she said sweetly.

He examined a perfectly manicured nail and sneered. "*Mrs. Casey.*"

She dropped a bundle of cash on his desk. *That ought to get the asshole's attention.*

He sprang to his feet. "Yes ma'am. What can I do for you?"

"I'll get directly to the point," she said. Then she had the lawyer draw up several legal documents.

She returned ownership of the Tillman house to Ben, and though she could never tell him his real daughter was dead, she told him she was happily married and planned to move to her husband's ranch. Some things about the past couldn't change, so

167

she asked him to give the house to William so her father could still inherit it in the future. At least now, the house wasn't haunted. Dylan hadn't died on the porch, and now that he'd been cleared of murder charges and Mary's remains had been laid to rest, perhaps her spirit could find peace as well.

As a final request, she asked the attorney to draw up papers giving Alberto and Anita the deed to the servants' quarters behind the house. They were to continue maintaining the Tillman house and farm until her *brother* arrived to take possession, but if William refused to hire them, at least he couldn't kick them out of their home.

"I don't know how long it'll take William to get here or even if he should want to live in Texas," she said as she signed the final papers and stood to leave. "So just as soon as you get an answer from my telegram, send it out to the farm. I'll be staying there until I hear back from you, and I want to know the minute my brother leaves Virginia."

"Your brother isn't in Virginia," Mr. Dudley informed her. "He's in Fort Worth looking for you."

Selena's heart slammed against her sternum. If William learned of his half sister's death, Selena could end up in jail.

The room spun and her legs nearly gave out. She sat heavily on the high-backed leather chair across from the lawyer's desk to keep from falling. Sean rushed to her side. Taking her hand and glaring at the attorney, he said, "Why didn't you tell her about her brother sooner?"

"She didn't ask," the lawyer replied churlishly.

"Why?" Selena whispered as Sean patted her hand. Why was William in Fort Worth? Surely, if the lawyer had known she was an impostor, he would have said something by now.

"I believe he was concerned about you," Mr. Dudley intoned in a bored voice. "He's heard nothing from you since your arrival, and I can only guess he suspects the worst."

"I sent a telegram to my father the day I got here letting him know I arrived safely." Ben's family had never accepted the bastard daughter of his mistress, so Selena assumed neither brother would care to meet her after she moved into the house, but if they'd stayed in touch and suddenly lost contact...

"After the letter you wrote upon learning you had brothers,

168

William assumed you'd maintain contact. Other than a brief telegram informing your father of your arrival in March, they've heard nothing."

She knew nothing of a letter. In fact, she knew nothing at all of her ancestors' personal lives other than the family stories she'd heard growing up and the meager information she'd dug up online. If William had already learned of her duplicity, she could be in serious legal trouble.

She swallowed her fear and tried to brazen it out. "I hope you told him I'm perfectly safe."

"He was informed you'd run off with an Injun and a half-breed. He assumes you're anything but safe. The army, of course, has monitored Casey, but once he returned to his post at Fort Davis, they informed your brother of your marriage and um, relative safety. However, I doubt he was greatly relieved."

If Dylan had reported to Fort Davis, he should have answered her letters or written to his parents, but he hadn't.

"I need to know where my brother is staying while in Fort Worth. I need to get word to him as soon as possible." She might be unable to do anything about Dylan's silence, but perhaps she could prevent William from learning the truth.

Within an hour of leaving the lawyer's office, she received an answer from William at the telegraph office in Canyon Creek. He'd been located at the Fort Worth Regency Hotel and would be arriving in Canyon Creek in two days to meet his sister. If her luck held, she could settle things in Canyon Creek and leave for Dylan's ranch in a week. If William believed she was his sister, she had nothing to fear. If not, she'd better find some way to explain the impossible, because no one in his or her right mind would ever believe the truth.

169

Chapter 23

The next day, Sean escorted Selena to Fort Davis in the hopes of seeing her husband. Dylan wasn't there, but they met the fort commander, Colonel Harper.

"Captain Casey was here two months ago," the colonel said. "He stayed the night and then rode out with a detachment of Buffalo Soldiers. I'm afraid your letters didn't arrive until after he was gone."

Her hands drifted to her stomach. Dylan hadn't gotten her letters and had no way of knowing she was pregnant or that she'd left Cheeratahge.

She and Sean thanked the colonel for his time and then left. As they approached the buckboard parked outside the garrison headquarters, they came face to face with Dylan's former friend and commander, Major Andrew Davis.

"Well, well," he said, brushing an index finger beneath his bushy mustache, "if it isn't our little crime solver."

"Major." She didn't have time for this, and she didn't have time for the major's petty barbs aimed at her or Dylan. She nodded and tried to walk around him, but he moved in front of her, blocking her path.

Sean bristled. "Let us pass."

"But I only wanted to offer my congratulations to the new bride." His smile was snide, his tone sarcastic.

"Tread lightly, major. The lass is my daughter-in-law, and I'll not allow you to insult her."

Selena patted Sean's arm, afraid his overdeveloped sense of chivalry would lead to bloodshed. Then she offered the major her sincerest smile. "I'm sure a gentleman like yourself would never intentionally insult a lady, whether he believed her to be one or not. Still, I thank you for your heartfelt warm wishes. Now, if you'll excuse us, we need to be on my way."

The major flushed but stepped aside. "You're right, Mrs.

Casey. I am a gentleman, but you chose a half-breed instead of giving me half a chance. Unlike your husband, however, I wouldn't have left you alone to fend for yourself."

Well, that explained a lot. The major *had* been overly solicitous when she first met him, but she'd only had eyes for Dylan. She'd also had other things on her mind at the time—like whether or not she was still sane.

"The heart wants what the heart wants," she said, not knowing how else to respond. "And I do appreciate your concern," she added when Sean puffed up like a peacock at her side. "But Dylan didn't abandon me. He left me in the care of his parents, and as you're well aware, he has a duty and responsibility to his country, the same as you."

"Casey is nothing like me," the major said through tightly gritted teeth. "White men don't pillage and plunder or rape and murder innocent women and children."

"No?" She raised her brows. "Even if you discount the Sand Creek massacre, how can you forget General Sherman's destructive pillaging of the South? You fought for the Confederacy and yet, you now work for the very army you once fought against." Sean tugged on her arm, trying to get her to climb into the buggy. She ignored him.

"A war was going on, Mrs. Casey," Davis replied, as though she was an ignorant child he needed to educate. "A war that is now over, and I'm proud to call myself a Texan and an American."

"There's still a war going on, Major, and innocents are always hurt in war. It's the nature of the beast."

"Maybe so, but no Yankee ever raped and murdered my mother and sister. The Comanche did," he said, and his eyes burned with hatred.

Gripping Selena's arm even harder, Sean turned her around and lifted her onto the wagon seat. "It's no use, lass. Some wounds are too deep to ever heal."

Before he could climb aboard himself and set the horses into motion, she turned to look over her shoulder at Major Davis. "I'm sorry about your family, Major," she said, before he could turn away. "But please don't blame an entire race of people for the actions of a few. Such hatred is a hard thing to live with."

171

Without bothering to reply, Major Davis turned on his heel and headed back to his office. With tears in her eyes, Selena looked at Sean and nodded. They rode back to the house in silence.

William Tillman arrived at noon the next day.

Selena was having lunch with Sean in the kitchen when Anita announced the arrival of their guest. Selena promptly ran out the back door and threw up. Sean blamed her pregnancy, but Selena knew it for what it was. Fear.

Before returning to the house, she stopped at the water pump out back to rinse out her mouth and wash her face. When she entered the kitchen, her skin felt flushed from retching, but she was cold and clammy. She wiped her damp palms on her dark cotton skirt and waited outside the living room, trying to control her breathing. Then she entered the living room and stopped dead in her tracks, clutching the doorjamb for support. She was living in a time nearly a hundred years before her birth, and the man she was supposed to pretend was her half-brother looked like the brother she never had.

"My Lord!" William exclaimed when he noticed her. "You look just like me, only you're beautiful."

"William." The first Selena had never met her brother, but William accepted her as his sister now without question. She was so relieved she felt lightheaded. Had Sean not rushed to her side and seated her on the sofa, she would have swooned like the Victorian lady she was pretending to be.

"I thought I'd find some green kid, but you're a married woman, and from what Mr. Casey tells me, you're going to be a mother."

"I'm twenty-five," she said, forgetting to lie about her age.

"Twenty-five?" William seemed flummoxed, and Selena started to panic. Then he smiled and kissed her fingers before releasing her hand. "Obviously Father didn't want to upset mother. He led her to believe you were much younger and were conceived only after—um—when they stopped. . ." He blushed. "Oh, dear. I'm so stunned I'm rambling. Let's just say mother suffered greatly after losing her last child—the third or fourth after me—and she didn't want to risk having more."

"I understand." Well, she understood the woman didn't let her husband in her bed after that, but she didn't understand how any woman could shut her husband out so completely.

Ben Tillman was starting to look just a bit more sympathetic.

William smiled, and the crease between his eyes disappeared. "I also need to apologize for mine and Bennie's lack of brotherly concern. Unfortunately, until we received your letter the day you left Richmond, we were unaware of your existence."

"And I didn't know I had brothers, before Ben—father— left me the house."

The twenty-something young man seated beside her was really her great-great-great grandfather, a man who should be long dead but wasn't. Now he was her brother. She had family again. Not that Sean, Melody, and Dylan weren't family, but William was blood.

Overwhelmed by the suddenness of the day's strange revelations, she burst into tears and threw herself into the unsuspecting arms of her new brother. He stiffened for only a second before pulling her to his chest.

"It must be the pregnancy hormones," she said, leaning back to wipe away the tears. "But I've missed my family so much, and now I have you."

"Now, lass," Sean added with an awkward pat on her back. "You're a Casey now, and you have Melody and me and a husband who loves you."

"Where is your husband?" William asked with a frown.

"He's a cavalry officer, and with all the local hostilities, the army needs him. He's trying to protect his family, his people, and his country by trying to prevent a war, but I'm afraid he can't stop the inevitable."

"You really don't have a problem being married to a man who's part savage?" He sounded more intrigued than prejudiced.

Selena smiled. He was probably one of those misinformed Easterners Major Davis warned her about. "Of course not."

"Savage!" Sean leaned toward the younger man and glared. Selena lovingly touched his arm before turning back to her brother. Sean reseated himself in the chair across from William and continued to scowl.

It reminded her of Dylan's dark, brooding looks.

"Are his people any more savage than the men who

173

massacred innocent women and children at Sand Creek in 1864?" Sean asked, a bit more controlled. "Colonel Chivington mutilated the Cheyenne, and he was a minister prior to joining the army. He was also white."

"That was in retaliation for what the Sioux did to Captain Fetterman and eighty-two of the finest cavalry men to grace this fine country," William countered. "With little or no provocation, I might add."

"That was in 1866, *after* Chivington's massacre and *after* the construction of the Bozeman trail across Indian lands. The Sioux were only protecting what was rightfully theirs."

William frowned. "But the trail was important to the settlement of lands west of the Mississippi. We needed that land."

"The government has enough land," Sean said through clenched teeth. "This obsession to own all the land from ocean to ocean has got to stop. It's no better than the bloody Brits greed for Ireland."

"Gentleman, please." Selena gripped her brother's hands. "I don't want to take sides."

The two men scowled briefly but reluctantly changed the subject.

While Selena got better acquainted with her new brother, Anita served refreshments in the parlor. Selena learned Bennie was the oldest and at twenty-nine, was still unmarried, as was William. Eventually, Bennie would marry and inherit Ben's property in Richmond. William was twenty-six and would stay in Texas, but his oldest son would eventually leave Texas and move to Fredericksburg where his wife would eventually inherit Willow Lawn—the home where Selena's great, great grandfather was born.

Lord, but it was just too bizarre, and trying to sort out her convoluted family tree was driving her crazy.

Pleading a headache, she kissed each man's cheek and went to lie down before supper. Once she was in Mary's old room, Anita pressed a cool rag to her forehead and promised to keep the men from starting a war while she rested. By the time the threesome sat down for supper, Sean and William had developed an uneasy truce.

Dinner conversation revolved around Selena's experience in the Comanche camp and the Cherokee town of Cheeratahge.

Sean added much to the conversation, jumping at the chance to further the Indians' cause and emphasize the differences in the various tribal cultures.

"The five civilized tribes are nothing like the plains tribes. Why, even after their forced removal west," Sean bragged, "the Cherokee formed a democratic society and education system far superior to the white man's."

"Come now, Mr. Casey," William said, "What kind of education are we talking about here?"

"A damned good one. Dylan attended the Baptist Mission School in Tahlequah as a wee lad and later, he went to the Cherokee Male Seminary. That was before he went to school back East," he said as he took another swig of the Irish whiskey he'd poured earlier.

"Dylan was going to go into the ministry?" Selena asked, surprised to hear he'd attended a seminary.

"No, lass," Sean chuckled. "The seminary is an institute of higher learning. It prepared Dylan for college back East. He attended the University of Georgia in 1859. He was only there for two years. He quit in sixty-one when most of the students and faculty joined the Confederate army. He spent some time with his Uncle Quinn before signing up with Stand Watie, and it broke his mother's heart. Not only did he not graduate, but his mother considered the time spent with her brother a betrayal. She never forgave Quinn for not walking the trail."

"The trail?" William asked as he spooned another helping of mashed potatoes onto his plate.

They passed the rest of the evening in comfortable conversation as Sean told tales he'd heard from his wife about the horrors encountered by the people along *Nunna daul Tsuny*, or The Trail Where They Cried.

After supper, Selena told William about saving the mayor's life and mentioned she might like to study medicine or possibly design products that could make people's lives easier.

"But you're a woman. What would you know about medicine or inventions?"

"Seriously?" Selena clamped down on her irritation, reminding herself that William was more than just old fashioned. He was Victorian.

"She did save a man's life," Sean reminded him.

"And I kind of came up with a design for a washing machine with a crank handle that spins so you don't have to wring out the clothes."

She'd worked on the designs while living with Sean and Melody. It wasn't as if she'd had anything else to do. And since she had no idea who invented the wringer washer or when, she didn't know if it had already been invented or not. But her washer included an inner tub designed like a colander with a crank handle that used centripetal force and gravity to spin the excess water from the clothes—kind of like the spinning salad bowl she used at home in the future when she washed lettuce.

She excused herself long enough to retrieve the designs from the suitcase she'd borrowed from Melody. When she returned to the parlor, she handed them to William. He and Sean both took a few minutes to study the washer design.

"I'm not much of an artist," she said with a shrug.

William looked at her sketches and whistled. "You're a genius, Sis. With your design and my contacts back East, we could manufacture and sell enough of these washers to make a fortune."

"I hope so, because I don't know what kind of financial position Dylan is in," she said as she rested her hand on her still-flat belly.

"Don't worry," Sean said. "Between his army pay and the ranch, Dylan has done real good for himself. He leases grazing rights to white ranchers running cattle along the Chisholm and Texas trails to the Kansas railheads. It's a good income and doesn't require his presence."

"I can't wait to see his house." She twisted her fingers together under the table. "And meet the ranch hands."

Dylan employed only five ranch hands, all half-breeds like himself, and the mother of one of the hands, a white woman named Mavis Poole, did the cooking and laundry. She lived in a one-room cabin between the bunkhouse and the main house.

"But don't get too excited," Sean said. "Dylan's cabin is ill-furnished and only a wee bit bigger than Mavis Poole's place—and probably not as clean."

"I'll make do. Believe me, Da, you'll never know just how adaptable I am." She'd already made unbelievable changes in her life.

       What was one more?

Chapter 24

Ill-furnished was an understatement, Selena thought as she stood in the doorway of the sod house her husband called home. Spartan was about the nicest word she could think of to describe it, though dump would have been more accurate.

The main room was small and dark with a soot-coated fireplace and a rickety rocking chair facing a stone hearth. On the far side of the room, a small, rough-hewn table, two ladder-back chairs, and a cupboard made up the kitchen's furnishings. The sink was a tin bowl, and the kitchen didn't even have a woodstove.

Drawing in one hot stifling breath, she strode across the room as Sean followed silently at her heels. Before she could even reach the back door, sweat had gathered between her breasts and trickled down her chest to her stomach. Her clothes were clinging and sticky and dust coated her skin like a second layer as she flung open the back door and stepped onto the stoop.

The house lacked even the basic amenities, but it sat amidst low rolling hills with, grasslands, cottonwoods, and natural springs all around. Situated between Fort Davis and Fort Stockton, it had an abundant supply of fresh water, making it ideal for cattle grazing.

The scenery was beautiful, but the house looked like shit.

"Don't fret, lass. Mavis does the cooking, and if I remember correctly from my previous visit, the bedroom is in a wee bit better shape."

"If it's any worse, I think I'll just go live in a tepee," she responded with a tired smile as she followed Sean to the closed door across from the fireplace.

Surprisingly enough, the room was fully furnished but every bit as dirty and dusty as the main room. The uncovered mattress looked sketchy, but at least the furniture was in good condition. Besides the bed, there was a single-drawer bedside table, oak washstand, and a double-door wardrobe. What really caught Selena's eye, however, was a covered piano sitting beneath the curtain-less window.

"A gift from his Uncle Quinn," Sean said as she crossed the room and reverently removed the dust-covered sheet. "I've never met him because of Melody not forgiving him and all, but Dylan thinks highly of him."

"You know, Da," she said as she sat on the piano bench and ran her fingers along the keys, "After all these years, you'd think she'd get tired of all the energy it takes to hold on to such an old grudge. Besides, it doesn't seem to have made much difference whether the Cherokee chose to fight or capitulate. The results were basically the same. I fail to see why Melody should hate her brother because he chose a different path."

"Aye, you're right, lass, and I'll be sure to tell Mel what you've said, but I don't know if it'll make a difference. She's a very stubborn woman."

Selena had to smile. "So's your son, Da. So's your son."

#

Later that afternoon, Sean introduced Selena to the ranch foreman, Joe, and his mother, Mavis Poole. Joe was a handsome man of average height with a lean, muscular build that lent him the appearance of someone much taller. His mother was a large, handsome woman with thick brown hair and hazel eyes.

Mavis didn't look old enough to have a son as old as Joe appeared to be, and he was part Native American. The combination of his age and heritage were telling, and Selena couldn't help speculating on the circumstances of his birth.

"I'm sorry the house is in such disarray, Mrs. Casey," Mavis said as she served her and Sean a large helping of thick, rich stew while they ate in the relative comfort of her small home. "The boss don't much care for anyone going into his place when he ain't home, and he don't spend much time here."

"I know, and please, call me Selena," she said before spooning up a mouthful of stew.

As she and Sean ate, Joe straddled a chair and talked about the ranch. Just before he left, he invited Sean to spend the night in the bunkhouse with the men. Then he cast a speculative glance in Selena's direction but spoke to his mother.

"Ma, you ought to let Mrs. Casey sleep here tonight.

179

Tomorrow will be soon enough to help her set the cabin to rights."

"That's exactly what I plan to do, Joe. Now you get your butt outside and wash off some of that trail dust. You're tracking up my clean house," she said, smiling affectionately at her grown son.

Sean bid Selena goodnight and followed Joe outside. And Selena spent an uncomfortable night having a sleepover with a woman she'd just met.

Early the next morning, she met the rest of Dylan's ranch hands. Curly was a half-black, half-Cherokee man in his late thirties. Jack Hawk was part Cheyenne, Ten Spots was half Comanche, and Ray Two Bloods was part white, part Creek, and part Comanche. The introductions were made outside the cookhouse before breakfast and afterwards, Sean reminded the men that Selena was the boss' wife. Then he gave Selena a hug and climbed onto the wagon seat. "If I had any doubts of your safety, I wouldn't let you stay."

"I know." Selena wiped away a tear. "Thank you for everything, Da, and give Mom a hug for me when you get back."

"Aye, and you take care of that wee one. We'll come for a visit around the holidays whether you've had the babe or not."

"You better." With tears in her eyes, she watched his wagon until it was out of sight. Then she set to work making Dylan's house a home.

She cleaned out the dust and cobwebs, and with Mavis' help, sewed curtains for the windows. Jack Hawk and Curly took the mattress out and beat the dust out of it while Mavis and Selena washed the sheets they'd found in a drawer and hung them out to dry.

The next morning, Selena found a beautiful quilt in a trunk and spread it over the bed. Then she concentrated her efforts on the living room. She hammered nails into the rickety old rocker and made a cushion for the seat. Since the rocker was the only furniture in the room, Joe promised to make her a matching rocker to go in front of the fireplace. He also promised that before the baby was born, he'd make a cradle.

After scrubbing everything from top to bottom, the old sod house finally looked like a home—not a nice home, but it was Dylan's home, and she didn't have to cook. Mavis prepared meals for the men and then delivered Selena's to the house in a picnic basket. Sometimes, Mavis asked her to come to the Poole house to eat. Once or twice, Joe joined them, and Selena now looked forward to his company. Thus far, he was the only ranch hand she'd gotten to know because Mavis didn't want her eating in the cookhouse with the men.

On the evenings when Mavis didn't invite Selena to share her meal, Joe stopped by the cabin to visit. He never stayed long and always left before his mother showed up with the supper tray. Selena got the distinct impression Mavis didn't approve of Joe making friends with the boss's wife. But it wasn't as if anything had ever happened, nor would it. Selena loved her husband.

Joe spent time with her every day. If he wasn't checking on her to see if there was some job that needed doing, he was stopping by to inform her of various ranch activities. They both knew she had no knowledge of ranching so there was really no need for him to consult her, but Joe was a considerate man.

Toward the end of the week, Selena had supper with Mavis. They were sitting at the table talking when Joe came in later than usual.

He hesitated at the door, but then smiled his usual smile and sat down to eat while Selena helped Mavis with the dishes. When Selena told them goodnight and turned to leave, Joe offered to walk her home.

"It's just a hundred yards away, Joe. I don't think she'll get lost." Mavis laughed, but there was also a warning in her tone.

"I know, ma." Joe laughed too, but he sounded nervous. "But I need to update her on some deposits I made into the ranch account. She needs to know how well her husband's ranch is doing financially." Then he chuckled and it sounded like a genuine laugh. "She might not believe it considering the shape of the house."

Selena rose awkwardly to her feet and followed Joe outside. "The house is fine. It's really shaping up. I just wish it had a bathtub."

Joe smiled and veered to the right, taking a path that led away from her back door. "Then you'll be happy to know there's a hot springs on the property well within walking distance. I know Ma's shown you around some, but I'll bet she hasn't taken you there yet. She don't much care for water."

Selena's heart did a somersault. If she could take a bath…
"Hot springs, as in hot enough to take hot baths in winter?"

With a smile wide enough to expose his dimples, he said, "Hot enough to be too hot for a bath in summer except on those cooler nights, but you'll love it come fall."

The springs were a half-mile from the house nestled beneath a canopy of low hanging branches in a copse of stunted live oaks. Selena imagined steam rising from the water on a cool fall evening and sighed. She could have stayed there all night enjoying the beauty of the landscape, but Joe shuffled his feet and cleared his throat, so she didn't tarry. He did little more than walk her to the springs before they turned around and headed back to the house.

"Thanks," she said as he walked her to the door and politely nodded his head.

"At your service, boss lady," he said with a smile. "With any luck, maybe the boss will be home soon, and the temperatures will drop enough for you to have that bath."

#

A week later, Dylan wasn't home, and Selena was still bathing out of a washbowl. She was hot, miserable, and tired of feeling helpless, and that needed to change. This was her life, and she would start living it with her eyes on the future instead of the past. She had her piano and now, her sewing, but she needed to do more—be more. She'd grown tired of Mavis's pampering and waiting for Joe to show her around the ranch. It was time to get out and see the property, with or without an escort, and both she and Dalmatian needed exercise.

She barely had a baby bump, but she could no longer button her jeans, so she put on a pair of Dylan's old pants and one of his old shirts she'd altered and headed for the barn. Unfortunately, Curly was there and refused to let her ride out alone.

She planted her hands on her hips. "Oh for Pete's sake. I'm a grown woman."

"This ain't the city, ma'am. It ain't safe for a woman to ride about the countryside alone."

She could saddle her own horse and ride out without his permission, but memories of what had very nearly happened to her on the trail gave her pause. "I hadn't planned on scouring the countryside, Curly. I just wanted to get out of the house for a while. Isn't there some place I can ride without an armed escort?"

Curly shook his head. "Nope. Ya, don't know the lay of the land, ma'am. Ya might get lost or what not, and the boss would kill me if'n I let ya go out alone."

"Go ahead and saddle her horse," Joe said, entering the barn. "I promised her nearly a week ago I'd show her around, so now's as good a time as any."

Her shoulders relaxed, easing the tension in her back. "Thanks, Joe."

Neither Curly nor Joe commented on her unconventional attire, although both men looked just a bit scandalized to see her in pants and a shirt knotted at the waist with the sleeves cut off, but she didn't care. It was easier to ride in pants, and it was too hot to cover her skin from her throat to her toes. She'd rather get sunburned.

After Curly saddled her horse, Joe showed her Whiskey Creek, a tributary of Musquiz Creek that ran through the middle of Dylan's property. The banks weren't too steep, and the current wasn't too swift. It would have been an ideal place to build a house in modern times. The view was breathtaking, and although the area didn't have many trees, they grew in abundance along the bank, and Selena spotted the perfect swimming hole.

Hot and sweaty from the long ride, she couldn't resist a swim. As her mount lowered its head to drink from the cool water, she released the reins and slid to the ground. Then she pulled off her boots and dove into the water fully dressed.

"Mrs. Casey, please," Joe sputtered as he climbed down from his horse. "Get out of the water before you drown yourself."

"Relax, Joe," she said, raking her wet hair from her eyes. "I've been swimming since I was five, and I'm not going to drown. And please, don't call me, Mrs. Casey."

"Yes, ma'am, but I'd still like for you to come out of the water. You're making me real nervous, Mrs. Casey."

"Selena," she said with a sigh as she climbed out of the creek. "I'm no older than you are, Joe, so just call me Selena. Okay?"

She spent the next two afternoons swimming at the creek

until she realized Joe wasn't getting any work done because he felt obliged to watch over her. He never swam with her and mostly sat on his horse like a knight of old, guarding his charge. So Selena reluctantly gave up her afternoon swims and spent the rest of her days and most of her nights seated at the piano.

Since coming to the ranch, she'd played every day, but after giving up her afternoon swims, she worked her frustrations out in her music. She was pregnant in a time without electricity, and she was miserable and lonely. It was too hot for the springs and too dangerous to ride alone or swim in the creek, so the piano was her only source of entertainment.

And Dylan still wasn't home.

Chapter 25

Dylan climbed from his horse, feeling every aching muscle. As he turned to lead the animal into the barn, movement in back of the house drew his attention. He glanced toward the bunkhouse. The lights were on inside, and he could hear his men laughing and talking, some arguing. It was poker night, and none of them missed poker night, but someone was behind his house, and he didn't think it was Mavis.

He tied Ishtabe's reins to the hitching post and patted his rump as a match flared to life. He tensed. His men took their smokes outside the bunkhouse. They wouldn't be sneaking around behind his house in the dark.

Crouching low, he pulled his knife and approached as the shadowy figure shook out the match and dropped it to the ground. Then in one swift movement, the man unsheathed his own knife and turned. Dylan froze. "Joe?"

The Comanche normally had quicker reflexes. No one got close to Joe unless he wanted them to. Something—or someone—had distracted him.

Dylan sheathed his knife and Joe did the same. Before Dylan could speak, an angel began to sing—a very sexy angel from the sound of her voice, and the words brought him to full arousal. He was suddenly rock-hard, and there was only one woman whose voice could cause such a reaction in him. His wife.

But what in hell was Selena doing at the ranch?

"Hey Boss. Welcome home," Joe said, his face flushing in the moonlight. Was he embarrassed he'd been caught unaware—or because he was caught spying on the boss's wife?

"How long has she been here?" Dylan looked over Joe's shoulder to the woman silhouetted in his bedroom window.

"A couple of months, I reckon. She sent a telegram to Fort Davis. Sent one to Fort Stockton too. Just in case."

He narrowed his gaze. How long had his foreman been

cozying up to his wife? Joe was obviously enamored of her. His eyes repeatedly strayed to the window.

As the haunting melody and lyrics of some unknown love song filtered through the open window, Dylan studied his foreman. "I haven't been back to either fort. I just left Crazy Horse and was out tracking Red Armed Panther. There's trouble brewing, and I don't think there's a damn thing I can do about it. Anyway, I was in the area and thought I'd check on things here. I had no idea," he continued before emphasizing his next words, "my *wife* was here."

"She sings like an angel, don't she?" Joe asked as his eyes strayed to the window again.

"Get lost Joe," Dylan finally growled. "I don't need an audience when I surprise *my* wife."

"Oh, somehow I don't think she'll be nearly as surprised as you." Joe smiled and lumbered off toward the bunkhouse.

Moments later Dylan reached for the front door only to have it pulled from his grasp by a stunned, Mavis. "Oh my!"

Acting quickly, so as not to alert Selena of his arrival, he placed a finger to his lips and winked. Immediately understanding his intent, Mavis returned the wink with a conspiratorial grin before dashing out the house.

Heart thumping too hard in his chest, he crossed the front room, noting the small but significant changes. The walls and floors were clean, and curtains hung in the windows. When he slipped into the bedroom, he noticed the quilt his Cherokee grandmother had made over the bed. His house looked like a home, and his wife was seated at the piano.

Her face was shadowed, her profile reflected in the window behind her. She ended the sad melody and slowly raised her chin, catching sight of him in her peripheral vision. She turned on the bench. Their gazes met. Her eyes widened, and she slowly rose to her feet.

"Dylan." His name was but a whisper triggering an ache in his throat he couldn't explain.

"What are you doing here?" He found himself whispering in return. Then his eyes traveled the length of her body as her hand dropped to her belly, and his knees turned to mush.

It may not have been obvious to just anyone, but to a man who'd spent the last four months remembering every curve of her body, it was. His beautiful wife was pregnant, and bastard that he was, he'd all but abandoned her when she needed him the most.

His heart dropped as he raised his chin to meet her steady gaze. Tears shimmered in her eyes, but before he could offer a word of apology, she hiked up her skirts and hurled herself at him. His first instinct was self-preservation. He raised his arm to block the punch he expected and caught a glimpse of her eyes. She'd already forgiven him.

He opened his arms, and she plowed into his chest, melting against him. Pulling her closer, their mouths fused in a kiss he'd remember until the day he died. She was here, and she'd forgiven him.

Her hands were everywhere at once, as he lowered his suspenders and shrugged out of his shirt. Then she reached for his pants, and he nearly went up in flames. Swearing softly, he wasted no time tearing open the bodice of her gown and plunging his hands inside to feel the firmness of her ripe, full, breasts.

He couldn't free them fast enough.

Lowering his chin, he took one taut nipple into his mouth and suckled gently. Then he seared hot kisses across her face and neck as she ran her hands over his sweat-slicked chest. She chanted his name like a prayer as he backed her against the bed and dropped her skirt to the floor. She wore nothing beneath her clothes but bare skin.

"You're not wearing any underwear," he panted as he felt his member fill to bursting.

"Too hot," she moaned, taking his erection in her hands as he cupped her mound and slid a finger deep inside.

"Make love to me, Dylan," she whispered. "Don't make me wait."

She was trembling with need, and he was on the verge of losing control when they fell onto the mattress. He entered her in one swift movement, and she opened for him like a flower welcoming the sun.

"God, I've missed you," she said once their breathing returned to normal. Lying within the circle of is arms she tentatively stroked his stubbly jaw.

It had been several days since he'd last shaved and just as long since he'd bathed. Staring into his wife's storm gray eyes, he was amazed to see the passion still lingering, despite his somewhat disheveled appearance and the total abandon with which he'd just taken her. Tensing, he also realized he'd held nothing back. He'd given everything he had to Selena, including his heart, and though he'd not said it, he loved her.

He pulled away both mentally and physically and rolled onto his back, draping an arm over his eyes to block her mesmerizing stare. She stirred beside him, and he assumed she was getting up to dress—until a cold cloth touched his skin.

"Hey!" He jerked in response, reflexively dropping his arm to trap the washcloth.

Selena giggled, her eyes dancing with mischief as she tugged the cloth free and slowly slid it over his chest and down his arms. He raised his head to nip at her exposed breasts and got a good whiff of the soap she used. Dropping his head back onto the pillows, he groaned. Thanks to his wife, he now smelled of horse, sweat, and…lilacs.

"Damn, Selena," he said snatching the cloth from her hands as the corners of his mouth turned up in a smile he couldn't suppress. "You can't bathe a man in lilacs."

Giggling, she grabbed the cloth again and deliberately dragged it over his face. "Why not? I like the smell of lilacs."

"I'm a hardened half-breed, woman. What self-respecting warrior wants to smell like a damned flower?"

Her giggles turned into full-fledged laughter as they began an erotically playful game of tug-of-war with the lilac-scented cloth. The playful game didn't last long after she dragged the wet cloth along the length of his now hardened shaft. Rolling on top of her, he would have taken her again, had he not suddenly remembered her delicate condition. Cursing his own thoughtlessness, he sat up and hesitantly touched the gentle swell of her abdomen.

"I didn't …I mean…we didn't hurt the baby, did we? I was a little rough. I wasn't even thinking. I'm sor –"

"Shh." She placed two fingers against his lips to halt his apology. "I'm fine and the baby's fine, but both of us could use a bath. Come on."

Bouncing off the bed again, she said, "Let's go down to the creek."

"The water might be too cold, but the water at the springs is hot and—"

"Good Lord, Dylan. It's got to be eighty degrees tonight. I swear I've never been so hot in my life, and you want to take a hot bath? I think not. Besides, hot tubs aren't good for the baby after the first trimester, and I want to cool off as much as get clean, so let's saddle up and go," she said, pulling him to his feet.

Standing in stunned silence, he watched her dress in the same torn bodice and skirt she'd just taken off. She didn't even bother putting anything on underneath.

She turned to hand him his dirty clothes and frowned. "What wrong?"

"Your bodice is torn," he said, casually crossing his arms over his bare chest.

"Oops." She smiled and took it off.

After carelessly tossing it on the bed, she strolled to the wardrobe and removed a sleeveless garment that vaguely resembled one of his old shirts. She slipped it on, buttoned two buttons between her breasts, and knotted it at the waist. Not only were her arms bare from the shoulders down, but he could see her navel, even after she put on a skirt without bloomers underneath.

"What in hell kind of getup is that?" he asked, staring at the shocking amount of skin she displayed.

She smiled sheepishly and shrugged her shoulders. "I'm not used to the heat, and this is comfortable. What's wrong with it?"

"You don't know?" How was that possible?

"Looks okay to me. Just a little baggy."

How could she not know there was a problem with the way she was dressed? No woman in her right mind would willingly dress the way Selena did. Then again, maybe she wasn't in her right mind. She was a liar, but perhaps she had bigger problems, and he just hadn't wanted to see it before. She might think his mother had coerced him into marriage, but his mother hadn't been able to force him into anything since he was eight years old. He'd wanted to marry her, and now she was his, for better or worse.

And he was damn scared it might get worse, especially now that she was pregnant. Some women went plumb loco after childbirth.

189

He lowered his voice and spoke in a soothing tone. "Selena, decent women don't dress that way. You know that."

She planted her hands on her hips and stared at him as though he were the one with the problem. "You're a hypocrite. You condemn those who judge you by the color of your skin, yet you have no problem judging me by the clothes I wear. That's not right."

"It's not the same thing, and you know it." He clenched his teeth, trying hard not to raise his voice. How could she even compare one to the other? He had no choice in skin color, but she had a choice in the clothes she wore.

"Isn't it? What have I shown? A bare arm? My navel? Boobs are sexual, Dylan, and mine are covered."

"Boobs?" She was trying to diffuse his anger again, but he wouldn't let her. "You're showing a half mile of your abdomen, and you're pregnant. You don't think that's scandalous? White women conceal pregnancy; they don't flaunt it."

"Oh for God's sake. I'm not ashamed to be pregnant. I'm thrilled, and you need to get over it already." With an exasperated huff, she spun around and marched to the door.

He reached for her and missed. Furious, he stormed out behind her, got to the front door, and realized he was buck-naked. *Damn it.* He hurriedly slipped on his dusty wool pants and sprinted out the door.

Just as he reached the barn, his lovely wife raced out on the back of her horse. Bareback. Thankfully, Joe had taken care of his mount while he'd been inside with Selena. Cursing aloud, Dylan threw open the door to Ishtabe's stall and flung himself onto the startled animal's back. He gripped the horse's mane, plunged his naked heels into the horse's side, and gave chase.

Damn fool woman, racing off across the plains at night. And damn her for making him rush out barefoot. He felt more naked without his boots or moccasins than he did sitting bareback on a horse with no shirt and his trousers unfastened.

When he entered the copse of cottonwoods, he slowed Ishtabe and slid from his back. He led his horse to a tree where she'd tethered the Appaloosa and gave the command for Ishtabe to stay. His wife was nowhere around.

"Selena? Selena! Damn it, answer me," he shouted, having

given her no time to answer had she been so inclined.

When he broke through the tree line, she dropped her clothes to the ground and sailed into the water without a backward glance. He stormed in after her, but she lowered her head and pushed off in the opposite direction. When she resurfaced, he was standing directly in front of her.

"Don't you ever walk out on me again," he said, gripping her shoulders.

"I'm not a child or a dog," she said calmly—too calmly, "and I don't respond well to commands. So, think hard. Think very hard Dylan Casey, but when we said our marriage vows, I left out the word, obey." She smiled. "On purpose."

Damned if she hadn't, he realized with a start. He'd attributed it to nervousness at the time, but it hadn't been an accident. His wife had never agreed to obey him.

Her gaze sought his. "I would never make a vow I couldn't keep."

"You made a vow to me once before, Selena. You swore you would never purposefully lie to me again, but do you keep your word?"

"Yes," she whispered straining to get closer, though he held her at arms' length.

"Who showed you where it was safe to swim in the creek?" It had to have been Joe, but he wanted to see if she'd lie.

"Joe," she said, giving up on the idea of trying to get closer to his body. As an alternate tactic, she began to run her nails lightly down his chest.

"I see," he said through tightly clenched teeth as anger heated his blood. Joe *had* been getting cozy with his wife.

"Oh for God's sake, Dylan, no you don't see either." She flicked a nipple with her fingernail. He flinched in response. "Joe and I are just friends, but I love you. Do you hear me? I love you." She emphasized each word by poking his chest and kept her eyes glued to his.

He wanted to believe her. God, how he wanted to. His arms relaxed marginally, and she stepped closer. He felt the instant erection through his sodden pants as she leaned into him. He knew she could feel it too, because she smiled slowly, and that angered him. She knew the kind of power she held over him.

191

Lilly Gayle

Well, he'd show her. He might be half-savage, but he wasn't an animal. He may feel lust, but he did not necessarily feel the need to act on it. He would not let her lead him around by the short hairs as her cousin had tried to do.

"*Oea-Yah*," she whispered in perfect Cherokee, and his anger dissolved instantly. She had first spoken those words during their wedding ceremony, and she did so now without hesitation. "I swear by God and all that's holy that I love you, and if I knew the words in Comanche or even ancient Celt I would say them. In whatever language you want to hear them, Dylan, I would say them," she whispered.

"Don't expect to hear those words form me. As long as there are secrets between us, I'll never say them," he responded hoarsely.

"But you feel them. Those feelings are there, deep inside of you. Aren't they?" She gently traced a heart shape on his chest with her index finger.

"I feel nothing," he lied as he lightly brushed her brow with a gentle kiss.

Then he scooped her into his arms and carried her to the moss-covered bank where he made slow, passionate love to her. They both knew he lied about his lack of feelings, but he'd vowed never to say those words as long as there were secrets between them.

And his wife had many secrets.

Chapter 26

As the light of a new day shone brightly through the bedroom window, Selena awoke with the certain knowledge her truce with Dylan had ended. Careful not to wake him, she shifted onto her side and studied his face.

He didn't look quite so fierce in his sleep. If anything, his relaxed countenance more closely resembled an archangel's than a fierce warrior's. Once he was awake, his expression would harden into a familiar scowl, and he'd be no more tolerant of her evasive answers today than he'd been the night before—or months before.

His eyes snapped open, and his expression hardened. The truce was over.

"Good morning," she said, forcing a smile. He didn't smile back.

"What are you doing here?"

Her stomach knotted. "I live here."

He had one arm curled beneath his head and the other draped across his flat, muscled abdomen. He raised his brows and waited patiently for a better explanation. She didn't comply. There was no good way to tell the truth. Even if she did, he wouldn't believe her.

She closed her eyes, fighting tears. The time had come when she could no longer put off the inevitable. But once the genie was out of the bottle, there was no putting it back.

He splayed his hand over the slight swell of her abdomen. She opened her eyes and met his deep, penetrating gaze.

"Did you leave the safety of Cheeratahge because of the baby?"

"Yes. This is my home now. I wrote you a letter explaining everything."

"I never got it." He sat up and placed both hands over her belly. The look on his face was all the proof she needed. Despite what he had or had not said, he was happy about the baby.

#

Dylan smiled when he felt the round bump below Selena's navel. His child grew in her womb, and the emotions swelling in his chest were unfamiliar but not unwelcome. Unbelievably, he was going to be a father, and his wife didn't seem to care that her child was going to be a half-breed.

But others would.

"Why did you come here, Selena? You were safe at my parent's house. Did you go back to Canyon Creek and find out a white woman with a half-breed child wasn't welcome there?"

"I did go back for a couple of weeks, but once William arrived and we got things settled, I saw no reason to stay. After all, it's his house now." She made the admission without remorse, and it felt as if she'd speared him with a flaming arrow.

He should have known his white wife would never choose to live on his Godforsaken, half-breed ranch if she'd had a choice. The only reason she was here now was because William Tillman had reclaimed his house and kicked her out on her ass—her very pregnant ass. Selena was in Whiskey Springs and in his bed for the same reason she'd stolen her dead cousin's house in the first place. She had nowhere else to go.

"Damn you, Selena," he said as he swung his legs over the side of the bed.

The searing pain in his chest was nearly unbearable as he stood to glare down at his treacherous wife. The look of pain on her face surprised him, but he quickly hardened his heart. He would not let her manipulate him again.

She scrambled to her knees. "I don't believe this. You're mad at me?"

"*Akinalvga*," he said, switching to the Cherokee words for, "I am angry." Returning to English, he said, "Not only did you disobey me by leaving Cheeratahge, but after you got to Canyon Creek and found out Tillman knew you were an impostor, you showed up here and set up housekeeping like nothing ever happened. You're damned lucky Tillman didn't have you arrested for impersonating his sister."

He looked into her beautiful, lying eyes and swallowed bile. "Did you think I had so little pride, I'd welcome you with open arms just because you're pregnant? Well, think again, sweetheart. You can stay until the baby is born, but then I want you out of my life, but the kid stays with me. You got that, Selena? My baby stays with me."

"Are you entirely off your rocker?" She swung her legs to the floor and stood to face him. "I *gave* the house to William. He didn't find me out, and he didn't throw me out. I'm here because this is your home. Damn you, Dylan Casey, I'm your wife!" she shouted, poking him in the chest with her finger.

He snatched the offending appendage in a vice-like grip, careful not to break it. This was not the first time she'd poked him like a damned pincushion, but it damn sure was going to be the last.

"Why in hell would you give William Tillman your house after you'd gone to so much trouble to steal it?"

"Technically, I didn't steal it." She pulled her finger from his grasp. "I inherited it, but I had to give it back to him. I couldn't risk changing anything. Don't you see?"

"No, Selena, I don't see. What do you think you might have changed?" She was talking crazy again.

She swallowed hard before answering. "If I didn't give William the house, he couldn't leave it to his grandson. You don't understand how important this is, Dylan," she whispered softly, raising her hand to touch his cheek.

"Don't!" He grabbed her hand and pulled it away from his face. The urge to inflict pain was great, but he didn't. She was his wife. And she was insane.

A shudder passed through him. He released her hand and raked his fingers through his hair. Then he stared at her and tried to push all those tender emotions aside.

"I'm glad you gave your cousin the house. If Ben knew his real daughter was dead, he'd want his son to have it. It was the right thing to do, but don't pretend you knew his father would give him the house or that he would move to Texas," he added in a steely voice. "You are not a psychic, Selena, no matter what White Deer thinks. And William Tillman isn't your brother."

With one last, hard look, he pulled on a pair of buckskins and quietly left the room.

#

It took a moment for Selena to gather her wits and her

clothing. She hurriedly buttoned the brown striped dress Mavis had altered to fit her increasing waistline and retrieved two letters from inside the drawer on the nightstand. If Dylan read the letters from William, he'd realize no one had ousted her from her home at gunpoint. The letters would prove she and William shared a genuine bond whether she was his sister, cousin, or…descendent.

Rushing out of the house with the letters clutched firmly in her hands, she prayed she would reach him before he saddled his horse and rode out of her life again. But when she entered the barn, she found him talking to Joe, who glanced nervously over his shoulder. He said something to Dylan and turned to leave. As he walked by her, he nodded once, gave her a sad smile, and quietly slipped out the barn.

Great. Dylan had probably told him she was unstable, and she'd never have any freedom. She sighed and took a step closer to her husband.

He lifted Ishtabe's hind leg and examined the animal's hoof, ignoring her completely. She shoved the letters between his face and the horse's leg. "Read them," she demanded.

Quizzically raising his brows, he lowered his horse's leg and took the pages from her hand. Selena watched his face as he silently scanned the contents of each page. She hoped to see a softening in his hard countenance, but his expression never changed. As stoic as any stereotypical Indian, he read without so much as a lift of his brow before handing the pages back to her and returning his attention to his horse.

How could he read William's letters and not believe her? They were proof she hadn't been evicted from her home. She'd even given William Mary's locket after removing Dylan's picture from inside. After all, William's son would one day be her great-great-grandfather, and eventually, her father would inherit the house, and Uncle Robbie would inherit the necklace. Of course, she didn't mention that to Dylan. He already thought she was nuts.

"Well?" she asked, once she'd gotten her emotions under control. "Do you believe me now? William didn't hunt me down. I contacted him. I wanted him to have the house because he's my flesh and blood relative. It doesn't matter if he's my brother or—a more distant relative."

"Dylan, we even look alike," she added when he continued

to dig beneath the horse's hoof with his long bladed knife.

Seeing the knife made her shiver. Whoever had wanted him dead might still pose a danger, but she couldn't worry about that now. She could only handle one crisis at a time.

"Say something!" she demanded when he continued to ignore her. "Don't these letters prove anything?"

He lowered Ishtabe's leg and absently patted the animal's flank. "What they prove," he said as he re-sheathed his knife, "is that you've managed to blindside another innocent man with your lies."

"Damn you, Dylan." She punched his naked shoulder with her fist. "What do you want from me?"

"I want the truth, damn it!" He grabbed her upper arms and shook her. The letters slipped from her fingers and floated to the straw covered floor.

"You want the truth?" She laughed humorlessly. "Fine, but you won't believe me, and if you do, you won't be able to handle it. I doubt you've even heard of time travel or science fiction."

He took a step back, concern and just a touch of fear shadowed his expression. He thought she was crazy. And maybe she was, but she couldn't avoid the truth any longer—and neither could he.

"The truth is, I'm not from around here. I'm not even from this century, and I *have* known luxuries you can't even imagine. You don't know about movies, or television, or cars, or planes, or microwave ovens. Hell, you don't even know about modern plumbing. You think your parents' set up in Cheeratahge is so damned fine and the mechanized shower in Dallas was so wonderful, but I had you beat when I was just a child. The house I grew up in had three full bathrooms with hot running water *and* flushing toilets. Even when I lived alone in Richmond in a tiny apartment, I had you beat. Not only did I have an indoor bathroom, but I also had access to a swimming pool."

"Ask me when I was born!" she demanded, stalking him as he silently retreated.

"Selena, please. Calm down." His eyes were wide, and his voice was rife with fear. "Don't get yourself all worked up. Think about the baby. You need help, and I swear, I'll get it for you. I'll get you whatever help you need."

Chapter 27

Dylan looked into Selena's eyes, and she didn't avert her gaze. She actually believed she was from the future. His heart cramped in his chest. His wife was as a mad as a March hare.

"Ask me," she demanded.

He retreated until he backed into the stable wall. He would do nothing to endanger Selena or the child she carried. He would rather die than bring harm to either of them.

"Ask me, damn you!"

Ishtabe danced nervously in the stall, and Dylan feared his well-trained mount might charge if he felt his master were in danger, so he quietly did as she asked. "All right, Selena. When were you born?"

"August 10, 1992. Do you understand what I'm telling you Dylan?"

"Sure. Sure I do, and everything is going to be fine, *adawehi*." He pulled her to his side and led her from Ishtabe's stall, latching the door behind them.

His heart raced fearfully, not for himself, but for Selena. God in heaven, what was he going to do? Standing in the aisle between the stalls, he gently patted her back. "I'll get you the help you need, and I won't abandon you. I promise."

"Don't you dare patronize me," She pushed away and glared up at him. "You wanted the truth, so here it is. I'm not a psychic. You were right about that, but I do know what's going to happen in the future because I've already lived it. I celebrated my last birthday nearly eleven months ago—in the year 2017. I'll be twenty-six next month, and I haven't even been born yet. I know it sounds crazy, but it's true. Where I come from it's a new century. Hell, it's a new millennium."

"You don't have to tell me anything else. I'll believe whatever you want me to believe." Perhaps he could confine her to the cabin and ask Mavis and Joe to care for her until he fulfilled his obligations to the army. Selena wouldn't like it, but at least she'd be safe. He couldn't lock her away in an insane asylum. It would destroy them both.

"Listen to me." She took his face in her hands and forced him to look into her perfectly sane eyes. "I'm telling you I'm from the future, and I know what's going to happen a hundred years from now because for me, it's already happened. I know there will be a gold strike in the Black Hills sometime this year or next. There will be a gold rush on Indian lands, and the Sioux and Cheyenne will join forces to try to stop it. In 1876, General Custer will lead more than two hundred men against the Sioux at the Little Big Horn River. More than 2,000 Sioux and Cheyenne warriors under Rain in the Face, Sitting Bull, and Crazy Horse, will surround and massacre all of them, including Custer."

Dylan's first thought was to indulge his wife and listen, but when she mentioned the names of real chiefs, chiefs who were even now joining forces, his chest tightened in fear. "How do you know this?"

"I told you. It's history to me. I learned this stuff in school and on TV. I also read a lot on third shift."

What in hell was a TV or third shift? "I don't understand. What you say isn't possible, and you know it. Give me a believable answer. Tell me the truth, and I'll understand. I swear."

"Dylan, this *is* the truth," she insisted, staring up at him with those storm gray eyes. "I've kept it from you because I knew you'd never believe me, but I don't want any secrets between us. Not now. Not ever again."

In the past, he'd been able to tell when she was lying. Those eyes were too honest by far, and she had yet to deceive him without his knowing she lied. Looking into those eyes now, he saw no signs of deception, yet what she was saying just wasn't possible.

"You know time travel isn't possible," he said as fear congealed in his heart. His wife was insane, and he had obligations that would prevent him from getting her the care she needed.

She took his hands in hers. "You're right. It isn't possible, but it's true. I was born in Virginia more than a hundred years from now. When I was ten, my uncle gave me a locket. Inside was a picture of one of my ancestors. Dylan, it was a picture of Mary.

Legend claimed she broke the heart of a half Native American army scout who wanted to marry her. Later, she disappeared, and no one ever found her body. Most people thought the scout killed her because she'd agreed to marry a white man instead of him. A year later, when no arrests had been made, someone shot the scout and scalped him with his own knife—on Mary's porch.

"Urban legends claimed Mary's restless spirit roamed the property because her body had never been found, and the scout's spirit sought justice—or revenge. I believed you wanted justice." She smiled, and it looked sad rather than mad. "Dylan, you were that scout, and I've wanted to save you since I was ten years old."

Although his pulse beat heavily in his neck, he said nothing. He didn't want to call her a liar, but he didn't want to reinforce her delusions either.

She released his hands and hugged herself as if warding off a sudden chill. "When I was little, I'd pull out my locket and look at Mary's picture, wondering how anyone so lovely could be so cruel. Your picture wasn't in the locket, and I now believe I removed it in this time period, but I knew what you looked like and dreamed of you often."

His mind raced, remembering every word Selena had ever uttered. From the beginning, she'd insisted a tornado killed Mary. She'd also claimed someone would murder him. He took a step back. "We both know I didn't kill Mary, and I wasn't murdered. If anything, I would have been hanged. So, your legends were wrong."

She ran her hands over her face and pushed her fingers through her hair as though *he* exasperated her. "But they wouldn't have been wrong if I hadn't pushed you to follow the path of the tornado. In my time, you had been murdered, and Mary's body had *not* been found. The house was passed from William to his oldest son and so on until my father inherited it."

"Selena—"

"When my father died six months after my mother, I inherited the house. My cousin, Jeff, knew about my dreams and believed Mary's spirit was attached to the necklace. He knew I needed answers and encouraged me to research the legends in person. So after a while, I quit my job in Virginia and flew to Texas."

"You flew?" He smirked, saddened and yet relieved her fantasy was starting to unravel. "What did you do, sprout wings? Or just hitch a ride on a phoenix?"

She rolled her eyes. "No, Dylan. I flew on an airplane. It's a mechanical flying machine that hasn't been invented yet. But as I was saying, I went to Canyon Creek, and the same tornado that killed Mary sent me back in time."

Woman with No Fear has ridden the winds of time, giving Long Blade a future once more.

Goose flesh pimpled Dylan's arms and made the hairs on the nape of his neck stand on end. Shaking off the chill, he continued to deny the possibility time travel existed. What sane man wouldn't?

"Listen to yourself, Selena. What you're saying is plumb loco."

"I know it's hard to believe. I have trouble believing it myself," she said, reaching out to touch his arm, "but it's true. I left my home in Virginia in March of 2017. I arrived in Canyon Creek, got caught in a tornado, was knocked unconscious, and woke up in 1872. I knew Mary died in a tornado because that same tornado jumped forward in time to bring me back to you."

For the rest of the morning, he listened to his wife talk about his death and how Mary's spirit brought her here to save him. If he believed her, then he'd have to believe she'd changed his life cycle as Dream Speaker predicted. But it was difficult to believe something so—unbelievable.

Around noon, Mavis brought cold chicken and bread into the barn. When she left, Selena gave him a history lesson. She couldn't always remember names or dates, but she continued to claim she was telling the truth, and her explanation of modern electricity and plumbing *didn't* sound crazy. It sounded like a believable possibility, as did the idea of a horseless carriage she called the automobile and a more modern telegraph contraption she called the telephone.

Her story became a little less believable when she started talking about cell phones, computers, and something called the Internet and social media, but she didn't just give vague descriptions. Her story was rich in details he couldn't ignore. It just wasn't possible. Still, the one thing that kept him from dismissing her completely was the last missive he'd received from Fort Davis.

Gold had been discovered in the Black Hills and though the military was trying to keep it quiet, such discoveries were hard to keep secret. Once it became public knowledge, miners would flock to the area, despite the white man's agreement to keep off Indian lands.

But it wasn't public knowledge yet. So how did Selena know?

Damn his promise to Colonel Harper. He needed more time with his wife to sort fact from fiction, but he was riding out first thing in the morning. He'd promised the colonel he'd track down Rain in the Face and try to bring the warrior in before he could negotiate with the other chiefs.

The situation with the Sioux and Cheyenne was reaching a boiling point. It was a doomed mission, but he couldn't give up without trying to bring peace to the nation. Thank God, White Deer had volunteered to help. Though he'd never agree to help the army, he had offered to help a friend—and his people.

"You cannot hold back a flood," he'd told Dog Ears before leaving the Comanche village for the last time. "You can only divert its flow. We must find a way to divert the flood of the white man or their numbers will drown our people."

The old chief would not bend, and so White Deer had left his tribe—this time for good. For the sake of The People, he'd said, warriors would need to survive when the white man destroyed those who would not submit.

Like a young sapling, White Deer would bend, and he would survive. Dog Ears was like an old pine. Because he would not bend, he would break. Dylan only prayed Selena wouldn't break as well.

Mavis and Joe promised to look after her, when he left the next morning, although Dylan couldn't bring himself to tell them why he feared for his wife sanity. He reckoned they assumed it was because he worried about her pregnancy affecting her mental state. But even after he kissed Selena goodbye, she didn't break down, and she didn't look crazy. His wife had stood on the porch with a determined look on her face and steel in her spine.

Crazy or not, she was the bravest woman he'd ever met.

Chapter 28

Selena held her breath as she watched the lone rider approach the house. It had been a month since Dylan left the ranch to search for Rain in the Face's camp. The morning of his departure, White Deer had ridden into the yard showing no hint of surprise at finding her pregnant and in Whiskey Springs. Dylan still didn't believe her revelations, but seeing White Deer again and knowing he'd have Dylan's back, had given her some measure of peace when they left.

As the rider drew closer, Selena shaded her eyes against the sun's glare, and hope faded. Her unexpected guest was a cavalry officer, but it wasn't Dylan.

"Better safe, than sorry," she mumbled as she went back into the house to get her gun.

When she stepped back out on the porch with her pistol hidden in the front pocket of her skirt, Joe came around the side of the house with a rifle cradled in his arms. He stepped onto the porch beside her. "Know him?"

"No."

When the man pulled his mount to a stop in front of the house, Joe eyed him suspiciously and said, "State your business."

"Where's Casey?" The officer's hand hovered above his revolver.

Selena's grip tightened on the gun hidden in the folds of her skirt. "He's not here, but I'm his wife. Is there something I can help you with?"

Joe glared at her from beneath his Stetson, but she ignored him. His long black hair was tucked beneath his hat, obscured from the visitor's view. When he swept it from his head and slapped it against his thigh, his long, dark locks tumbled about his shoulders. The stranger tensed and thumbed his holstered weapon.

"This breed bothering you, ma'am?"

"Does it look like he's bothering me?" She made no

attempt to temper her sarcasm. "Joe's my foreman," she continued as Mavis and the other men came into view. "And these other men are my ranch hands—and friends."

Mavis, Curly, Jack Hawk, Ten Spots, and Ray Two Bloods, all formed a half circle at the bottom of the porch. The men were all armed, and Mavis held a rolling pin as if it were a lethal weapon. Selena didn't know where they'd come from or how they'd known she felt threatened by the stranger's appearance, but she was glad for their support.

"I'm getting' down off this horse, ma'am, so you best tell your men to lower their weapons." He slung his leg over the saddle horn and stepped to the ground.

He was of medium height and build with dark blond hair, pale blue eyes, and a patrician nose. As he stood waiting, he withdrew a linen handkerchief from the front pocket of his woolen pants and wiped the sweat from his brow. He then readjusted his military hat and neatly refolded the handkerchief before putting it back in his pocket.

Large sweat rings were clearly visible beneath each arm, yet he refused to loosen even one button on his shirt. However, he had removed his woolen uniform jacket.

Selena kept her eye on their visitor but spoke to the others. "Lower your weapons, but keep them close. Mavis, could you please get our *guest* a cool glass of lemonade?"

While Mavis left to fill a tray with lemonade, Curly led the man's horse to the water trough, and the soldier stepped as close as Joe would allow.

The stranger nodded. "Ma'am, my name is Lieutenant Walters. I'm a surveyor for the United States Army, and we're checking out all claims made by Indians in an attempt to ensure the reservation system is preserved. We don't want any of them claiming reservation land as their own."

Selena's blood froze in her veins, and her knees threatened to buckle. She dropped to the porch step and tried to calm her racing heart. Dylan was no longer a murder suspect, and Mary had been properly buried. So, there was no reason for Lieutenant Walters to want him dead. Yet she couldn't shake the uneasy feeling he was lying about his reasons for wanting to speak with Dylan.

Her hand shook when she accepted a glass of lemonade from Mavis. After Mavis handed a glass to Lieutenant Walters and each of the ranch hands, she set the tray down and stepped back onto the porch—with her rolling pin. The Pooles, mother and son, flanked Selena like a pair of guardian angels as the other men stood guard on the ground.

Selena eyed the lieutenant. "My husband's land isn't on the reservation."

"Maybe not, but some Cherokee, like your husband, make money off the cattle drives by leasing grazing rights to white ranchers driving their herds east. The army just wants to make sure none of the whites are taking advantage of the Indians or trying to buy their land at prices below current market value."

His explanation sounded reasonable, but what did it have to do with surveying Dylan's land?

"So, you think my husband is just another ignorant Indian." She smiled sweetly, suppressing a shiver. "He's not. He's also as much white as he is Native American, so why do you care if he owns land or not?"

Mavis and Joe looked at her askance.

"Selena, Dylan is part Cherokee. That makes him an Indian," Joe said, ignoring Walters' raised eyebrows. He obviously didn't approve of Joe using her Christian name.

"Dylan is no more Cherokee than he is white." She wouldn't let anyone deny her husband's duel heritage, not even her husband.

"Ma'am, being from back East," Lieutenant Walters began as if he were talking to a small child, "you're probably unaware of how things are done out here. If a man is part Indian, then he's all Indian."

"And you sir," she said trying to tap down her rising ire, "are unaware of a basic, fundamental knowledge of genetics. My husband is as much white as he is Indian, but regardless of his racial make-up, he has the right to lease his lands in any way he sees fit. If he makes a profit off the cattle drives, then I'd call him an astute businessman, not a gullible Indian ripe for swindling."

"Perhaps I should wait until your husband returns or discuss these matters with your foreman. Being a woman, I don't think you quite understand the financial and political implications

205

of such things," he said as he handed Mavis his empty glass.

Selena stood, and her anger and her mouth got the better of her. "Being an idiot, you'd be unable to recognize intelligence if it bit you on the—"

"Selena!" Mavis and Joe shouted in unison, abruptly cutting her off before she could embarrass herself further.

Mavis led her inside, making excuses for her temper by blaming the heat and her pregnancy, while Joe spoke with Lieutenant Walters.

Later, Joe told her he gave the army permission to survey.

"But they don't need it. They can do whatever they want on Indian land, even if it ain't on the reservation." He shrugged as if it made no difference. "Dylan's part Indian so asking permission to survey is a courtesy, not a requirement."

#

The next day, Joe and the other men killed a steer and cooked it over an open pit. They dragged a table and benches from the cookhouse and invited Mavis and Selena to join them for supper. It seemed a bit awkward at first, but then Mavis relaxed, and the men settled into conversations about cattle and ranching.

Selena looked around the table and smiled. For the first time in a long while, she felt like part of a family—a big, diverse, multi-racial family. She was just starting to relax and enjoy her meal when the conversation turned to more serious matters.

"The army done set up camp on the north pasture," Ten Spots said.

"Is that bad?" She'd never been to the north pasture and had no idea how far away from the house it was. She wasn't even sure how much land Dylan owned.

"It ain't good," Ray Two Bloods said. "Especially since I ain't seen no surveying equipment. You seen any Ten?"

He shook his head. "No sir. I sure ain't."

Joe propped his elbows on the table and leaned forward. "What bothers me more than the lack of equipment is the number of soldiers they seemed to need for the task."

Curly had tied his hair back with a rawhide strip, and the frizzy curls puffed out behind his head like a pompom. He shook his head and the pompom bounced. "That major didn't say nothing about surveying. He said they was here to prevent Indian attacks."

"We ain't never had a problem with renegades around here." Ten Spots' freckled face made him look much younger than thirty-eight, so he'd grown a beard in an attempt to look older. With his Comanche blood, it never grew in and was little more than scraggly scruff. "Besides, what's the army doing protecting a bunch of half-breeds like us from renegades for anyway? Don't make no sense."

Selena's heart beat just a little faster. "Then why did they send so many men?"

Ten Spots shrugged. "Don't know, 'cept I think they up to no good."

"Ah, don't you worry none, boss lady," Jack Hawk said, flashing his handsome smile. "Ten Spots just don't like white men, but some of 'em ain't so bad, not even Major Davis, once ya get passed his problem with Injuns and breeds."

"Andrew Davis?" Her pulse jumped, thinking of all the possible reasons for Andy Davis to be camped on Dylan's property—and none of them were good.

"Yeah. That's the one," Jack said. "I served with Captain Casey before he was assigned to the Special Services Unit. Ran into him once after that, and he introduced me to Davis. They was friends back then."

Selena's heart thumped just a little harder against her ribs. Major Davis was assigned to Fort Davis, not Fort Stockton. Then again, so was Walters. "Why is a survey team from Fort Davis camped on our doorstep when Fort Stockton is closer?"

Joe frowned. "I been wondering that myself."

Images of Dylan's scalped body filled Selena's head, and she had difficulty tapping down the terror rising in her throat. Dylan never thought Davis hated him enough to commit murder, but Lieutenant Walters probably did. Even if Dylan hadn't killed Mary, he'd slept with her, and Walters knew it.

"You all right, boss lady?" Jack Hawk asked. "You look a bit green around the gills."

She swallowed the lump in her throat. "I think Ten Spots might be on to something. The army is up to no good—or at least Lieutenant Walters is, and I don't trust him."

Without going into details, she told Joe to send a rider out to find Dylan and warn him of the possible danger, expressing the importance of calling Walters by name. Ray Two Bloods volunteered.

"Ray might not live among the People anymore, but he's the best man for the job," Joe assured her. "If anyone can find Dylan and warn him of the army's sudden interest in his land, it's Ray."

#

Selena had never been a patient person, and by late the next afternoon, she was a nervous wreck. She was hot, tired, and restless, and she needed to get out of the house or she'd go stir crazy. With so many soldiers patrolling the property, she shouldn't be in danger from renegades or drifters. So she grabbed her gun and a change of clothes and went to the barn to saddle Dalmatian.

It was already late September, but the daytime temperatures remained in the eighties, despite the cool, almost chilly temperatures at night. The water was still warm enough for swimming, and she needed to relieve the stress and work off some of her anxiety.

When she reached the copse of trees near the water, she slid from Dalmatian's back and hobbled the animal in the rich, green grass that grew along the bank on this side of the creek. Then she slipped through the trees that shaded her favorite swimming hole…and stumbled to a halt.

Her private beach was occupied.

She slid her hand into the front pocket of her skirt and carefully withdrew her revolver. The trespasser had on pants, and he was reaching for a shirt hanging from a branch when Selena steeled her nerves and steadied her aim. "I believe you're trespassing, major, and if you don't have a damned good reason for being here when your regiment is camped a mile away, I might just shoot you."

Andrew Davis jumped as he was poking his head through his clean white shirt. Then he spun around to face her, and his color deepened. As his shirt fell into place over his chest, he raised his hands, but his gaze dropped to the gun belt lying on the ground next to his boots.

"If you so much as twitch in the direction of that gun, I'll blow your head off." Her pulse quickened and sweat beaded her brow, but to her relief, she wasn't visibly shaking.

Davis lowered his hands and fingered his bushy mustache, raking droplets of water from the thick facial hair. "Looks like I found your private swimming hole."

Ignoring his attempt at small talk, she said, "I thought you and your men were camped out on the north pasture, but it seems you've strayed a bit. Haven't you?"

"True, but the water farther up-creek is too shallow for swimming, and it's not as secluded. I take it that's why you're here." He inched closer.

"Don't move." She steadied her aim, but her muscles strained, and her arms were starting to burn. "I asked you a question. What are you doing so far from your regiment?"

"I was taking a bath. Now lower your gun or I'll take it from you."

"No. Answer my question." There was iron in her voice, but the gun wavered. She couldn't hold up her arms much longer. Even if she could, she wasn't sure she could shoot an unarmed man.

The major looked into her eyes and then dropped his gaze to the gun. Her arms were now visibly shaking. He stepped closer. "Lower your gun or shoot. They're your only choices."

"Don't make me shoot," she whispered on a shaky breath.

"You won't," he said. Then he reached for the gun and pulled it from her limp fingers.

Her arms fell to her sides. "You should have threatened me. Then I could have pulled the trigger."

Davis held the gun by the barrel, and his expression softened. "I'm sorry," he said gently. "But I can't let you hold a gun on me. I know you don't trust me, but you didn't feel that way the day we met, did you?"

"Of course not." Why would he ask that now? It definitely made her uncomfortable, but it still wasn't a threat. Even if she still had her gun, she couldn't shoot him. The twenty-first century had made her too civilized. Too soft.

A touch of sadness shadowed the major's eyes. "Then why did you choose Casey? Most women find him attractive, but they'd never overlook his Indian blood. Even your cousin was ashamed of her attraction to him, but you married him knowing he was a breed."

Dylan was once his friend—a good friend according to Dylan—but Davis destroyed that friendship when he learned Dylan was half Cherokee. Now he was questioning her reasons for marrying him in spite of his Indian heritage, but he sounded more curious than envious. Maybe he just wanted to understand how a woman could rise above social bigotry when he'd been unable to.

"A man's character shouldn't be defined by his race, creed, or color but by his heart and actions," she said at last. "So the color of Dylan's skin doesn't matter."

"But a damned breed?" He flushed crimson, but she was unsure if it was due to anger or humiliation.

"He's a good man. You should know that," she said, unable to tamp down her frustration. "You were friends once. Remember?"

"I remember being deceived by a damn half-breed. Nothing else matters."

As long as he held onto his anger, nothing else would. Experience and perception shaped opinions, and Comanche renegades murdered his family, tainting his perception of an entire race of people. The experience was so brutal it prevented objective consideration of anything related to Native Americans. Until he opened his heart and mind, nothing anyone said could change his opinions.

"Why are you here, Andy?" Calling him by his given name startled him.

"Not you personally, but the army," she added when he seemed too stunned to answer. "If you're really surveying Dylan's land, why haven't we seen any survey equipment?"

His brows came together, creasing his forehead. "I don't know what you're talking about. The army's not here to survey."

"That's not what Lieutenant Walters said."

"Walters? You must be mistaken. The army isn't conducting any surveys in the area. Like I told your foreman, we're here to ward off possible Indian attacks."

"But Walters said the army was surveying land." He might have an ulterior motive for being here, but he was a surveyor, and he was in Davis' unit.

Andy frowned, looking genuinely puzzled. "Walters isn't here."

The truth was evident in his direct gaze. He wasn't lying. He didn't know Walters was here, which could only mean one thing. Walters wasn't here to survey. His motives were purely personal—and probably deadly. But that didn't explain why the army was camped out on the north pasture when an Indian attack could come from any direction.

Fear knotted her stomach, and her hand drifted to her baby bump. The reflexive action didn't go unnoticed, nor did her condition. Andy's eyes widened, but he didn't comment.

Selena swallowed hard and took a deep breath, trying to hold the fear at bay. "If you're not here to survey, then why are you here?"

He shuffled his feet and lowered his gaze. "I'm here to arrest your husband. We know he's on his way home, and when he gets here, I have orders to bring him in."

"Why?" Her throat cramped, and her knees threatened to buckle.

Sympathy shone in Andy's eyes when he finally met her gaze. "Our mission was to meet with the Sioux chiefs and relay the terms of their surrender. Dylan went to act as interpreter and to advise us on their customs."

"And?" She tapped her foot. Blood roared in her ears.

Davis avoided eye contact. "On his advice, our regiment made camp a few miles away from the Sioux while Captain Casey and that Comanche friend of his took a small contingent of breeds and Buffalo Soldiers to meet with the chiefs and relay the terms. If the chiefs refused to accept our terms, your husband was supposed to bring them in or return to base camp for reinforcements. He failed to complete his mission. When the chiefs refused to surrender or negotiate, he told his troops he'd seen enough bloodshed, and he and that Comanche just rode off."

He slid her gun into his waistband and shrugged. "I'm sorry, but he refused a direct order. By not arresting the renegade chiefs or returning to his unit to assist in their forced removal, he opened himself up to a court-martial."

Fear, anger, resentment—all those emotions and some she couldn't even identify—churned in her gut, quickening her pulse. She threw up her hands, completely exasperated with nineteenth century mentality. "What in hell did you people expect? Did your superiors really think Dylan would turn traitor to his own people? He's compromised himself enough already, or can't they see that?"

"We're talking about the Sioux, not the Cherokee."

"They have a shared heritage. Dylan would no more take the army's side against the Sioux than you'd have taken the Indian's side at Sand Creek. No, the army asks too much of him this time."

"I'm sorry, but I have my orders."

"Fine, you have your orders, but does it take the whole damned army to arrest one man? And what about Walters?" she demanded. "Why is he here?"

"The army is here to bring in the Sioux after we arrest your husband." He flushed, looking chagrined. "We had no idea there were so many of them, so Dylan was right not to engage at that time, but he shouldn't have deserted. As for Walters, he's here without the army's knowledge, and I have no idea why."

Chapter 29

Damn the army, damn the Sioux, and damn his own stupid pride for thinking he could make a difference. Dylan ground his teeth. By walking away from his regiment, he was no longer sanctioned by the US government. Any help he gave the Sioux now would be considered an act of treason—if he wasn't arrested for desertion first.

It didn't matter that he wasn't regular army or that his terms of service had officially ended months ago. He was a half-breed, and he'd refused a direct order.

Dylan looked out at the rain and scowled. He and White Deer had erected a lean-to an hour ago to shelter themselves and the animals from the raging storm, and the weather aptly reflected his mood. He'd ranted and raved while White Deer held his tongue.

Seeking shelter beneath a tarp pulled between two cottonwoods was foolish. Hell, it wasn't as if they could get any wetter, but he'd insisted, and White Deer hadn't argued. The Comanche was smart enough to know Dylan was using the weather as an excuse to delay his reunion with Selena.

It no longer mattered if she was from the future or not because she'd been right. He couldn't do anything about the Indian situation, so he'd just walked away. Now, he had to face his wife. And anything he said would just widen the rift between them.

She'd begged him not to go on this damned assignment, but he'd chosen his People over her. Yet when it came down to choosing between his People and his country, he'd been unable to make the choice and had walked away instead.

So, where does that leave us?

When the rain tapered off, he and White Deer took down the lean-to. As they put away the tarp and wiped down their animals, the parched soil soaked up the moisture, and the ground cracked like old potting clay. By the time they remounted, the sun had come out from behind the clouds, and Dylan's thoughts turned once more to Selena.

The things she'd told him were unimaginable, yet when he'd confided in White Deer, the only other person he'd ever tell his wife's bizarre story to, White Deer had believed without question. Then again, White Deer had always been more spiritual than Dylan, but of all the things Selena had told him, the one thing Dylan found hardest to discount was her knowledge of the differing tribes coming together in defense of the white man.

One of the reasons Dylan refused to follow orders and arrest the Sioux chiefs was because Crazy Horse and Rain in the Face were heading to the Oglala Sioux camp to meet with Red Cloud. The Cheyenne scout, Red Armed Panther, was with them, and the war councils were already planning strategies for dealing with the yellow-haired general, Custer.

Selena's prophecies about Custer's death sent chills racing down Dylan's spine. If he were to believe his wife, then he'd have to believe the Sioux and Cheyenne would defeat Custer in a little more than two years. If Selena was right, then Quanah Parker would surrender within the next two years, and the entire Indian Nation would give up the fight by the turn of the century.

He closed his eyes, torn between wanting the truth and needing his wife to be sane. If Selena were telling the truth, he'd have proof within the next two years.

But how did he deal with her until then?

Lost in his own turbulent thoughts, he failed to notice the dust cloud on the horizon until White Deer rode up beside him.

"Rider coming."

Turning his mount, Dylan stopped and watched as the rider headed toward them at a gallop. He rested his hand on the grip of his Colt revolver. White Deer caressed the rifle butt lying across his lap. Tensed and ready, they waited until the rider was close enough for them to make out his identity. Ray Two Bloods.

The hairs on the back of Dylan's neck stood on end, and the burning sensation in the pit of his stomach intensified. Something had happened at the ranch, and he wasn't there to protect Selena.

Unable to wait for Two Bloods to reach him, Dylan kicked his mount and spurred the animal forward. Ishtabe's hooves kicked up clods of mud as he thundered across the prairie, but Dylan didn't let up until he was almost on top of Two Bloods.

Both animals snorted and tossed their heads when Dylan sawed on the reins, bringing Ishtabe to a halt. His mount pawed the ground, and Dylan's heart rose into his throat.

Ray Two Bloods nodded. "It ain't good, boss. The army's camped out on your doorstep, and your wife said to tell you that weasely surveyor, Walters, is sniffing around. She don't like it none and says for you to be careful."

His mind and pulse raced. If Andy had taken a regiment to his ranch to arrest him for desertion, he wouldn't need a surveyor. Walters was up to something, and Selena could be in danger.

Damn it to hell and back. If he and White Deer hadn't doubled back to the Comanche encampment to beg Dog Ears to send the women and children back to the reservation, he would have been home when the army arrived. Instead, he'd made one last attempt to convince the old warrior to comply with the army or risk bloodshed.

He hadn't expected Dog Ears to return to the reservation, but he'd hoped the chief would send the women and children. He should have known better. Dog Ears wanted to make a stand before all his People, not just the warriors.

He'd failed in his mission, he'd failed White Deer's tribe, and he'd failed his wife. She was in danger because he wasn't at the ranch to protect her.

"How long since you left?" He held his breath.

"Just a couple of days," Two Bloods replied. "I headed toward Fort Davis but picked up your trail late yesterday afternoon and doubled back. Didn't know you was already headed home."

Relief loosened some of the knots in Dylan's stomach. "Apparently, I didn't head home soon enough. What in hell is the army up to?"

"Don't know for sure," Two Bloods said, shaking his head. "They say they're surveying, but it don't make no sense. Major Davis is with them, and they don't got no survey equipment."

They weren't there to survey. Andy was waiting to arrest him, but there was no reason for Walters to be at the ranch, so it had to be personal, and the army probably didn't even know he was there.

215

Fear knotted his stomach—not for himself but for his wife and unborn child. "We got to get back. Now."

He turned his mount around and urged the horse into a gallop. Ishtabe stretched his long, dark neck and raced like the wind for home, leaving the other two men to catch up on their own.

As the sun dipped lower on the horizon, Dylan pushed Ishtabe harder, needing to get home—needing to get to Selena. He didn't let up until the report of a rifle brought him to a skidding halt. Ishtabe pranced as he sawed on the reins and brought the animal under control.

A second rifle shot sent Dylan to the ground, rolling for cover behind sagebrush as his horse took off at a gallop. He fired blindly into the rocks. The shooter held the high ground and had the advantage of cover.

And I have a damn bush.

He fired again. If he didn't pop off a lucky shot, his only hope for survival was if White Deer and Ray arrived in time to get a jump on the shooter.

"Did you think you wouldn't have to pay, half-breed?" a disembodied voice shouted down from the rocks.

Dylan's pulse jumped. Walters! Selena had sent a warning, but he'd been too concerned with saving her to pay attention. "What's your problem, Walters? You know I didn't kill Mary."

By now, he had to know—but he also knew Mary never loved him. She'd confessed as much, and Walters had overheard. Dylan remembered the look on Walter's face. He'd been furious, and apparently, he'd been nursing a deep-seeded hatred, born of intolerance and jealousy, ever since.

"Hell, half-breed," Walters shouted. "You think that matters to me? I wanted you dead from the moment I learned you defiled a white woman."

He fired another shot, and Dylan tensed, waiting for impact. The bullet hit the dirt to his left, kicking up a cloud of dust, but his luck wouldn't hold forever. Walters was a surveyor, not a sharp shooter. But even a bad shot could hit his mark if he fired enough times, and Dylan didn't have adequate cover. Walters did, but he wasn't moving between shots either. He wasn't trained to know the disadvantage that posed.

216

The next time he fired, Dylan could pinpoint his position. He just had to draw him out.

"I didn't defile her," Dylan shouted. "I loved her, and that really burns your biscuits, doesn't it? That, and knowing she loved me and not you."

"Shut your mouth, half-breed!" Walters fired off another shot, barely missing Dylan's shoulder. He felt the breeze as it whizzed by and hit the ground behind him.

"The truth hurts. Doesn't it, Walters?" Dylan tried pinpointing the direction from which the bullet had come and the trajectory it had taken before impact.

If he could just get a bead on Walters position...

"I was there the day you found her body," Walters shouted before firing again. "Hell, I knew where she was months ago, you dumb breed. But I didn't tell. I wanted you to hang. Since you didn't, I'll kill you myself."

Was that four shots or five? It didn't matter. Walters had plenty of time to reload.

"It's over, Walters. Give it up," Dylan said as he aimed in the direction of the previous gun blast and pulled the trigger. The bullet hit a rock and ricocheted.

"I want you dead, half-breed. If you hadn't left Canyon Creek when you did, I would have killed you months ago. Instead I had to wait and follow Davis to this Godforsaken place."

"Not much of a surveyor if you can't find your way around without a guide," Dylan said, attempting to infuriate Walters and draw him out of hiding. His strategy worked. Walters came out from behind his rock in a blaze of profanity and rifle fire.

Dylan rolled to his feet and fired off two shots, but the sun was in his eyes, and the first shot went wide. The second found its mark, but as Walters went down, someone approached from behind. When Dylan turned to protect his back, Walters fired off another shot.

The impact of bullet hitting bone sent Dylan to his knees. As he went down, he tried raising his weapon, but the searing agony in his back and shoulder made it impossible. Before his face hit the dirt, he looked up.

Andrew Davis sat on his horse, and the gun in his hand was still smoking.

Chapter 30

Selena was sitting on the porch, trying to turn a pair of Dylan's old long johns into a gown for the baby when a cloud of dust drew her attention. She dropped her sewing and rose to her feet, shading her eyes against the afternoon sun as riders topped the ridge.

White Deer led the group. He held a man in front of him in the saddle, and the second man's head slumped forward. They were still too far away for Selena to identify the unconscious man, but that didn't stop her blood from running cold.

Andrew Davis rode behind White Deer, and Ray Two Bloods rode behind the major, holding a rifle across his lap. A fourth horse brought up the rear carrying a canvas-wrapped body draped over the saddle.

Selena's heart slammed against her ribs. The fourth horse was Ishtabe. "Dear God, no."

With tears blurring her vision, she jumped from the porch and ran toward White Deer's horse. When the man seated in front of him moaned, she stumbled and nearly fell.

"He lives," White Deer said as Ten Spots and Jack Hawk ran up from the barn and reached for Dylan. White Deer lowered him to the ground and then dismounted.

Blood stained Dylan's shirt, and his head lolled between his shoulders. Selena raised a trembling hand to his face. His eyelids fluttered but didn't open. Her throat tightened. "What happened?"

Ray Two Bloods dismounted and pointed a rifle at Andy Davis. "This bastard shot him—in the back,"

Andy dismounted at gunpoint. "I told you. I shot Walters, not Casey."

"Ya shot him tryin' to arrest him, didn't ya?" Jack Hawk said as he and Ten Spots struggled to hold Dylan upright.

Selena wiped the tears blurring her vision. "We have to get Dylan inside and see to his wounds, and someone needs to ride to

Fort Stockton to get the doctor. Everything else can wait."

"I'll fetch the doc." Jack Hawk stepped back so White Deer could get beside Dylan and help Ten Spots carry him inside.

"Take my horse." Ray Two Bloods handed him the reins. "He's already saddled."

Jack Hawk leapt onto the saddle and was already galloping away before Ray could tie the other three horses to the hitching post.

As White Deer and Ten Spots half dragged, half carried Dylan inside, Selena followed, her heart saying prayers her mind couldn't put into words. It would take time for Jack Hawk to get to the fort and get the doctor—time Dylan might not have. She wasn't a doctor or a nurse, but she was a medical professional, and she and White Deer could be Dylan's only chance at survival.

Fighting tears, she squeezed by White Deer and Ten Spots to clear the kitchen table. They staggered forward and placed Dylan on his back as Ray came through the door, prodding Andy Davis inside at gunpoint.

He pointed to the rocking chair. "Sit your ass down and don't move."

When White Deer cut away the remains of Dylan's shirt, Selena sucked in a sharp breath. She'd x-rayed patients with gunshot wounds and open fractures, but bullet removal and suturing weren't in her job description. But she didn't have a choice. Dialing 911 wasn't an option, and emergency rooms didn't exist yet.

She swallowed the fear that rose like bile in the back of her throat and turned toward the sink. Her hands shook when she reached for the homemade lye soap and began scrubbing from her fingertips to her elbows.

"White Deer, I'm going to need your help," she said over her shoulder, hoping she didn't sound as terrified as she felt. "Once I'm done here, you're going to have to wash your hands and arms just as I'm doing."

"What about me?" Ten Spots said.

"You'll need to hold Dylan still while we clean the wound." She closed her eyes, blocking the tears that threatened to fall.

When she finished washing her hands, White Deer washed

his while she assessed Dylan's condition. His breathing was ragged, his face pale, but he was still alive—and unconscious. Normally, that wouldn't be a good sign, but without pain medicine...

She took another deep breath and removed the blood soaked bandage White Deer had applied on the trail. Blood oozed through a thick paste of pungent herbs covering a raw, jagged wound just above Dylan's left collarbone that looked like a through and through. Thank God. She wouldn't have to dig a bullet out of his chest.

"This is an exit wound. I need to see where the bullet entered." Her voice shook with relief and a hint of fear.

White Deer placed his hands under Dylan's shoulders and Ten Spots grabbed his hips. As they carefully rolled Dylan onto his stomach, Ray Two Bloods poked Andy Davis with a rifle barrel.

"He dies, you die," he said as Joe, Curly, and Mavis rushed into the room.

Joe glanced at Dylan and then Selena. "I'll heat the fireplace poker so you can cauterize the wound."

"No." Selena cringed just thinking of the smell of burning flesh and the pain it would inflict. "The risk of infection would be too great."

Mavis touched her son's arm. "Why don't you fetch a bottle of whiskey from the bunkhouse? Then you and Curley need to take care of the horses and Ishtabe's grizzly cargo."

After Joe and Curley left the room, Mavis put water on to boil and then turned to Selena. "What else do you need, sweetie?"

"A clean, sharp knife, a heated needle, sewing thread, and tweezers," she said as she examined the small hole just above Dylan's left shoulder blade. It was definitely an entrance wound, but if the bullet nicked an artery or punctured the top of his lung...

She put her ear to Dylan's chest. Air moved through his lung so it hadn't collapsed, but without a chest x-ray, there was no way to assess the damage. When she touched the hole in Dylan's back, he flinched.

Ten Spots gripped his legs tighter, and White Deer held his shoulders to keep him from thrashing while Selena probed the wound. "The bullet went in at an upward angle and exited through the front, just above his collarbone."

Mavis handed her a warm, soapy rag and then began cutting a sheet into strips to use for bandages while Selena cleaned the wound. When Joe returned with the whiskey, he handed it to his mother and then went back outside to help Curly with the horses. Selena finished washing the entrance wound as best she could and then poured whiskey over it while Ten Spots held him down.

When Dylan settled down, she reached under his shoulder to feel the pad covering the exit wound. She wasn't a forensic investigator, but she knew anatomy, and the bullet had traveled at an upward angle. "The entry wound is lower than the exit wound."

"What's that mean?" Ten Spots asked.

"It means Dylan was shot in the back from below." And he could have died, as was his fate before her arrival in this century.

Her chest cramped. Had she changed his destiny—or just the time and location of his death? She bit her lip to stop it from trembling.

Ten Spots glared at Andy. "You shot him off his horse, didn't ya?"

Ray Two Bloods frowned. "The boss won't on his horse. He'd already got down and killed the surveyor when the major shot him in the back."

Andy stood. His hands fisted at his sides. "I was still on my horse, ya damned fool, and I didn't shoot Casey. I shot Walters. Walters shot Casey."

Selena looked at Davis and then turned her attention back to Ray. "From the angle of the entry wound, he wasn't shot by someone on horseback."

Andy curled his lip. "Like I said, I didn't shoot him. I shot Walters."

"But the boss shot Walters," Ray insisted.

"If you'd bothered checking Walters' body, you would have seen *two* bullet holes," Andy said, clenching his teeth. "Casey shot him in the shoulder, heard my approach, and turned. Walters went down but managed to fire off another shot a second before he died of a bullet wound to the head. The head wound was courtesy of me, asshole."

Ray re-holstered his weapon and left the cabin. He took Andy with him. Selena breathed just a little easier. She didn't need the drama or the audience when they worked on Dylan's more serious wound.

After White Deer and Ten Spots rolled Dylan to his back, Selena washed Dylan's chest and shoulders. The wound started bleeding again, but it didn't bubble when Mavis poured whiskey over it, and Dylan wasn't gasping for breath. If his shoulders hadn't been so thick and muscular or the bullet had exited under his collarbone instead of over it, he probably would have had lung damage—or worse. The bullet could have struck his heart or nicked a major artery.

When Selena pressed on his collarbone as she was cleaning the wound, Dylan nearly came off the table. She leaned on his good shoulder. "I think his clavicle is broken. He needs something for the pain."

Ten Spots pressed down on his thighs while White Deer removed something from his medicine bag and slipped it between Dylan's cheek and gum. "This will take away his pain; take him to the spirit world."

Peyote? It didn't matter. As long as it eased his pain, Selena didn't care if it was magic beans.

When Dylan stopped thrashing, Selena picked up the tweezers and plucked a blue shirt thread from his wound. Any foreign bodies left behind when she stitched him up could cause infection. Before she could ask, Mavis handed her a needle and thread and White Deer assisted her with the tedious task of matching the torn ends of Dylan's flesh and stitching it back together. By the time Selena tied off the final stitch and clipped the thread, her back ached, and her shoulders burned.

White Deer opened his medicine bag and sprinkled a yellow powder over the wound. "My People believe everything on earth has a purpose and every disease, a plant or herb to cure it. The sulfur will prevent infection." He dipped his finger into a metal tin and spread a salve over the stitches. "This is pinon resin. It will help him heal."

It might help, but Dylan needed an IV, antibiotics, and possibly a blood transfusion, but it wasn't even a remote possibility. Intravenous tubing and blood transfusions didn't become a part of modern medicine until the Second World War, and antibiotics didn't exist yet. So she said a prayer, covered the wound with a thick pad and immobilized Dylan's arm with strips of torn sheet. Then White Deer and Ten Spots crisscrossed the rest of the strips around Dylan's chest and shoulder to hold the padding over both wounds before carrying him into the bedroom.

Selena followed them into the room, her heart in her throat. Mavis stood beside her and wrapped an arm around her shoulders. "You need to rest."

"I'll rest when I know Dylan is going to be okay."

White Deer and Ten Spots stripped him down to bare skin and covered him with a sheet. He looked so pale and lifeless. If he'd lost too much blood or developed an infection, he could die. As if reading her mind, White Deer handed Mavis a small pouch. "Make a tea from the black willow bark. It will relieve his pain and reduce the fever."

Mavis took the pouch and headed to the kitchen. Then White Deer handed Selena a small jar. "Courtesy of the white man," he said with a smile. "Inside is a salve made from bear root. Put it on his wound when you change the bandage." Then he handed her a small burlap bundle. "If the wound becomes warm or swollen, boil this blue flax root and make a compress."

Selena accepted his gift with a shaky hand and watery smile. "Thank you."

As she was placing the medicine on the bedside table, Jack Hawk entered the room. "I'm sorry. I failed."

She turned, swallowing the lump that rose into her throat. "What do you mean?"

"The doctor from Fort Stockton. He ain't coming. He said he don't treat breeds and Injuns. I could of forced him to come, but I figured it'd just make things worse for you."

It didn't matter now. The doctor probably would have just poured whiskey over the wound and cauterized it with a hot poker the way Joe had suggested.

"Apparently, that kind of racist attitude isn't uncommon. So I guess White Deer will just have to teach me about herbs and medicines so I can become a doctor who doesn't discriminate. Maybe the folks around here will accept a woman doctor better than the white people of this century would."

Jack just smiled, looking a bit befuddled, and quietly left the room.

Chapter 31

Dylan's mouth was so dry, it felt as if he'd eaten sand, and he could barely lift his lids. When he finally managed to pry open his eyes, Selena was lying on her side with her head propped in her hand. Her eyes widened.

"You're awake," she whispered.

"Yeah." He smiled weakly. He didn't know how he'd gotten into bed with his wife, but he couldn't think of anywhere he'd rather be.

He tried to lift his left hand and brush away the tears, but his arm was tied to his body, and his attempt to move it brought a tearing agony to his shoulder. He gritted his teeth and broke out in a cold sweat. Closing his eyes against the pain, he tried to recall the last thing he remembered.

His eyes flew open. Tommy Walters shot him.

"Don't move, sweetheart." Selena touched his good shoulder and then scrambled out of bed to light a lamp.

She checked his wound and then leaned over to kiss his brow. "You're still a little warm, but at least you're not burning up with fever." She crossed the room to get something off the dresser. Glancing over her shoulder, she added, "You need rest and fluids, and if we can keep you from getting an infection, I'll take those sutures out in six or seven days."

He didn't even know what day it was or how long he'd been laid up in bed. Hell, he didn't even know how he'd gotten into bed or who tended the bullet wound.

"Who?" He wanted to know who'd treated his wound, but his throat wouldn't cooperate, and he couldn't get out the words. The doctor at Fort Stockton would never treat a half-breed. So it must have been White Deer or Joe. But Joe would have cauterized the wound and then let White Deer treat it with herbs and salves afterward, but since Dylan's skin didn't burn, someone must have stitched it.

Selena held a cup to his parched lips. As he drank the herbal-laced tea, she described his wound and treatment. Her medical skills didn't surprise him. He'd been there when she saved the mayor's life at the spring gala, but he couldn't believe she'd trust Indian medicine.

He finished the tea and let his head drop back down onto the pillows stacked under his shoulders. "Surprised...you...listened to White Deer."

"Why does that surprise you?" She sounded hurt rather than defensive. "I respect White Deer and his knowledge of nature and herbs. If not for Medicine Men, the white man would never have discovered insulin. Well, they'll discover it in the future at any rate."

When he just stared, unsure of what to say, even if he had the breath to say it, she flushed. "Sorry. I didn't mean to ramble on about the future. I know how much it bothers you."

He closed his eyes and saved his breath. What was the point? Whatever knowledge he gained in the future would be knowledge she'd had before he was even born. Hell, it was the main reason he didn't want to believe she was from the future. If it were true, then she'd lived with technology, medicine, and luxuries he couldn't even imagine. She'd never be happy living a simple, *old-fashioned* life with him.

It was bad enough they were from two different worlds racially and culturally, but they were also from two different centuries. Not even love could bridge that wide a gap.

Keeping his eyes closed, he drifted into an uneasy sleep filled with dark dreams and disturbing images. He awoke the next morning to find Selena and White Deer re-bandaging his wound. He didn't encourage conversation.

He could no longer deny his wife was from the future, and if she ever found a way back to her own time, he'd have to let her go. He just didn't know how he'd survive losing her.

"Just because you don't want it to be true doesn't change anything," Selena said after White Deer left the room.

"What are you talking about?" Talking was easier this morning, but that didn't mean he had anything to say.

She sat on the edge of the bed and touched his hand. "My being from the future. I'm sorry you can't deal with it, but facts are facts. You think it changes things, but it doesn't. I love you, and I'd rather stay here in the past with you than return to all the luxuries of the future without you."

He closed his eyes, praying it was true, fearing it wasn't. He raised his lids and met Selena's gaze. "If, and I do mean if, what you say is true, it changes everything. You don't need me, Selena. You never have."

She gave him *that* look. The one that made him feel like an ass. "I'm not with you because I need you to take care of me. I'm with you because I love you more than any man I've ever known, past, present, or future. And just because I know about the past, doesn't mean I know how to live in it. I wouldn't have survived that first week without Anita and Alberto. Yes, I know about technology and the future, but I need you to help me make a home for our child—together—in this century."

"Dylan," she added, tracing the side of his face with the back of her fingers, "I traveled back in time to find you, a man who should have died on March 31, 1872. It's nearly October now, and you're still alive. That's got to mean something."

"All it means is that you've apparently saved my life more than once," he said bitterly. "In my time, a man takes care of his woman, not the other way around."

She huffed. "You big doofus. Women have been taking care of men since Eve. Historically, we take care of hearth and home while you men do the hunting and protecting. But if a woman can hunt better than her husband, or the husband is better with the children, why shouldn't they utilize those skills to best serve the family?"

"That's not how it's supposed to work." Did she not understand that a man was defined by his ability to care for his family? "I don't want a woman who can take care of herself better than I can. Hell, I can't even take care of myself."

She stood, glaring down at him with a mixture of anger and sadness. "Let me know when you're done with the pity party and maybe we can have a civil conversation."

With another huff, she stormed from the room. Footsteps outside drew his attention to the open window. While he and Selena had been arguing, Andy Davis had ridden into the yard and was now mounting the porch steps. When Selena stormed out the

226

house, she nearly plowed into him.

Dylan couldn't see his wife's face, but he could hear her. Everyone for five counties could probably hear her as she took her anger out on his superior.

"Don't you even think of trying to arrest him," she said with enough heat to scorch Andy's ears. "I'll shoot you before I let it happen!"

Andy held up his hands as if surrendering. "Whoa, I just want to talk to him. I need to know what he's learned about the Sioux and Cheyenne."

"The Sioux have left their summer camp. Dylan won't tell you that because he won't turn against his People, but I have no such loyalty right now. Do you know why?" she asked, leaning toward Andy until he stepped down. The back of her head now blocked Andy from view, but Dylan could now see the back of Selena's head through the open window. "Because it won't make a damn bit of difference. The army ran the Cherokee out of Georgia years ago. They stole their land and marched them west. Over a fourth of them died, but those who refused to march were treated even worse.

"During the Civil War, the Cherokee lost more men than either the north or the south, yet their sacrifice was never recognized. But do you know what true irony is? It didn't make one damned bit of difference. No matter what path the Cherokee have taken over the years, war, accommodation, capitulation, surrender, or flight, their fate has remained the same. So, do you really think it makes a damn bit of difference now, which path my husband chooses for himself?"

"But . . ." Andy dropped his hands and Selena brushed by him and stormed off, out of view. Andy shouted at her| retreating form. "But we're not talking about the Cherokee."

Dylan could no longer see his wife through the window, but he heard her yell. "Do you think that matters to the army? To you people, all Indians are the same."

Lying in bed listening to the exchange outside his window, Dylan smiled sadly. Selena had not only defended him but his People. She had spoken with such passion he could no longer deny she really loved him. So maybe she was right about the two of them. Maybe he didn't need to take care of her. Maybe they needed to take care of each other.

Andy cleared his throat. He was still standing on the porch, probably trying to decide how to retreat with his dignity still intact. Dylan knew exactly how he felt. Selena had a way of giving as good as she got, and it usually left a man wondering what the hell had just happened.

He wasn't looking forward to another confrontation, but he couldn't avoid the one with Andy. His service to the army was complete, but until Andy signed his discharge papers, he was still accountable for his actions. And Andy still outranked him.

"Come on in, major," he shouted toward the open window. "I'm awake."

Looking a bit awkward and more than a little embarrassed, Andy avoided eye contact when he entered the room. He glanced toward the open window and grunted. "I guess you heard, huh?"

"The whole damn county heard," he said with a grunt, but pride swelled his chest.

Andy smiled but then his eyes drifted to the floor. "Well, I'm not here to arrest you, but I do need an official report on what you learned from the Sioux."

"What I learned is that I've been a fool," Dylan said, disgusted with himself, the Sioux, and the entire US Army. "I can't make a difference. So whatever I did or didn't learn won't change anything. The army and the Indians have set a course that can't be altered—by anyone—and both sides will fight until the other surrenders or there's no one left standing."

"It won't get that far, and for the record, you have made a difference." Andy scuffed his feet and still wouldn't meet Dylan's gaze.

Dylan grunted. "You defending a half-breed now, Andy?"

"Give me a break, breed. I'm trying to be nice," Andy smiled, and for just a second, it felt like old times, but too much time had passed for Dylan to completely let down his guard. Still, if Andy could make the effort, then so could he.

He smiled, and it didn't feel forced. "Well, you did save my life. So, thanks for shooting Walters when you did. I guess I owe you one."

"Hey," Andy said looking directly into his eyes for the first time since entering the room. "If I'm not mistaken, we're not even yet. I still owe *you* one."

"Well I won't hold my breath waiting to collect. I don't think I like your repayment methods. You're too slow. Any slower and I'd be dead," he added with a laugh. The sharp pain in his shoulder made him wince.

"Yeah, well . . ." Davis shrugged off the awkward moment before stepping forward to offer his hand.

Dylan accepted the handshake, and the tightness in his chest loosened. It felt as if a weight had been lifted, and for the first time in years, he could breathe easily. He didn't delude himself into thinking it changed everything, but it felt good knowing some minds could be changed. He and Andy might never friends again, but they were no longer enemies either.

"Andy, I can tell you in another eighteen months or so you won't have to worry about the Comanche. Once Quanah Parker surrenders, the Sioux will too. Then you'll just have the Apache to deal with." He refused to warn the army about the threat to Custer. If ever a man deserved to die at the hands of the red man, it was General Custer.

Andy's eyes narrowed. "Did Rain in the Face tell you this?"

"Let's just say I have a reliable source." Andy would never believe the truth. Hell, he wasn't sure if he believed it himself, but after the faith and support Selena had shown, he was determined to accept what she'd told him as fact. In truth, it didn't matter. Whether it was true or not, he could no longer live without her.

Chapter 32

The army headed out the next morning. Dylan was sitting in the rocking chair by the bed when Andy came in to bid him farewell. Selena hovered in the background, just waiting to pounce if the major made a move to arrest him. She looked calm and accepting, but she hid a Colt revolver in the folds of her skirt, and Dylan didn't doubt for a minute she'd use it if she had to.

Andy extended his hand. "Thank you for your service, Captain Casey. You've been a true asset to the unit, but your services are no longer needed."

Dylan nodded and released his hand, but his gaze strayed to his wife. She stared at the back of Andy's head with such heat in her eyes it was a wonder the man's scalp didn't catch fire.

"I did my best, Major, but I couldn't bring in that many Sioux chiefs without bloodshed, so I walked away." If Andy were going to arrest him, now would be the time. He just hoped Selena kept that damn gun in her pocket.

"We were outnumbered, and you made a judgment call. I now support that decision, but there's still the desertion charge we need to address," Andy added in a stern, authoritative voice. "I'm going to document that you took a French leave to check on your wife and planned to return afterward, but Lieutenant Walters shot you in the back before that happened. Since Walters wasn't supposed to be here and didn't have the authority to arrest you, his shooting was unjustified. He'll receive a posthumous dishonorable discharge, and you'll get a verbal reprimand in your army record for taking an unauthorized leave. Then I'll sign those discharge papers, and this matter will be settled."

"I appreciate that," Dylan said, finding no joy in having the charges against him dropped. "But it won't be finished for the army or the Indians until every warrior surrenders tribal membership, returns to the reservation, or dies."

"There is that," Andy said. Then he turned to leave, but

Selena blocked his exit.

"So, Walters tried to murder my husband and all he gets is a dishonorable discharge?"

"We can't arrest a corpse," Andy said, and Dylan could hear the smile in his voice.

Selena scoffed. "But his historical record will say he attempted to arrest Dylan without authority. In the future, that could look as if Dylan got shot evading arrest, and that's not what happened."

"Neither you nor I were there, and since your husband was on unauthorized leave at the time, it's his word against a man who can't defend himself. This is the best I can do, Mrs. Casey."

"Will you at least see to it that the official record states he shot Dylan in the back?"

Andy sighed, "I'll do my best. That's all I can promise."

He placed his hat back on his head and left without a backward glance. Selena tried slipping out the room behind him, but Dylan wasn't going to let her get away so easily.

"Selena," he said more harshly than he intended.

"Yes?" She paused and turned in the doorway to face him.

"We need to talk, if you don't mind." His wife thought she was tough, but she'd always worn her heart on her sleeve, and she was worried future generations might still think he was a savage. Why else would she be so concerned with what Davis put in his and Walter's military records?

She eyed him with no small amount of suspicion. "About what?"

"Just come here so I don't have to shout, and for God's sake put away that gun before you accidentally shoot someone." *Like me.*

"Why should I listen to you?" she asked, putting the revolver on the washstand. "You don't need me. You don't need anybody. You wall yourself off from the world and refuse to let anyone get close to you, including your own mother."

She visibly struggled to keep her voice down and maintain the cool facade she'd presented earlier, but his wife was a passionate and opinionated woman. He would have laughed at her failed attempt to feign indifference had it not been for the remark about his mother.

231

"My mother?"

She placed her hands on her hips and stepped in front of his chair, putting him at a disadvantage because he had to look up to meet her gaze. "Yes, you idiot, your mother."

So, he was an idiot now, was he? Was that better or worse than being a doofus?

Sighing, he gave up any pretext of having control over his wife or the conversation. "What about my mother?"

"Dylan, I know you're a warm, caring man, but in your pigheaded attempt to protect yourself from hurt, you shut people out."

"I'm not shutting out anyone," he said with a groan, "but neither you nor my mother will ever understand what it's like to have your loyalties divided between two races so culturally different they've been at war since the Pilgrims landed at Plymouth Rock. But that isn't even what I wanted to discuss with you."

"We understand a lot more than you think," she said, turning her pert little nose up in the air.

"Look," he said, shifting his hips in the chair and trying to get comfortable. He was damn tired of recuperating. "I can't be someone I'm not. I can't be all white or all Indian depending on the direction of the wind, and I can't sit around and talk about my feelings all day."

"What feelings? You're a rock, an island even. You want me to sing the lyrics?"

Jisa! What in hell was the woman talking about now? "Look, I said I don't want to talk about my feelings. I wanted to discuss—"

"What feelings?"

She leaned forward. Her breath was a whispered caress against his skin, stirring emotions he didn't want stirred. Then she kissed him, sweet and tender with so much love it melted his heart.

When she pulled back just enough to meet his gaze, she whispered again, "Tell me how you feel."

"I love you, damn it. Is that what you wanted to hear?"

"Yes." she whispered, and tears glistened in her eyes. "Say it again."

"You heard me the first damn time," he said, looking down at the bandage crisscrossing his bare chest.

"Oh Dylan," she said as she squatted before him and laid her head in his lap. "I've waited so long to hear those words. Would it really hurt to say them again?"

He caressed her hair and back with his good hand. "I do love you, but that doesn't mean it's going to be easy. That's what I wanted to talk to you about."

She lifted her head to meet his gaze. "About life not being easy? Life is life, Dylan. No one ever said it was supposed to be easy."

"Selena, it's not that simple, and you know it." Damn, was it so easy in her time that no one noticed skin color? If that were true, then he wanted her to go back to the future and take him with her. "We come from two different worlds, and if you're to be believed, two different centuries. What makes you think either of us will ever fully understand the other?"

She furrowed her brows but then her face just seemed to crumble with grim acceptance. He still couldn't admit aloud that she was from the future.

"Does anyone ever fully understand another? But despite what you believe or don't believe, there is a child to consider," she said, standing and wrapping her arms protectively around her middle.

"Do you think I haven't thought of that?" It was all he ever thought about—well that and making love to his wife, but now was definitely not the time to mention that. She might decide to retrieve the gun from the washstand and shoot him in the other shoulder—or lower. "This isn't about my mother, or our child, or anyone else. It's about you and me."

"Whatever you say, Dylan." She pulled a blanket from the bed and placed it over his lap, tucking it around his legs as if he were a feeble old man. Her eyes twinkled, and he could have sworn she was trying to hide a smile.

His pulse jumped. "Don't you dare patronize me."

"I'm not. You're right. This isn't about your father or your mother, because they'll never fully understand what it's like for you to be a part of both worlds. That's why you should tell them and not shut them out. I'll never understand how you feel because I'm a white woman from the future, but it doesn't mean you can't talk to me. I love you, and I want to understand everything you think and feel, but I will never know what it feels like to be part Indian."

She stepped closer, and he had to arch his neck to meet her gaze. Tears glistened in her eyes when she said, "And that's why you'll need to be there for our child. You'll be able to understand what it's like to be biracial so our child will have an advantage you never had."

He reached for her with his good arm and pulled her onto his lap. Then he kissed her with all the feelings he'd kept locked in his heart for so long. When she ended the kiss and leaned back, he cupped her face. "I want you, but..."

"I know." She leaned down to kiss his forehead and somehow, that relayed her emotions more convincingly than any kiss on the lips ever had, so he was surprised to feel a tear drip onto his face.

"What's wrong? Don't cry *Adawehi*." He ignored the tear that rolled over his cheek to thumb away the one rolling down hers.

Selena sniffed and then smiled. "You always slip into Cherokee when you're emotional. Did you know that?"

"Why are you crying?" He wasn't touching that statement.

"I know you want me, the evidence speaks for itself," she said glancing down at his erection. With a sad smile, she added, "You even say you love me. So why can't you think of reasons why our relationship *will* work instead of focusing on all the reasons it won't?"

So, this was what was bothering her. He'd moved on to other concerns—like when he'd be able to make love to her again—and she was still dwelling on his lack of enthusiasm over their living happily ever after.

"Do you have any idea how rough it can be on a white woman in Texas who marries an Indian or a half-breed and then gives birth to his child?"

"I read *Ride the Wind*," she said, haughtily. "It's the story of Cynthia Parker and her husband, Nocona. He was a Comanche chief and Quanah Parker's father."

"I know who Nocona is. I've met the man...in person. I just can't believe you know of him or that you've actually read a book about him." Or that a book was actually written about a

Comanche war chief who kidnapped a white woman and made her his wife.

"I read about him and the great love he and his wife shared, despite their differences. When the soldiers took her away from him, she wanted to die, and when she learned of his death, she did." Sorrow shadowed her face as if she actually believed it, but he doubted anyone else did.

"The whites believe she died because of her ill treatment at the hands of the Comanche and the grief she suffered when her daughter died."

"In the future, people will believe she died of a broken heart."

"Either way, Selena, she died. Their story did not have a happy ending." Didn't that make his point for him?

"No, Dylan," she said with a smile. "They lived. They may not have lived long, but they did live, and they loved. They made the best of the short time they had together. That's all I'm asking of you. I don't expect guarantees. I just want us to live and to love for as long as we're together. That's all anyone can ask in this century or the next."

"I will love you, Selena, *igo hi dv*. Forever."

Chapter 33

Christmas came and went. Family and holiday preparations kept Selena from dwelling on everything that could go wrong during childbirth, but when the holidays were over and Dylan's parents and William went home, she began to panic.

Having a baby was unnerving in any century, and she would be delivering at home without pain meds or a doctor. She trusted Mavis. She just didn't trust her to deliver a baby. Mavis wasn't even a midwife, and Selena didn't think calf delivery qualified as prior experience.

Joe had made a cradle as promised, but there'd be no baby showers, no cute outfits, and no disposable diapers. Her child would wear diapers made from flannel and drawstring gowns made from every scrap of material Mavis could find. There'd be no cute rompers or matching outfits from a children's store. There wouldn't even be baby pictures.

Maybe it was hormones. Maybe it was fear or even homesickness, but for the next week, Selena moped around the house or cried herself to sleep. She was breaking Dylan's heart, but she couldn't help it. She was terrified—not just of childbirth, but of raising a child in the nineteenth century. People still got small pox here, and they hadn't invented childhood vaccinations yet.

By the second week in January, Dylan was tiptoeing around her as if she would break. So, it surprised her when he rushed into the house late one afternoon and lifted her off her feet. "You're never going to believe it, but Whiskey Springs finally has a doctor."

He was still smiling when he lowered her feet to the floor. Selena wasn't. The baby she carried was still biracial. "Is he a bigoted ass-hat like Dr. Reams?"

Dylan's disapproving glare at her choice of words quickly gave way to a smile. "No. The new doctor is Doc Adams. Ross left the army to start his own practice in Whiskey Springs, and he's stopping by in a couple days to examine you."

"Are you serious?" Her knees nearly buckled. God had answered her prayers. Ross Adams might not be an OB-GYN, but he was still a doctor.

She threw her arms around Dylan's neck and kissed him until her knees went weak a second time.

Two days later when the doctor stopped by the house, Selena was already in labor. After only six hours, she gave birth to a beautiful baby girl with dark hair and gray eyes. Selena had never been more relieved, and Dylan had never looked happier.

"You did it. We have an *ageyutsa*, a daughter," he said with a catch in his throat.

When Doc Adams placed the baby on her stomach, Selena momentarily forgot about the pain. Looking into her child's angelic face, her fears faded away, and a love like no other filled her very soul.

The doctor smiled. "What will you call her?"

"That's up to Selena," Dylan said, his heart shining in his eyes. "Mothers name their daughters."

"She's our daughter, Dylan, but if you don't mind, I'd like to name her after my grandmother and mother. I want to name her Sara Jane Casey."

At the time, Selena thought she'd never have another child. The pain and fear of delivering a baby in this century had been too much. But two months later, she looked down at her sleeping child and knew she'd do it all over again, but not until Dylan added another room onto the house.

He and his ranch hands had added one room already. They'd also upgraded the kitchen so Selena now had a woodstove. She still wasn't the cook Mavis was, but at least she wasn't totally dependent on the older woman for all their meals. Although, she still relied on Mavis for help with the laundry.

Hand washing diapers was a bitch, but Dylan was helping William build the crank-handle washing machine she'd designed, and William had already started on the paperwork to start a family-own manufacturing company. In the meantime, Dylan still had a ranch to run.

Leasing grazing rights had become a profitable business for the Cherokee, especially along the Cherokee Strip. It wasn't illegal, but the government frowned on such enterprise, and Selena told Dylan the commission on Indian affairs would stop it. He hadn't argued. Then again, he still acted as if she was just another nineteenth-century housewife.

After putting the baby down for her nap, Selena returned to the kitchen. She stirred the soup and then moved the cast iron pot to a shelf on the back of the stove. Woodstoves didn't have off buttons, so moving the pot was the only way to keep it from boiling over or scorching until the fire went out and the embers cooled. She'd also have to put up with the heat. It was early March, but it was already getting too hot to cook in the house without fans or air conditioners, and Mavis didn't allow her in the summer kitchen.

Selena smile to herself. She'd definitely come a long way in the wrong direction technologically, but she wouldn't trade this life for her old one, even if she could.

As she was pouring two glasses of apple cider, Dylan came into the kitchen waving an envelope. A frown creased his brow.

"It's from Andy," he said as he pulled out a chair for Selena. As always, he didn't sit down until after she was seated. "I never expected to hear from him again."

Nerves and curiosity fluttered beneath Selena's ribs. Or maybe it was just hunger pains. "So, read it already."

He read the first page, shook his head, and scanned it a second time. "Andy says Colonel Harper was satisfied with my assurances that Chief Quanah would soon surrender. I guess he assumed the information came from Rain in the Face, because he removed the unauthorized leave charge from my file."

Selena's pulse leapt. "You have a clean military record?"

"I have a clean record," he said with a smile before finishing the letter. The smile slowly faded. "The army is also reassigning Custer to the Dakota Territory to protect railway surveyors and gold miners crossing onto Sioux land."

Selena wanted to tell him she'd told him so, but it would do no good. He still couldn't admit she was from the future.

He crumpled the letter in his fist and slammed it on the table. "I can't help them. I won't choose sides again. I'd die before I put on another uniform."

"I'm sure no one expects you to." She certainly didn't want

that for him. The hostilities between America and the indigenous people would only get worse.

He met her gaze, and his face paled. "Everything you ever told me was true. You really are from the future."

"Yes." He finally believed her, without a doubt or a single reservation, but knowing the truth didn't lessen his anguish. He still felt torn by divided loyalties.

As she was trying to think of something to say to ease his pain, hope sparked in his eyes, and his face brightened. "You know what the future holds for the Indian Nation, but we both know the future isn't set in stone. It can change."

"Some things, yes, but not everything. At some point, you have to believe in fate. It's what brought me to you. Otherwise, you'd be dead." And she had to wonder if anything had really changed at all. If neither Dylan nor Mary haunted the Tillman house in the future, and Mary's spirit wasn't attached to the necklace, then Selena would have had no reason to go to Texas to look for answers. Yet here she was, almost a year later.

"But I'm not dead," he said, excitement tingeing his voice. "Which means we can make changes."

"Minor changes."

Her reservations didn't lessen his enthusiasm. "I want to set up a scholarship fund for Indians and help White Deer get into Princeton. The world can change, Selena. We can help it change."

White Deer was supposed to have died. There could be catastrophic repercussions if he went to Princeton, and racism still existed. "I think that's a find idea," she said, despite her lingering fear.

Finding schools that accepted Indians was difficult, but Dylan had already contacted Princeton. He'd even convinced his mother to reconcile with her brother, Quinn. His parents, Uncle Quinn, and William were all coming to visit Easter, which happened to be on the one-year anniversary of Selena's arrival in the past.

"Aren't you afraid of changing the future so much that I'll just disappear?" If that happened, Sara would cease to exist.

"No," he said with a reassuring smile. "You're exactly where you're supposed to be. It was your destiny to come to me from the future, so why waste your knowledge if it can benefit mankind in the present and possibly create a better tomorrow?"

"But what if my being here changes so much it causes some kind of paradox? Not only are you still alive, but you're married, and we have a daughter who should never have been conceived." It was the one fear she couldn't shake.

"I no longer doubt you're from the future, but if something is meant to be, nothing we do can change it. Which means you were sent back in time to right a wrong. I should never have died when I did, and you should never have been born in the twentieth-first century."

"Actually, I was born in the twentieth century—in 1992," she said, trying to let go of any lingering doubts about her existence in a time before her birth. If she believed fate had brought her here, then she had to believe this was where she belonged, and any changes she and Dylan wrought would be for the better.

"And you will become a doctor in 1875. Maybe a bit later," he added with a smile.

"I'm not sure that's possible now." White Deer had been teaching her about herbs and holistic medicine. William had even ordered medical books from back East so she could study the *latest* advances in medicine, but Dylan hadn't been as supportive.

He shoved his untouched soup aside and reached for her hand. "I know I said no medical school would accept a woman, but I just didn't want you to leave me."

Her shoulders tensed. She tried to snatch back her hand, but he held firm. She ground her teeth. "I would never leave—"

"I know. I know," he said, squeezing her hand. "But it doesn't matter. You don't have to go away to medical school to become a doctor. I talked to Doc Adams, and he says he'll set up a proprietary program that will eliminate the need for medical school. You'll have to take a sixteen week course of instruction in anatomy, midwifery, and chemistry before you can apprentice under him. The apprenticeship will last two or three years and once he signs the certificate of completion, you can sit for the medical boards."

Selena's head spun, and her pulse leapt. She already knew anatomy. She knew every bone and organ in the body. She didn't remember as much as she should about the nervous system or circulatory system, but she probably knew more about infection and diseases than most doctors in this century. She just didn't know much about pharmaceuticals or midwifery, and the drugs she did know about probably didn't even exist yet.

"Where would I practice if I did become a doctor?" She certainly couldn't compete against Doc Adams. No one in this century would see a woman doctor if a man was available.

Dylan pushed back his chair and tugged her hand until she moved onto his lap. He wrapped his arms around her waist and pressed his cheek to hers. "Ross wants you to go into practice with him. He was there when you saved Mayor Huddleson's life, and he doesn't doubt your abilities for a minute."

Dylan chuckled, and Selena felt the vibration in his chest when he added, "Hell, you could probably teach him a few things."

She turned her head and met his loving gaze. "You know I wasn't a doctor or a nurse in my time. Right? I took x-rays."

A smile chased the frown from his eyes. "Nobody else even knows what x-rays are. So, I'm betting you know a lot of other stuff nobody else knows about, even doctors."

He had a point. Still..."But what about Sara? There's no such thing as daycare in this century."

He bent his head to hers, their foreheads touching. "We'll figure it out, *adawehi*, Together."

"Together," she whispered as her lips touched his. At last, everything made sense. She wasn't living in the past. This was the present, and Dylan was her future.

She was finally home.

Epilogue
Canyon Creek, Texas. Present day

The flashing blue lights of the patrol car cast strange shadows on the old house where the young woman from Virginia had disappeared. She'd come to Texas to claim her inheritance and found trouble instead.

"So how do you know her? Is Selena Tillman some sort of kin?" the deputy asked, glancing at the name on the rental agreement he'd found in the abandoned car's glove compartment.

Blade Casey glanced over the deputy's shoulder to the abandoned house. Thomas Tillman, a distant cousin, should have sold the place years ago. The land was valuable, but the house was worthless.

He returned his attention to Deputy Jim Hines. "She's a distant cousin from back East. Mom asked me to meet her out here today and show her around. The car was here when I got here, but she wasn't."

"Did you look for her?"

"I did, but nothing is here but her car."

Hines scribbled something in his notebook. "So, what is she doing in Texas?"

"She's a stockholder in Tillman-Casey and was doing some genealogy research on the family. This house once belonged to a mutual ancestor, Mary Tillman, who was killed by a tornado on the property back in the 1870's. My great, great, great grandfather, Dylan Casey, was accused of killing Mary until he found her body. Later, he married Mary's cousin, the first Selena, who was also the half-sister of the missing Selena's great, great, great grandmother, but a DNA test suggested a closer relationship between the two Selenas. Since Mom is also into genealogy, she wanted me to meet Selena and answer any questions she might have about the Casey side of the family."

"They didn't have DNA back then," Hines said with a

snort. "So how'd a DNA test suggest a closer kin to a woman long dead? She dig her up or something hinky like that?"

Jim was idiot, but Blade wasn't surprised. He'd gone to school with Jim some ten years back, and the man wasn't any smarter now than he was then. He still couldn't find his own ass if his head were tied between his knees. "DNA is passed down from generation to generation, Jim. Selena Tillman didn't have to test the first Selena's DNA. My father is a direct descended of Dylan and Selena Casey, and he had his DNA tested. The match was closer than expected." And the DNA results didn't make sense.

Jim smirked. "Still think you're smarter than everybody else, huh Casey?"

Blade arched his brows, unable to hide a smile. "Is that relevant to the investigation?"

If Jim's uncle hadn't been sheriff, the county never would have hired him. Blade's dog had more sense than Jim Hines did, but he was the first officer on the scene. Blade didn't have a choice but to respond to his idiotic questions.

"I'll ask the questions," Jim snarled. "How long were you here before you called 911?"

"About an hour. I saw the car, searched the house, and came up with nothing. I thought maybe she'd taken shelter from the storm somewhere on the property, but I couldn't find any sign of her."

Jim looked up from his notepad. "What storm? There won't no storm today."

"Yes there was. It looked like a tornado. It briefly touched down behind the house and then was gone as quickly as it came."

"I'm telling you there won't no twister today," Jim insisted. "There won't nothing on the news, the wire service, or the emergency broadcast channels. Hell, just look at the sky, Blade. Ain't hardly a cloud in sight."

Blade looked up at the expanse of blue overhead. The setting sun cast long shadows, washing the horizon in shades of pink, mauve, and orange, but there wasn't a black cloud in sight.

So if he hadn't seen a tornado, what the hell was it?

An uneasy feeling settled in the pit of his stomach, and goosebumps pimpled his skin. He rubbed his arms to ward off a sudden chill. "Maybe you ought to put out an APB on her, Jim.

You might want to organize a search party too."

"No shit," Jim said, sarcastically.

Blade whipped out his cell phone and punched in his mother's number. "I'll call Mom and get Robbie Tillman's number in Virginia. He's Selena's uncle. Maybe he can fax you a picture or a description."

"Hot, damn!" Jim rubbed his hands together. "I finally got a real crime to solve."

Blade groaned. "Just get some damn men out here."

But six months later, Selena Tillman was still missing.

Her body was never found.

About the Author

Award winning author, Lilly Gayle, is a wife, mother of two grown daughters, a grandmother, and a breast cancer survivor. She lives in North Carolina with her husband. When not working as an x-ray technologist and mammographer, Lilly writes paranormal and historical romances. She is the newsletter editor and VP of Communications for her local RWA chapter, Heart of Carolina Romance Writers.

Look for all of Lilly's books online and in print at your favorite online retailer.

Historical Romances by Lilly Gayle

Wholesale Husband
Slightly Tarnished
Slightly Noble
Helpless Hearts
Wilder Hearts
Winds of Time

And her paranormal romances:

Out of the Darkness
Embrace the Darkness

www.ingramcontent.com/pod-product-compliance
Lightning Source LLC
Chambersburg PA
CBHW071855220626
47052CB00002B/125